THE SILK'S

CW00471180

Volume 8 of The Silk Tales

A NOVEL BY

JOHN M. BURTON KC

FOR MY LATE FATHER, MALCOLM LESLIE
BURTON, A GOOD MAN, A GOOD HUSBAND
AND A GOOD FATHER

TABLE OF CONTENTS

INTRODUCTION

This novel is a work of fiction. It refers to a substance known as 2,4 Dinitrophenal, (DNP). DNP is a genuine substance often described as a fertiliser, a dye, or a munition. It should not be thought for one moment that any of the arguments advanced in the novel during the course of the fictional trial are intended to encourage anyone to take DNP. The expert evidence is that it is a poison unfit for human consumption and can result in serious illness, organ failure and death.

Sadly, several people have died from taking the substance and the death statistics referred to in this book are accurate at the time of writing.

CHAPTER 1

THE BODY BUILDER

Jensen Willmott took another look in the mirror. He did not like what he saw. He was twenty-five years of age, 1.8 metres tall, 5 feet 11 inches tall as his mother would say, weighed 70 kgs and when he attended a gym, most people who saw him thought he had a perfect male physique, the body of a fit, if not, super fit athlete.

To Jensen though, he saw himself as fat, flabby, ugly and with the physique of a seventy year-old man who had led a debauched life and never exercised. Jensen had tried everything. He had taken virtually every slimming product on the market; he attended the local gym at least five times a week, he used weights of various sizes, parallel trainers, rowing machines, running machines, he swam at least a kilometre each time he got into the pool, but as far as he was concerned it was all to no avail.

He had tried steroids and protein powder to build up his muscle to achieve a wonderful physique that he saw in others, but not in himself. In his eyes there was nothing out there that could help him. He had even removed all the mirrors in the house as he could not stand looking at himself.

He had never approached Doctors about his condition, never thinking that he might be suffering from Body Dysmorphic Disorder. He had never even heard of the condition.

He continued with his life being miserable about his body, but then, just a few weeks ago, he saw the advert on a website that would change his life forever. A company called Slimming, Limitless Inspiration and Motivation UK Ltd (SLIM UK for short) was selling a new super slimming pill whose ingredients were based on an East Asian recipe that was over a thousand years old and had only just been rediscovered.

Of course, he was sceptical at first, he had tried so many different pills and other dietary remedies, but he decided to give it a try and he used his email to contact the director of the company, a man who went by the name, Nashad. Eventually he spoke directly with Nashad over the phone. He seemed genuine, he had an extensive knowledge of East Asia having apparently lived there for most of his life and he had studied with many fantastic gurus out there.

Nashad was a great believer in East Asian culture, and he had enthusiastically described ayurvedic medicine and the wonders of East Asia that were simply not appreciated by Westerners and generally not available in the cynical over regulated Western world.

Nashad went on to tell him the recipe for this slimming pill was only recently discovered by accident by his colleague Lee Han Ong, a Chinese collector of ancient manuscripts. Lee purchased a very old manuscript in a Hong Kong Street market and found that it revealed an ancient formula for a slimming aid. A formula that had been lost for centuries.

According to Nashad, Lee had instructed a friend who was a chemist to follow the recipe closely using ingredients that were not readily available on the market. He produced a batch of pills that he took himself. Lee Han Ong was a large man who had overindulged in rich fatty food all his life. He was clinically obese but within four weeks he shed fifteen kilogrammes of weight, restructuring his body perfectly and allowing him to resume a healthy lifestyle after years of ill health. Now Lee Han Ong wanted to offer the miracle pills to the world so that others could benefit.

Nashad explained that, sadly, the pills were relatively expensive because the ingredients were difficult to obtain and the chemical processing was complicated, but he emphasised that the expense was definitely worthwhile when compared with the results.

Nashad advised Jensen to buy a test batch of just ten pills for £30 and take them one a day for ten days. If Jensen didn't notice a large drop in weight over ten days, Nashad would refund him his money in full, no questions asked.

Jensen felt he had nothing to lose, he had tried everything else, maybe this would work. If it did not, he would lose nothing as he would get his money back. He ordered the pills on Sunday 8th September 2019, and they arrived just four days later on Thursday 12th September 2019. He was a little surprised to see that the package that arrived was labelled 'Food Colouring Pigment.' He assumed there had been a mistake and he immediately phoned Nashad.

Nashad did not answer the phone but did return his call within the hour. He pointed out that the company was waiting for the product to be properly licenced in the United Kingdom as it was in other countries and to avoid unnecessarily restrictive EU and UK regulations, the pills had to be labelled in this way. He assured Jensen that these were the pills that he had ordered.

After the call Jensen opened the package and noticed it contained ten blue and yellow capsules. There was a note stating only take one a day, but Jensen wanted to ensure that they worked quickly, so he had taken two a day for five days.

He did think about discontinuing them after two days as he felt nauseous and had almost vomited several times. He also noticed how dizzy he felt, how his heart pounded much quicker than normal, how he became extremely sweaty and had an almost constant headache.

Slightly worried by these signs he had again phoned Nashad who told him not to worry, these signs were perfectly normal. The pills increased the metabolism meaning that more energy was used than normal and therefore the pills burnt more fat even when there was little exertion. Nashad told him these side effects were normal but to ensure he only took one pill a day. Jensen lied in response and said he had only been using one pill a day and would keep to that. He then immediately used the internet to order another batch of ten pills on 15th September 2019. They did not arrive until 18th September 2019 which meant that at his rate of consumption, he had run out two days earlier. He was not going to make that mistake again so he quickly ordered ten pills that day.

He thought about Nashad's instructions to take one pill a day, but he could not see any harm in increasing the dose to two pills. He knew his own body better than anyone and was sure it would not cause any problems.

He continued to take the pills and he had found at the end of the first 5 days he had lost 2 kilos of weight despite doing less exercise and not changing the amount he ate. After ten days he had lost 3.5 kgs. To him this was a good start, and the side effects were worth suffering for the weight loss and the consequent body sculpturing. He had even purchased a small mirror so he could see the changes the pills were making to his body.

Jensen acknowledge that he soon became hooked on the 'miracle' pills and the next batch arrived on 22nd September 2019. He still hated his body, but at least he was losing weight and eventually he was sure he would have the body he wanted.

It was now 4pm on Friday 27th September 2019 and the weekend was upon him. He took his last two pills last night and had a rough night, feeling very ill. He had decided to order 30 pills on the last occasion, so he did not need to order so frequently. He looked at the brown paper package that arrived that morning with thirty pills for a total cost of £75, supposedly a month's supply, though he knew it would last him less than two weeks.

It was an important weekend for him. He met Zoe Slater just a month ago and for some reason she seemed to like him despite his revolting weight and barrel figure. Although they had only known each other a short time he believed she was the one. She was one ray of hope in an otherwise depressing life. He had even given her a key to his flat and they planned a romantic weekend together.

He was both scared and overjoyed with his new relationship. He had not had a regular partner for two years. In those years he had a few one-night stands, but he had found them deeply unsatisfying. He wanted to make this weekend extra special as it could be the start of a meaningful future.

He took another look in the small mirror he had recently purchased. He could not belief how fat and pale he looked, he even looked a little yellow. He needed to look his best for Zoe. He broke open the package and looked at the thirty yellow pills inside. He would take a few, maybe they would have a quick effect upon him, and he would shed more weight before Zoe arrived.

He opened the plastic packing and took four pills out. It was twice his usual dose, but he needed to lose weight rapidly. He swallowed them all with a large glass of water and then sat down hoping they would take effect.

Within a few minutes he felt hot and again started to feel sick. Good he thought, the pills are working. He should be able to shed a few more kilos over this weekend.

However, he was alarmed to note that the room began to spin, and he had a terrible burning sensation in his throat stretching all the way down to his stomach. He knew he should lie down, maybe four pills were too many in one go. He would only take two in future.

He recalled that he felt ill the night before after taking just two pills, so it was not surprising that he felt ill after taking four pills. Perhaps that was too many.

Slowly he moved towards his couch and lay down. He really did not feel well, and it was obvious to him that he needed to rest. Although the room was well lit with extra bright lights, he suddenly felt a darkness descend on him. He knew he would soon be asleep. That was all right, a couple of hours nap was surely good for him and would make him feel much better. He would still have time to get ready for Zoe who was arriving at 7pm that night.

CHAPTER 2

THE GIRLFRIEND

Zoe Slater dabbed at her eyes with a soggy piece of tissue. The tears had flown freely for over an hour now and she used up all the tissues she had brought with her in her handbag. She looked at her new handbag and at her new dress. She had bought them both for this weekend. It was supposed to be so special, a lovely weekend planned with her boyfriend. The rather strange but exciting Jensen Willmott. He was strange because he seemed to have no confidence in himself despite being, 'drop dead gorgeous', the words she used to describe him to her friends.

They were supposed to be going out dining tonight, seeing a play tomorrow, a walk planned in a park on Sunday and generally they were just going to enjoy being together. However, here she was seated in the Accident and Emergency department of the Southampton General Hospital. Around her were an assortment of patients, quite a few with nasty looking wounds, looking drunk and making lots of horrible noise. It was far removed from what she expected for that weekend.

She looked at the clock on the wall, it was already past midnight. She arrived in the hospital almost four hours earlier. Jensen had invited her round to his flat at 7pm that night. She phoned him at 6pm just to make sure everything was alright and to ask if he wanted her to bring anything. She was surprised that he had not answered her call even though she had phoned several times.

Eventually she went round to his flat at 7pm as arranged. On arriving she noticed through the windows that the lights were on, but Jensen did not come to the door when she had rung his doorbell repeatedly. Eventually, she used the key he had given her to gain access. The scene she saw on entering the flat terrified her. Jensen was spread out on the sofa asleep, he looked pale with a ghastly yellowish pallor to his skin, and he was breathing heavily, making a throttling, or choking sound.

There was a pile of foul smelling vomit at the base of the couch near to his head. There were a couple of yellow and blue pills in the middle of the vomit and some more nearby on the floor coming from a metallic looking bag that protruded from a ripped brown package. She did not know what the pills were but assumed that he had taken an overdose.

She was shocked, she did not know he had a drug habit. She knew he attended a gym regularly and he was always talking about trying to achieve a healthy weight and maintain a healthy lifestyle. She never imagined for a moment he would take drugs and she could not fathom why he would take an overdose on the night he was expecting to see her!

She desperately tried to wake him but was unable to do so. Within a few minutes she realised there was nothing she could do with her basic first aid training and she phoned 999 and asked the emergency services to send an ambulance.

The ambulance had taken almost 20 minutes to get there. The paramedics were thorough, and they worked on Jensen for another 30 minutes or so in the flat. However, they were not able to wake him although he was still breathing, and they managed to make him look a slightly healthier colour. They placed him on a saline drip and took him to hospital in the ambulance with their emergency lights flashing. She was allowed to sit in the back of the ambulance on the journey, holding Jensen's hand. She heard him make a few noises through an oxygen mask they placed over his nose and mouth, but the sounds were unintelligible and it was clear he had not regained consciousness. Now the doctors were working on him, trying to keep him alive.

The doctors in the hospital assumed naturally that he was suffering from a drug overdose but at first, they had been unable to tell what drugs he had taken. Then one of the younger doctors suggested that it was something called DNP, 2,4 Dinitrophenal. He told Zoe he had only recently qualified and he had come across it in his recent studies. Zoe had never heard of DNP and certainly Jensen had never mentioned it to her, so she could not assist as to whether they were right.

After 30 minutes or so a chemical test proved that the young doctor was right. The medical staff then administered a drug they told her was called dantrolene, as it had some success with 'DNP poisoning'.

She was shocked when she heard the word, 'poisoning' and she collapsed onto the bench behind her.

They tried to make her feel better by telling her that it was good that Jensen had vomited, as he had got rid of some of the DNP, but they could not tell how much he had taken, nor whether he had been regularly consuming it. Whatever the situation, he was in a serious state and they told her he needed constant monitoring. A few minutes later a senior doctor came up to her and added that they could not predict what the outcome would be and it might be better if she prepared herself for the worse.

She realised she had passed out herself for a moment and came to with a nurse close in attendance. Once she seemed all right, the nurse left her but the medical staff checked on her and updated her regularly.

There was no good news. Jensen had not recovered consciousness and it was not clear if he was getting better or worse. They did tell her he was 'burning up' at one stage and that they were applying cold compresses and ice to bring his temperature down.

At 2:10am Zoe was falling asleep in her chair. She had heard nothing more from the doctors in the last two hours and she could only hope that was good news.

She started to dream and Jensen was there holding his hand out to her but for some reason she could not touch him. She was woken suddenly by a loud noise and she looked and saw a door opening slowly and a young doctor, wearing scrubs, peering out. He looked towards her, she saw that he was not smiling and her heart missed a beat. He slowly moved forward to where she was seated, a slight frown on his face.

"Ms Slater?" He asked.

"Yes." She replied nervously.

He swallowed loudly.

"I am so sorry to have to inform you that although we did all we could, Mr Willmott has passed away."

He paused looking at her closely, expecting a reply. He was trained for this, to give bad news to patients' families but it was not easy in real life. He thought he must add something.

"The death was certified at 1:55am as a result of DNP poisoning."

He did not add that the doctors spent the last five minutes deciding who would break the news to the distraught woman. Eventually the senior doctor on duty decided this task should go to the most junior member of the team, 'as you need the experience'.

Zoe collapsed into her chair and burst out crying again. She had only known Jensen for such a short period but she had grown very close to him, she might even be in love with him. He was so good looking, but he doubted himself so much he was like a little schoolboy on his first day at school, so unsure of himself. That endeared him to her. He was not bombastic, arrogant, or cringingly possessive like so many of her boyfriends had been.

She hoped for great things between them but now, that was all over because of some stupid yellow and blue pills. Why, oh why, did he take these pills? Why did he take them that night? They had planned to do so much together that weekend. What was wrong with her that made him take an overdose rather than be with her?

CHAPTER 3

TRADING STANDARDS

It was a cold morning on 15th October 2019 and Roger Lovesay was in a foul mood. He was Head of the Trading Standards department for Salisbury and the surrounding area. There were several subordinates in front of him and as he had just been appointed to the role, to the consternation and annoyance of others, he wanted to show he was up to the job.

"I have heard of DNP poisoning before..."

Actually, he had not heard of it, but he did not want to admit that fact in this company. A file had arrived on his desk from the local NHS with a police report suggesting he investigate any potential Trading Standards offences relating to the death of a young bodybuilder and as a result he had asked Deborah Shaw in the office to conduct some extensive research.

"... Unscrupulous people in this country offer miracle slimming aids to people who have psychological disorders such as Body Dysmorphic Disorder."

He paused to look around the room to see if anyone other than Deborah looked like they knew what he was talking about. Satisfied that they did not he continued.

"These people make massive profits and yet their customers die. We have a case like that now and I want to make sure we don't have anymore.

A young man, Jensen Willmott with almost his entire life before him, had an undiagnosed psychiatric disorder that made him feel fat when in fact he was a good healthy weight. He was persuaded to take a so-called 'miracle sliming pill' and as a result he died. I have told our legal department to instruct a Queen's Counsel, Gerard Smedley QC, who has some experience in similar cases, to advise on prosecuting the purveyor of the filth that killed this young man, with the offence of manslaughter!"

He paused to see the effect of his words on the room. He was disappointed to see the blank expressions on the faces in front of him. He looked to Harvey David. Harvey had been expecting Roger's job and was a potential troublemaker in Roger's eyes. He was the one who needed to be singled out in this meeting.

"Harvey, you are our most senior man here, what do you think we should do?"

He hoped he had left Harvey with no options but to support him. After all, a young man died, what possible argument could there be?

Harvey grimaced at being singled out. He had wanted the top job and, in his mind, he deserved it, and he confidently assessed others felt the same. Roger was not up to it but had simply been promoted because he had spent his career brown nosing the people who mattered.

Whatever his opinion, he was going to disagree with Roger.

"Roger, surely if we are considering manslaughter charges, we should be consulting the Crown Prosecution Service. Manslaughter trials are expensive and I am not sure that our budget can afford such an expense. If we lose the case, we will pay our own costs and maybe the defendants if he pays privately for his defence lawyers. If we win the defendant will go to prison so we will probably never see any contribution to our costs. Either way we are likely to lose a very large sum of money from a constantly overstretched budget."

Roger's eyes narrowed, this was an earlier challenge to his authority than he had imagined. His eyes narrowed even further when he heard a few murmurs of approvement from the group. He had to put an end to this quickly.

"Obviously, I have already considered that Harvey. However, this is a product that has been pedalled in our area and a young man has died because of taking it. Our duty is to protect the people in this area from unscrupulous business practices."

He paused to see if he now had the room's attention, satisfied that he had, he continued.

"This was not only unscrupulous business practices, but they also caused a young man's death. Of course, I intend to liaise with the Crown Prosecution Service and hopefully receive some of their resources and indeed we will need the police to conduct arrests, but I feel duty bound for the protection of the public in the Salisbury area to take this case on, whatever the cost.

Are there any more comments?"

No one had anything further to add and Harvey decided he had said what he could, so Roger set the team several tasks. He told Harvey that he would be the 'lead' on the case and would be responsible for liaising with the police and the Crown Prosecution Service. That should keep him quiet for a while he thought. If things went wrong, Harvey's 'I told you so' would look particularly self-serving. Nevertheless, he was surprised to see Harvey with a beaming smile.

Harvey was smiling at the prospect of overseeing this case. He wanted the position as soon as Roger had mentioned the prosecution for manslaughter, it was so much better that dealing with the drudgery of prosecuting companies for breaching some opaque and probably unnecessary regulation.

His comment about the Crown Prosecution Service was just in case the costs of a prosecution became prohibitive and he could tell the powers that be that he had pointed this out at the very start. If there was a successful prosecution everyone would forget the comment except for Roger. Now Harvey could make himself indispensable to this prosecution and it would certainly help him into Roger's job when Roger inevitably failed and had to stand down, or more likely, be moved sideways to another department.

Two days later Harvey contacted the Crown Prosecution Service who were happy to assist providing no part of the costs of the prosecution came from their budget. He also contacted the local police who were similarly willing to help.

Now all that was required was to put together a team to properly investigate and prosecute the matter. He already knew who he would approach. The brightest person in the unit was Deborah Shaw and Roger had suggested that she be involved. She would be an ideal person for this job, but he had no intention of asking her to assist. She had shown far too much loyalty to Roger and had not even commiserated with Harvey on the fact he did not get the top job. No, he would approach Kerry Williams, Peter Wilson and Jenny Seaton. They had all approached him and told him they thought he should have been given the top job. They would make an ideal team to prosecute this case, in more ways than one.

CHAPTER 4

A KNOCK ON THE DOOR

Nashad was in a quandary. It was 6am on Monday, 4th November 2019 and he had not slept well. He had not slept well for some weeks now. He was heavily involved in the 'slimming' business. He had invested what little savings he had into this business, about £4,000, all he had at the time having spent the inheritance he obtained on his mother's death. He was the one who came up with the company name 'Slimming, Limitless Inspiration and Motivation UK Ltd (SLIM UK)' ditching the original company title of 'Slimming Inspiration UK Ltd' which he felt was simply not long enough and did not fully convey the aim of the organisation. Lee Han Ong had been happy to go along with the change and indeed had been happy to leave the day to day running of the company to Nashad.

Nashad had never run anything in his life having spent many years trying to find the, 'meaning of life', rather than involving himself in the mundane process of living a life, so he had found his new role both challenging and exhausting.

At first the company had done incredibly well and in just three months Nashad had received a three-fold return on his investment. He had been paid back his initial £4,000 and had another £8,000 on top as pure profit. This was even though Lee Han Ong took 25% of the profits; 50% went to some 'sleeping partner' in Hong Kong who he only knew as an unnamed 'main investor' and Nashad only took the remaining 25%.

There was a massive internet demand for the product and Nashad had been extremely busy dealing with the import of the slimming product, taking orders, filling the blue and yellow capsules and arranging packaging to send the product around the World, ironically including Hong Kong, where the slimming product came from in the first place. He had thought of hiring someone else to fill the orders as he was spending most of his day on the business but hc had not had the time to interview anyone.

Everything had been fine until that idiot boy had decided to overdose on the pills. Nashad had made it plain that this was a strong pill and no one should take more than one a day, but this boy apparently took twice that amount and according to press reports probably took four pills the day he died!

Nashad only found out about the death as a result of reading a local newspaper article which was followed almost immediately by a desperate phone call from Lee Han Ong. Lee had phoned Nashad from Heathrow airport about a week earlier telling Nashad that he had to visit Hong Kong on 'important business'. He asked Nashad to continue with the business and transfer the funds in the normal way from the company bank account.

Nashad was concerned to hear about the death of the boy, but he felt no personal responsibility. Lee had said it was 'unfortunate', but they had nothing to worry about. They had made it plain that customers should not take more than one tablet a day and they could not be responsible for some idiot who had taken more than that.

Nevertheless, Nashad was worried. He did not know how the United Kingdom authorities would react and the fact that he was on his own now and Lee was not answering his phone or emails, gave him a horrible feeling in the pit of his stomach. The authorities might even close his business and it was so lucrative he had hoped to retire soon and move back to India with sufficient funds to keep him in a good lifestyle for the rest of his life!

He turned over in bed and tried to sleep some more but to no avail. Perhaps he should ask his niece Wendy about his situation. He could even approach her husband David, although he was loath to ask for any assistance from him. David never accepted Nashad's constructive criticism and always made Nashad feel unwelcome in their home. No, he would not ask David for help, but he would phone Wendy later that evening.

He started to fall asleep, but he was awoken by a loud knock on his front door. He glanced at his clock, it was 6:23am, who on Earth would be knocking on his door at this time?

Within seconds he received an answer to his silent enquiry.

"Police, police, open up or we'll break the door down."

Nashad was shocked, why were the police here?

He froze to the spot temporarily unable to move, but coming back to his senses he shouted, "I'm coming'.

Almost immediately he heard a splintering of wood.

"Stop, I'm coming," he yelled, but it was too late, the police had already battered the door down. Nashad was standing in the hall of his two-bedroomed flat at 6A Ashton Street, Milford, near Salisbury. He moved there five months earlier just before starting the business. He looked at the door of the flat and was surprised to see the door open quickly revealing a police officer holding a small one-man battering ram. Looking at the damaged door Nashad wondered how he was going to explain this to the landlord.

Whilst he was wondering about this, a burly police officer shouted at him, "Stay where you are, don't resist arrest or it will be worse for you."

Nashad looked surprised, wondering who he was talking to. Before he figured it out, two other large officers grabbed him by his arms and forced him to the ground.

"What is going on?" he asked.

One of the officers, PC Roger Wilson, told him, "I am arresting you for the manslaughter of Jensen Willmott, you do not have to say anything, but it may harm your defence if you do not mention when questioned something which you later rely on in Court. Anything you do say may be given in evidence."

Nashad could only reply, "What?"

PC Wilson grabbed hold of him and forced him to the floor, "You are being arrested because you caused the death of a young lad, you don't need to say anything, but if you do, it will be written down and maybe used against you in a Court of law. If you later want to say something in court that you have not said now, that fact may be used in court as well."

The officer put his face very close to Nashad's, "Do you understand now?"

Nashad did not have a clue what was going on and did not understand what the officer had said, everything was a daze. However, he had not liked the officer getting so close to him smelling unpleasantly of stale smoke and cheap coffee and he nodded. All he could think of was why was he being arrested for killing the young man. He had never even met him! He tried to make this point to the officers, but they did not seem at all interested.

PC Wilson applied handcuffs to Nashad's wrists which dug deep into his skin.

"Is that really necessary?" he asked.

DC John Colhoun appeared at the door next to Harvey David, Kerry Williams, Peter Wilson and Jenny Seaton from Trading Standards. DC John Colhoun addressed Nashad, "It is for now. We will take them off when we get back to the police station."

Nashad sighed, he was in a complete state of shock and had no idea what to say.

DC Colhoun turned to three other uniformed police officers and told them to search the flat. "Remember lads, we are looking for anything important, drugs, chemicals, documents, computers, you name it."

Nashad watched as the police came into his house and started pulling out drawers and throwing his belongings onto the floor. As soon as he could, he must contact his niece, Wendy, maybe, in the circumstances, he should talk to her partner, David, as well.

CHAPTER 5

THE INTERVIEW

Six hours later Nashad was seated in an interview room at Salisbury station, nursing a hot cup of tea and nibbling on a rather stale biscuit. Next to him was Henry Granger, a local solicitor who had been called in to assist Nashad as he did not know any solicitors in the area. Across from them was DC Sonya Sharpe and DC John Colhoun and seated behind them was Harvey David.

Sonya was the most senior officer present and she was the lead interviewer.

"I understand you go by the name Nashad, can I call you Nashad?"

Nashad put his cup of tea down almost spilling it as it was quite full.

"It is a name that was chosen for me, so I am happy for you to use it."

Sonya smiled, "How are you feeling Nashad? Are you alright to be interviewed?"

Nashad nodded, "I am fine, thank you. I am happy to be interviewed and assist in any way I can. I would like to get this over with as soon as possible and return to my flat and arrange for the damaged door to be repaired."

His solicitor, Henry, grimaced at this comment. He had tried to explain to Nashad that he was facing a serious charge, carrying a maximum of life imprisonment and he would probably not get bail. He had advised Nashad to make no comment during the interview and reserve his defence until they knew the strengths of the prosecution case against him. Nashad had looked at him aghast and then performed a long soliloquy about having nothing to hide and being happy to help the authorities. Nevertheless, Henry would try again,

"Mr Pritchard, my advice to you is to make no comment to any questions asked as there has been very little disclosure in this case and until the police give us proper disclosure of their case it would be better to make no comment to any question asked."

Nashad looked at him as if he was crazy.

Sonya quickly tried to reassure Nashad, "Don't worry about your flat. Police officers waited there until temporary repairs could be carried out and the premises were left secure."

Nashad smiled, "I am so happy about that. I have many artifacts from the East which I have collected over the years and which have fond memories attached to them all. I would be devastated if any of them were stolen by criminals or damaged in any way.

Sonya nodded again making a mental note to check whether Nashad may have breached any import control regulations, such as the one she had read about the other day in a police magazine concerning 'tainted' objects under an act called the Dealing in Cultural Objects (Offences) Act 2003.

Sonya put the thought out of her mind, she had enough to do in this case. She declared, "Well let's get started then."

She opened a large file in front of her that she had read before coming into the interview. Most of the contents had been supplied to her by Harvey and contained all the information that he and his team had collected over the last few weeks. In addition, there were a few documents that had been found in the search of Nashad's flat which had been photocopied and added to the file.

"Nashad, can you tell us what you know of DNP or 2,4 Dinitrophenal, to give it its proper name?"

Nashad looked blank, "I have never heard of it."

"But you were selling literally kilos of it on the internet as miracle diet pills?"

Nashad shook his head.

"I assure you good lady that I was not. I was selling a diet pill that came from an ancient formula that has only recently been rediscovered."

"So, you are claiming that you didn't know you were selling DNP?"

"I have never heard of DNP."

Sonya turned to the file in front of her and picked out a document that had been found in Nashad's flat.

"Nashad, this is a document found at your flat. It's an invoice for a drum of chemicals imported from Hong Kong. It has Chinese writing on it that I don't understand, we will get that translated, but there is some English writing underneath which refers to 'fertiliser'. Underneath that is a reference to, 2,4 Dinitrophenal, i.e., DNP.

There was also an empty drum found in your residence that was labelled in the same way.

I also have a photograph that was taken in your business premises of a drum which had the word 2.4 Dinitrophenal stencilled on it and underneath the word, 'fertiliser'."

Nashad looked surprised. He quickly asked, "May, I see that document and the photograph of the drum?"

Sonya handed over them both, "Have you seen these before?"

Nashad looked carefully, "Oh yes, I have."

"The document clearly states that a shipment of 2,4 Dinitrophenal was sent to an address at 10 Coventry Street, Salisbury. We understand that is an address associated with your business."

Nashad nodded, "Yes, that is right. That is where I placed the slimming product into capsules and then packaged and sent them to customers."

"This invoice clearly states that a drum of 2,4 Dinitrophenal was sent to your business address."

"Yes, I see that."

"If you look closely at the invoice, its states at the top, "For the attention of Nashad Pritchard."

Nashad looked closely at the invoice, "Yes, yes, it does."

"If you look at the photograph of the drum, you can clearly see the words, '2,4 Dinitrophenal' and 'fertiliser'. So, you knew you were importing 2,4 Dinitrophenal, a fertiliser which you were then putting in capsules and selling as a slimming aid."

Nashad shook his head again.

"Dear lady, you have got it all wrong. The product that was ordered was the miracle slimming drug that came from China via Hong Kong. It was this substance that has been labelled 2,4 Dino something or other.

Our problem was that we had not been licenced to sell the product. We knew how effective it was and its great potential health benefits to consumers, but we could not afford to wait years or possibly decades for formal licencing, so we did use a subterfuge. We pretended that the drug was fertiliser so we could avoid licencing offences. I accept we shouldn't have done this, but we wanted to get this slimming aid onto the market as soon as possible in order to help people."

Sonya stared at him, "Are you really saying you did not know that you were supplying a 'fertiliser' or a 'munition', as some describe it, and advising people to put it in their bodies?"

Nashad shook his head slowly in a frustrated way.

"My dear lady, you have got it all wrong. This was not a fertiliser or a munition. It was a chemical composition that replaced natural herbs that were used in a slimming product. It was labelled 'fertiliser' simply to allow the product to get through Customs."

"Nashad, the substance found in Jensen Willmott's body was analysed and found to be 2,4 Dinitrophenal, commonly known as DNP. It was a poison, not a slimming pill and it killed him."

Nashad stared at her intently.

"My dear, dear lady, my solicitor has informed me that is what you were going to say but I dispute that. It was a slimming pill. I would not sell fertiliser or munitions as a slimming pill. I suggest this Mr Willmott has taken something else that has killed him, or he has taken far too many of these pills and that has killed him. I suggest you have the contents of his stomach analysed again and meanwhile analyse the powder you found at my business address. You will find it is a combination of specific herbs which have a remarkable slimming effect."

Sonya looked at a further page in her notes.

"When you supplied these 'pills' to customers, you supplied them in packaging that stated that they were 'Food Colouring Pigment.' Why did you lie about the contents if you thought they were just slimming pills?"

Nashad looked increasingly frustrated.

"My dear lady, it is the same reason as to why the drums were labelled 'fertiliser'. We were posting these pills around the World, we needed to label them as something that would not attract the unnecessary attention of local Customs. Those packages all contained slimming pills."

Sonya stared at him again before passing him a two page document.

"Please read this. The first page is a chemical analysis of what was found in Jensen Willmott's body and the second page is a chemical analysis of blue and yellow capsules found in his flat in an envelope, sent by you and labelled, 'Food Colouring Pigment'. You will see that the analysis of both states the pills contained approximately 92%, 2,4 Dinitrophenal, DNP."

Nashad took the document and read both pages quickly. He paused and then read the second page more slowly before looking up at Sonya.

"This cannot be right, the pills I sent need to be analysed again. Lee assured me they were slimming pills and I believe him. They may have a similar composition to this DNP, but they are definitely a slimming aid."

Sonya looked into her bundle again and took out another document.

"I see that Lee Han Ong was involved in this business. Where is he now?"

Nashad looked slightly alarmed.

"I don't know, the last time I heard from him was about a week ago. He was in Heathrow airport on his way to Hong Kong."

"Have you heard from him since?"

Nashad shook his head.

"No, I have tried to contact him, but his phone always goes to voice mail. It is quite frustrating to tell you the truth."

"Is that because he has done a 'runner'?"

Nashad gave her a questioning look.

"A runner?"

"Has he flown out of the jurisdiction in order to avoid being charged with manslaughter?"

Nashad hesitated, "No, that cannot be right, he was adamant that this was a slimming product. He has no reason to 'do a runner'."

"He knew that a young man died after taking these pills?"

"Yes, but ...."

But you have not been able to contact him?"

"No, I have tried."

"He is not in this country?"

"As far as I am aware."

"And he is not contactable?"

"No."

"So, he has 'done a runner'?"

Nashad stared at her, opened his mouth as if to speak but then thought better of it and remained silent.

CHAPTER 6

THE SILK'S DIET

David Brant flopped into his armchair, he had just finished a perfect Sunday lunch. It was Sunday, 8th December 2019 and he had cooked a traditional Sunday dinner, roast beef and added all the trimmings, roast potatoes, obligatory Yorkshire Pudding, broccoli, carrots, sprouts, red wine gravy, a feast for a King, washed down with a few glasses of good Burgundy.

It was now time for a good rest in front of the television. He rubbed his stomach that protruded from his trousers a worrying amount, but soon put any negative thoughts behind him. Better a barrel than a six pack he told himself.

As he smiled at his own attempted humour, he looked across at Wendy who had Rose on her lap. Wendy was looking at him strangely and it looked like Rose was looking at him that way to.

"What's wrong?" He asked.

"Nothing." She replied.

"Come on something's wrong. I can tell, you are unusually silent!"

She narrowed her eyes, "All right, I was wondering how much longer you were going to be around."

David's eyes widened with surprise. "What?"

"Well David, Rose and I want you around a long time, but I'm not sure you are going to make it."

David sat upright, all he could do was repeat, "What?"

"Stop looking like a Goldfish David. You know what I mean. I suggested we have a light lunch but once again you wanted a gargantuan lunch washed down with a bottle of Burgundy."

David looked shocked. "But it's Sunday, am I not entitled to a Sunday lunch?"

Wendy sighed, "Of course you are. The trouble is that because you haven't been in court for a few weeks, you've been having a Sunday lunch every day!"

He thought for a moment before replying.

"Not every day."

"Every day, David!"

He involuntarily breathed in and consciously tried to make himself look thinner.

"There's no point doing that, David."

He looked surprised, "Doing what?"

"Breathing in."

"I'm not."

Wendy sighed again.

"You know your father was overweight and he had diabetes. When you last had an examination two years ago, you were told you were prediabetic and the doctor told you, you had to lose some weight if you were to avoid diabetes. It's obvious from looking at your trousers that instead of losing weight you've put weight on and it's highly likely you are diabetic."

David looked down at his waistline, surprised he could not make out a waist he quickly replied, "It is possible my trousers have shrunk a little, I told you I wasn't impressed with that dry cleaner."

Wendy frowned, "David, the dry cleaner could not have affected our weighing scales! You said the other day that you had put weight on. There's a serious chance that you are diabetic and you know, that can affect your health badly. You can go blind, lose limbs, or even die.

You will remember I once represented a bouncer who was 40 years of age, drank 10 pints of lager every night and lived on a diet of fried food. He was charged with causing Grievous Bodily Harm with intent and the trial had to be adjourned because he was diabetic and had to go into hospital for an emergency operation to have his ulcerated leg amputated."

David's considerable enjoyment of his Sunday lunch had now evaporated and he involuntarily looked at his legs. For some reason they were both very itchy at this moment. He looked up and caught Wendy's eye.

"You're exaggerating a little Wendy, I feel fine."

"You don't look it and I am getting concerned about you. The bouncer felt fine as well until he saw a small spot on his leg and the doctors told him he had to have a leg amputated! You need to go for blood tests to check whether you are diabetic or about to become diabetic and, in any event, you need to lose some weight!"

David frowned, "Well I'm not taking one of Uncle Robert's remedies!"

Wendy scowled at him, "That's not funny David."

David realised he had gone too far with that comment. They had learnt on 8th November, four days after he had been arrested, that Uncle Robert had been charged with manslaughter for selling DNP as a slimming aid. On 22nd November 2019 David had been asked to represent him, even though the vast bulk of the papers had not been served yet and there was no Silk certificate in place to cover David's remuneration. He decided it was in his interests to withdraw the comment.

"Sorry, that was inappropriate."

Wendy nodded, "I meant you should exercise and cut down on your food, don't eat anything fatty."

"Surely you mean eat less fatty food?"

"No, I mean don't eat anything, fatty!"

David grimaced at the old joke, but Wendy had made her point. He knew he should contact his local GP and embark on blood tests, just in case.

David's age helped with the NHS and he managed to arrange a blood test within a few days. The result was given a few days later and was not encouraging. He had a blood glucose reading of 7.4 and although the doctors could not tell definitely from one test, he was told there was a real danger of diabetes if he had a reading over 6.5. He was sent for a HbA1c test to specifically test for diabetes.

After an anxious few more days his GP, Dr Thornton, phoned him on 19th December 2019. She was very matter of fact as she always was.

"Mr Brant, we have the results of your HbA1c test back, you have a reading of 7.2 which means that you have diabetes 2. I have prescribed metformin for you, one a day and you can pick up the prescription from your local chemist."

She did not wait for a response before adding in a disinterested voice, "Have you any questions?"

The verdict was devastating to David as was the manner in which it was delivered. Diabetes 2, taking a pill every day for the rest of his life, risks of hypoglycaemia, blindness, loss of a limb or maybe two, all these worries went quickly through his head in a series of disturbing images. Surely there was something else he could do?

He felt that the doctor was about to put the phone down, so he quickly asked, "I thought it was possible to manage diabetes 2 with diet?"

Dr Thornton paused before answering, probably looking up the answer in her book. David had seen her several times over the years and had never been impressed with her medical knowledge or the manner in which she dealt with patients. If he had ever raised an issue with her, she would more often than not tell him to, 'learn to live with it!'

"No, your reading is too high, and a prescription for metformin is the standard recommendation. Of course, there will be a review in six months. I suggest you organise that through the surgery. Thank you."

With that the call ended leaving David in a state of shock. He had felt quite healthy, alright he was a little, well maybe a lot, overweight, but he had not noticed any signs of ill health. He was a little out of breath walking upstairs in the courts that he visited but he had put that down to getting older. Now though, he was going to spend the rest of his life taking this horrible drug.

He thought for a few minutes, he supposed the first thing to do was to look up metformin on the internet. It might not be that bad. He opened his laptop and searched online for any literature about metformin.

Half an hour later he was not happy with what he saw. Possible side effects included weight loss or weight gain. He did not mind losing weight, but he certainly did not want to gain any more. Further effects could be bloating and diarrhoea and feeling sick. None of this sounded good, but then he read there was a possibility of 'hypos'.

'Hypo' he read was simply short for hypoglycaemia. It was a condition you could get if the medication was too effective and reduced your blood sugar level by too much. The symptoms included; feeling shaky, disorientated, irritable, fast pulse, blurred vision, lack of concentration, night sweats. The list went on.

More disturbingly, the article advised that metformin should not be taken if there were any liver or kidney problems or a person drank a lot of alcohol. None of this sounded good to David. He did not think there was anything wrong with his kidneys or his liver but then again, he never thought he had diabetes and he had to accept that over the years he had consumed a large amount of alcohol and although he had cut down, he had to acknowledge that he still consumed too much. He might have hidden liver and kidney problems. Surely the doctor should have sent him for a test before recommending metformin? Then again, it was Dr Thornton, she probably did not want the cost to her practice when the simplest approach was to prescribe a drug and then ignore the patient.

The only remaining piece of research he could do was through his son, Robert, who was a doctor. He was always loath to contact Robert about medical matters as Robert always seemed to consider the worse possible scenario and make David feel even worse. Nevertheless, there currently seemed no real alternative.

Two hours later he was on the phone to Robert who answered his query about metformin. "Hi dad, you know this isn't my field, I specialise in respiratory matters. However, I know something about it and your HbA1c results weren't that bad. If you can go on a diet, do some exercise and cut back on the alcohol you probably won't need medication."

After the call David sat back in his chair and looked at the large glass of Malbec that he had poured for himself. The lunchtime bottle of burgundy had somehow disappeared.

He had no choice. He had to go on a diet and do some exercise. It was somewhat annoying as Christmas was rapidly approaching. He regretted that he had not waited until after Christmas to have the blood test, but he had no alternative. He knocked back the glass of Malbec and then put the glass down. He would not refill it. He was determined, that was the last one of those for a few weeks.

Over the next few days, David became almost obsessive and read all he could about diets. He even went out and bought cookbooks for diabetics. He also read about the 'miracle pills' on the market and dismissed the idea of a 'quick fix', wondering if these online companies sold a similar product to that sold by Uncle Robert. He shuddered for a moment. If it wasn't for Uncle Robert being arrested for manslaughter, he might have been persuaded to take some of his 'miracle' slimming pills and ended up in hospital, or even dead! He realised he must not think like that, he was going to represent Uncle Robert soon!

David's research took him to all types of diet and exercise plans. He looked at the Keto diet which suggested cutting down drastically on carbohydrates and decided he should try something similar. From doing a basic calculation it was clear that he had a very large carbohydrate diet. Wine, beer, potatoes, bread, rice, cereals, chocolate, had been part of a stable diet for years.

The books all suggested that carbohydrates were the villains. The body needed them for energy but if you had too many the body could not adequately process them and they turned to fat and worse could cause diabetes if the body did not produce enough insulin to help break them down.

His further research showed him just how many carbohydrates there were in potatoes, bread, cereal and chocolate bars. Those were the first items off his menu. He also noticed how many carbs there were in beer and wine. He did not drink that much beer but cutting down on his red wine was a heavy sacrifice to contemplate.

Christmas came and went in the flicker of an eye. David cut potatoes, bread and cereals, chocolate, completely out of his diet, save for a few roast potatoes on Christmas Day. He cut back a little on red wine determined to try out a dry January for the first time in his life but enjoying a few drinks over Christmas and New Year and consuming an expensive bottle of Malbec that Wendy had bought him for a present.

He noted that extra dry Champagne contained very few or no carbs and had wondered if to change his tipple from good Malbec to extra dry Champagne. Cost was however a driving factor on that one, but he did manage to purchase a few bottles of good extra dry Champagne which Wendy and he consumed over Christmas.

From 1st January 2020 to 1st February 2020, David was determined to manage his dry month. He had never tried this before. He had never seen the point in taking one month off if you overindulged the remaining eleven months, but in the first few days, he started to note a change.

Although he had of course said nothing, he irrationally resented Wendy during this period when she opened a bottle of wine and consumed a couple of glasses in his presence as he sipped at his sparkling water, but after a few days, he had barely noticed what she was drinking and had started to feel distinctly healthier.

David also managed to cut his carbs down dramatically and took up swimming twice a week at his local gym. He started at swimming 25 lengths of the 20 metre pool, but after a couple of weeks he increased this to 50 lengths when he began to feel stronger.

In just three weeks he impressed himself and lost 7 kilos. He distinctly felt lighter, however, he also felt colder, more lethargic, suffered headaches and felt dizzy if he got up too quickly. He decided that dieting and exercise were not things he enjoyed and were not really that good for him!

David realised as he subjected himself to this regime, just how difficult it was to make such lifestyle choices and how understandable it was that people wanted a 'quick fix' like one of Uncle Robert's miracle pills!

In mid-January 2020 David took another HbAc1 test and then arranged an appointment with his local GP. He demanded that he be seen by someone other than Dr Thornton, who he was determined never to see again.

On Friday 24th January 2020 he had a face to face meeting with Dr Rachel Best at his GP's surgery. Dr Best was the 'Diabetic Lead' at the surgery. He waited 15 minutes from his listed appointment, which was not unusual in his experience.

Finally, he was invited in through the GP's door to her room. Dr Best was in her early thirties, relatively newly qualified, surrounded by new medical books and looked a great deal more knowledgeable and keener than Dr Thornton. She was also more attractive which made the whole experience more palatable for some unfathomed reason.

She greeted David with a smile, "And what can I do for you Mr Brant?"

David returned her smile and told her he was there for his diabetic blood results. In response she grimaced slightly which concerned him some concern. She then looked at her screen and said, "Let me print this out for you. I want to show you something."

David's heart missed a beat, was this bad news, would he need Metformin after all, was he doomed to take the horrific pills for the rest of his life?

Dr Best presented him with a graph. David looked at it closely. He did not follow the numbers but could ascertain that it showed a steep rise over two years followed by an even steeper fall over a few weeks.

Dr Best had a big beaming grin, "Well done you."

She pointed at the graph. "We measure blood sugar in what are called mmol these days. 41 and above and you are pre-diabetic. You had a reading of 44 two years ago and were pre diabetic. Your reading in December was 58 which signalled diabetes 2, after the HbA1c your reading was 56 but your reading from last week was 46. You are down to the pre-diabetic stage!"

She pointed at some figure that was meaningless to David. Nevertheless, he could not help grin. He had been very worried that his strict regime was making no difference to his general health save for losing some weight. Now he could relax. However, before even a minute passed Dr Best announced, "You'll need to carry on doing what you are doing, but if you keep this up, you'll be down there the next time you have a blood test."

She pointed to a part of the graph that was below the pre-diabetic range. David inwardly groaned but nodded. He wondered how long he could keep this self-torture up! How he wished there was a miracle slimming pill out there!

CHAPTER 7

A CONFERENCE WITH UNCLE ROBERT

David kept to his no alcohol diet until Saturday 1st February 2020 but as it was the weekend, once Rose was in bed, he relaxed and opened a bottle of extra dry champagne which he shared with Wendy.

It had been David's turn to put Rose to bed and read to her and when he returned to the living room, he noted that Wendy was avidly reading the newspaper. She quickly steered the conversation to a little known epidemic in China called Covid 19. Wendy seemed to find it concerning, David was far more sanguine about it.

"It sounds like it's no worse than flu. According to today's newspapers, the first person to die from it died on 11th January this year, they say to date 213 people have died from it in the entire world and there are only two cases in the UK. Seasonal flu in this country kills far more. There's nothing to worry about."

Wendy was not convinced but left the subject and turned the conversation to Uncle Robert.

"So, when are you going to see my Uncle Robert?"

David was dreading meeting Uncle Robert, but a case was a case.

"This week, as you know he lives in Milford, near Salisbury these days and has chosen a local firm of solicitors, Granger and Heath, to represent him. I've arranged an all-day conference with him on Thursday next week starting at 9:30. I'm going to stay in Salisbury the night before as I can't face travelling at five in the morning."

Wendy gave a knowing nod before asking, "Is Sara staying in the same hotel?"

David was used to this topic of questioning.

"Yes, Sara's booked her own room. I suspect we will have dinner together and discuss the case before the conference."

Wendy frowned at him, "I bet you will."

David raised his eyes slightly before replying.

"I have told you that Sara is back with her fiancé, Charles after that hiatus with Gavin."

Wendy looked almost bored as she replied.

"Yes, you did, oh well enjoy your downtime with Sara and do give my best to Uncle Robert. Are you sure we can't invite him to stay here for a few weeks before the trial?"

David was alarmed, Wendy kept bringing this subject up, probably to annoy him as she knew the answer to the question.

"You know we cannot invite Uncle Robert here until the trial is over."

Hopefully not even then, he thought.

"Firstly, one of the conditions of his bail is that he lives at his home address in Milford. Secondly, it would not be good idea for him to stay in his counsel's home. It might be thought I am far closer to him and less objective than I am."

Wendy grimaced slightly, "I don't think you could be more objective when it comes to Uncle Robert!"

David nodded in agreement but in reality, he was probably more subjective about Uncle Robert than most clients. He could not stand the man. Nevertheless, in his career he had come across many clients he could not stand, mostly sex offenders, particularly paedophiles, but he had still done his best. As he would tell anyone who was interested, he was a professional and it was important to him to do his best however revolting the crime or obnoxious the defendant was.

Thursday soon arrived and both David and Sara were seated in the offices of Granger and Heath in central Salisbury, sipping coffee and discussing the case with Henry Granger, Nashad's solicitor. David learnt that Henry was the firm's senior partner. David had a pleasant evening the night before with Sara having a large steak, far too many carbohydrate overloaded fried potatoes and they shared a bottle of Malbec. He and Sara had discussed the case for about twenty minutes before having the 'downtime' that Wendy had predicted, with chats about chambers, legal aid and other far more interesting matters.

Henry Granger was a man in his late forties. He had taken over the practice from his father who had run it for thirty-odd years before retiring in 2010. Henry had the jaundiced view of a great number of criminal solicitors and spent most of the pre-conference moaning about, what he called, 'the perilous state of legal aid' and how difficult it was to run a practice these days.

David did not disagree, but he wanted to discuss the case. If he wanted to have any further discussions on legal aid, he could spend the evening in Briefs sharing a couple of bottles of wine with Graham or another member of his chambers.

After half an hour, Uncle Robert entered the room. He looked at the gathering, gave a nod to David and then a great beaming smile to Sara. He took Sara's hand, bent to kiss it and told her it was such a delight to meet her.

David found the whole tableau revolting but saw no need to express his thoughts. Uncle Robert still thought he was in his twenties and could charm the ladies, not a man nearing eighty with the charm of a Boa Constrictor.

It actually annoyed him to see Sara apparently enjoying the attention of this fraudster.

After spending time chatting to Sara and admiring her 'business-like suit', he finally turned to David.

"David, it is good to see you, it looks like you have lost a little weight since I last saw you."

He paused before adding, "Though I can see you still have some way to go!"

Before David could reply, Uncle Robert asked, "How is my darling niece Wendy, and my wonderful little niece, or is it grand-niece, Rose."

David really did not want to be involved in small talk. There was a lot to cover in this conference as the trial had been booked for Monday 13th April 2020 and David did not want to make numerous trips to Salisbury in the next two months, certainly not to see Uncle Robert.

"They're fine Robert, now there are a few subjects I want to cover with you today about your case."

Nashad frowned, "David, we are in a professional setting now, I do wish you would use my chosen name, Nashad."

Henry Granger intervened, "We all refer to our client as 'Nashad' as it is his preferred name."

David loathed calling him Nashad, it was a reminder of how insufferable the man could be, but he did not want to appear churlish, especially in front of the solicitor.

"Of course, I temporarily forgot, Nashad. Now let's start by you telling me how you came across this mystery person, Lee Han Ong?"

CHAPTER 8

A MUCH NEEDED BREAK

The conference took most of the day with a break for lunch. In that time David was able to take Nashad through all the evidence that had been served to date including expert reports. Satisfied that he had received all the information he needed for now, Sara and he returned to London.

He knew from experience that the prosecution would serve extra evidence, but he felt he had enough instructions to deal with, or at least confront, all the evidence that had been served to date.

The trial was listed for 13th April 2020 with a two-week time estimate. David had another week's trial listed on Monday 23rd March which was a very well privately paid driving case. A rich businessman Roger Cooper was charged with causing death by careless driving whilst under the influence of drugs. He had approached a firm of solicitors who had a reputation for representing people on driving charges and charged accordingly and David had been fortunate enough to be briefed in the matter. The case would be nowhere near as complex as Uncle Robert's case, would take half the time but would pay at least four times as much. How he liked private cases, how he wished, like just about every other criminal barrister, he could attract more.

He had little to do in February and was not really looking for work. He did not want to take a case on that might run into his driving case and force him to return it. As a result, Wendy and he decided to take Rose abroad on a trip to the island of Madeira for a week. After his own diabetic scare and Wendy having dealt with Rose's poor health over parts of December and January, they both felt like they needed a holiday.

Wendy had chosen Reid's Palace in Funchal in Madeira and they had booked flights for 15th February. It was going to be expensive and strain their finances, but David thought they deserved it and he would soon be involved in a series of trials that would certainly help pay for the luxury.

Saturday 15th February 2020 came and went. Up until midnight on 14th February, David and Wendy were informed that the flight would still go ahead despite a pending storm, but shortly after midnight they were told there would be no flights because of 'Storm Dennis'. A ferocious storm that was going to ground all flights in Gatwick.

They were devastated. They had so looked forward to a break partly to celebrate St Valentine's Day but mainly because David had a series of trials over the next couple of months and might not get another chance for a break until much later in the year.

It was clear that obtaining a flight that week would be difficult but they were still keen to have a holiday and so they settled for a break in

Disneyland Paris which they could visit by the Eurostar. They could not get into one of the main hotels but could get into one that was a short distance from the park. In reality they thought Rose would probably prefer the experience of going to Disneyland Paris than visiting Madeira and that was some consolation.

They arrived in Disneyland Paris on Tuesday 18th February 2020 and had a fantastic break with Rose. Rose loved the basic children's rides, the Flying Dumbos, Pinocchio and Peter Pan and she loved having lunch in the 'Agrabah' Moroccan style café and then with a selection of Disney Princesses in the 'Auberge de Cendrillon'.

In all it was a great break but all too soon it was Friday, their last full day, as they had to catch the Eurostar at lunchtime on Saturday.

They had a late day in the Disneyland Park and then returned to the hotel. Although they were all tired, they decided to go into the hotel bar for a couple of drinks after dinner.

They seated themselves by the large window of the room looking out over the expansive hotel gardens complete with fountains. On the next table was a group of four British tourists with their children. They were quite loud and although David did not want to listen to their conversation, he could not avoid it.

He started to be more interested when one of the two women in the group said, "I lost 8 kilos of weight in just 4 weeks. I never dieted, I didn't reduce the amount I ate, didn't do any exercise, I just took a pill every day for four weeks."

The other woman in the group who was clearly overweight replied, "I need to take that pill, I've tried every diet out there, I joined a gym and have gone at least once a week for six months and I haven't lost any weight at all. In fact, I think I've put some weight on!"

She paused as she took a bite out of a large cream filled cake that was on a plate in front of her. Having devoured that piece of the cake she continued.

"Where can I get these miracle pills from?"

The first woman beamed as she replied, "I got them from a company called SLIM UK Ltd."

David was very interested in the conversation now. The second woman finished another bite of her cake and then asked, "Do you have an address for this company, I think I'll try them out. I cannot lose weight by dieting and exercise alone!"

She took another bite of the cake as the first woman looked at her and smiled.

"I do have an address at home, I know the company is in Salisbury, but I have to say, I tried to contact them recently but my email bounced back and the phone line seems to be dead."

The second woman finished off the cake. "That's a pity, I am so sure that pill would have helped me."

David raised his eyes. This was supposed to be a holiday and putting work behind him, but to find someone in Disneyland Paris, who might be able to assist Nashad's case was too good an opportunity to miss. Afterall, she seemed an example of someone who had taken the pills and had a success story, losing weight and not having any obvious side effects.

It was a strange world where if there had not been a storm preventing them from going to Madeira, followed by a decision to go to Disneyland Paris, a decision to go for a drink tonight and a decision to sit by the window, he might never had heard this. He supposed that was life. He turned around to face the woman.

"Excuse me, I wonder if I could have a quick word with you?"

The woman turned suddenly and looked shocked, her husband more so, but David quickly reassured them. He pulled up his chair to their table and joined them, explaining why he had approached them. He then asked if the lady might be willing to give evidence in court.

The shocked expressions that they wore when he joined them now changed into the looks of abject horror of British tourists abroad, suddenly confronted by a stranger talking to them.

CHAPTER 9

PANDEMIC

The holiday was over much too quickly and David, Wendy and Rose returned home the following day. David passed the details of Margaret Thompson, the lady he had met in Disneyland onto Nashad's solicitors, Granger and Heath so they could contact her and take a full statement.

Satisfied that he had done what he could he turned his mind to his driving case. The defendant, Roger Cooper, was a Chartered Accountant. He had a busy workload and often worked late into the night and then got up early to face the next day. He lived in Hove in East Sussex. On Wednesday 15th May 2019 he had got up at 6:15am and travelled to work at 7am. The journey should only take him about 30 mins to his offices in Worthing but unfortunately the journey required him to cross a mini roundabout. He had not expected anyone to be crossing the road at that time in the morning but sadly, Joshua Grant, a sixteen year old schoolboy had chosen to go to school early to be with some friends in an early morning club and he decided to cross the road just at the end of the mini roundabout rather than travel 20 metres down the road where there was a Pelican Crossing. Roger had taken the roundabout at 30mph and collided with Joshua throwing him

10 metres into bollard near the crossing. His head had hit the bollard and he had died at the scene.

The police had arrived and breathalysed Roger. That had proved negative, but a drugs test had proved positive for cannabis. Roger later gave blood and had a reading of 2.3mg/ml of blood which was over the prescribed limit of 2mg/ml of blood but because of analytical uncertainties the prosecution could not charge him with being over the prescribed limit and had charged him with being unfit.

Roger maintained he had one cannabis cigarette the night before at about 10am before he went to sleep. He also maintained that Joshua had stepped out in front of his car and there was nothing he could do.

The prosecution's accident reconstruction expert disagreed with the latter and the prosecution provided a drug expert's report to suggest that because Roger's reading was so high, he was unfit to drive through drugs at the time of the accident and therefore he was guilty of causing death by careless driving whilst unfit through drugs. It was not going to be an easy case.

The case was fixed for Monday 23rd March 2020 in Lewes Crown Court. David had advised early in the case that his solicitors should get their own experts, firstly an accident investigator and secondly an expert on the effects of cannabis. The first expert, Reginald Trainer had proved disappointing. He had a look at the initial papers in order to give a quote for a fee. He stated then that he believed that he could come up with some interesting points that might help the defence. However, once he was instructed, he took ages to come up with a report and when he finally did it simply agreed with the prosecution. The drugs expert was not much better although there was one paragraph in a twenty page report that might prove useful dealing with readings of heavy users of cannabis. It had stated that the active ingredient in cannabis was THC. In alcohol cases the elimination rates of alcohol from the body were usually the same in all people. This meant that a back calculation could be done from the time a reading was taken back to the time of the accident and thus an approximate reading could be obtained at the time of the accident to see whether someone was over the limit. However, in cannabis cases, THC elimination rates varied so much in people that it was not possible to do back calculations. That might assist David's cross examination of the prosecution's experts when the case came to court.

Since their return David had followed the news on covid 19 with increasing interest. He had changed his opinion about the virus as it had slowly taken a hold in the World. He read how on 29th February there were now over a thousand cases in Italy. On 1st March there were 36 cases in the United Kingdom which did not seem too many, but it looked like cases were increasing at an exponential rate around the World.

On 2nd March he read there were now 40 cases in the United Kingdom, but 89,000 cases in the World and 3,000 deaths. He now considered that covid 19 was nothing like the flu at all. It was far more deadly.

As the month progressed the news became more concerning. On 6th March the first death in the United Kingdom was recorded. By 12th March over 1,000 deaths were recorded in Italy. By 15th March the United Kingdom Government was taking the pandemic seriously and gave advice to self-isolate if you had symptoms. There were then 1,400 cases in the United Kingdom and 35 deaths.

On 15th March 2020, the Prime Minister announced, *"now is the time for everyone to stop non-essential contact and travel."*

Clearly this was getting serious and worrying.

On 17th March 2020 the news David had expected was announced, at first the Lord Chief Justice had stated that it is, *"of vital importance that the administration of justice does not grind to a halt"*, but on 17th March 2020, he made the announcement, that, *"no new trial should start in the Crown Court unless it is expected to last for three days or less. All cases estimated to last longer than three days listed to start before the end of April 2020 will be adjourned"*.

David was devastated. It was one thing to put Uncle Robert's case back, but to put back his privately paying driving case was potentially disastrous to his finances. He hoped that the cases would only be put back by a month or so, but he doubted it as Covid 19 did not look like it was going away.

On 18th March 2020 at 7pm evening, David received a phone call from his son, Robert. Robert was a doctor working in St Thomas' Hospital on the Covid ward. It was so rare that Robert phoned him that he was worried something had happened until Robert reassured him.

"No, I'm alright dad, I'm phoning about the coronavirus."

David was concerned again, "Why have you caught it?"

"Not yet, but it's probably a matter of time. We are running out of suitable PPE in the hospital."

David was getting used by now to his son using terms that David had no idea about.

"PPE?"

"It stands for Personal Protection Equipment, special masks, disposable gowns etc."

"Oh, so why the call? It's lovely to hear from you but I rarely get a call these days."

"I'm worried about you dad. This pandemic is really straining if not breaking the system. In South London on 6th March, we had just seven cases in ICU, the intensive care unit, but by yesterday, we had increased that number by thirteen fold to 93 in just 12 days. It all began last weekend and has just exploded since then. We've been told 86 of those 93 are on ventilators or have been intubated. Four of those are receiving, ECMO!"

David was definitely lost now.

"And what is that?"

"Extra Corporeal Membrane Oxygeneration. It's where blood is taken out of the body, oxygen is added to it and then it is put back into your body. It allows you to 'breath' without using your lungs.

David had never heard of this before, "And does it work?"

"We don't know yet."

Although fascinating, David was beginning to wonder why Robert had phoned him.

"This is fascinating Robert but why are you telling me all of this?"

"I'm worried about you dad. You are at risk, 62, you have asthma, you are overweight (David involuntarily looked down at his stomach and breathed in). It's dire out there dad, we have run out of protective gear, we are probably all infected, we lost a consultant to coronavirus the other day. He was only 40 and we intubated him and he died. Young people, in their 20s and 30s who were previously fit are on ventilators. Some of them won't survive.

We don't have enough beds, ventilators etc. Ventilators are barely good enough for one person, but we are running tubes from them to 2 or 3 patients! Dad you must avoid London, you must avoid crowds, you must avoid social contact."

The call had a sobering effect on David. It must be serious for Robert, who normally spent months ignoring him, to phone him. On the following day, 19th March 2020, David looked at the newspaper again, there were now 103 deaths in the United Kingdom with 2,640 cases, there were 8,800 deaths in the World with 218,000 cases. This was no longer merely serious, it was potentially catastrophic. The Prime Minister was now giving regular briefings. He stated on this day that the United Kingdom could, *'turn the tide of coronavirus'*, in 12 weeks. Having read the newspapers thoroughly, David started to think that was wishful thinking.

David started to worry less about his finances, despite their parlous state, and more about his health. Then on 23rd March 2020, the Prime Minister announced that people should stay at home and the Lord Chief Justice announced that there would be no new jury trials even ones of three days length or less. Existing trials would continue until they ended but there would be no more trials until further notice.

In a strange way, David was quite happy about this. It meant he was less likely to catch covid 19 by having to go to court. However, it also meant that he was not earning. He was still being paid because it took ages for the fees from his cases to come in, but soon there would be no new money coming in and yet bills still had to be paid.

He hoped the Prime Minister was right and this Pandemic would be over soon. However, it did not bode well when the Prime Minister was taken into intensive care on 5th April 2020 when he succumbed to what would prove to be a very bad case of covid.

CHAPTER 10

THE RELUCTANT BARRISTER

David looked at the clock on the wall in his kitchen. It was 17:04 on 11th May 2020. He wondered where the day had gone. He had stayed away from the courts and chambers meaning to do all those jobs at home which he had put off, "because I am too busy with cases".

That line had never really worked with Wendy and he could not use it now as there was really very little to do on his cases which had not even been given new dates yet.

The lockdown had been extended for three weeks on 16th April, which had not assisted David's waistline. He had listened to the prime Minister on 30th April when he had announced, *'we are past the peak'* of the pandemic. He had not really believed him. He had also listened to him the day before on 10th May 2020 when he announced a 'conditional' plan for lifting lockdown, encouraging people to go back to work but not take public transport. At least there was talk of vaccines being produced soon.

David wondered about the backlog of cases. The backlog had been growing pre-pandemic, in his opinion, because courts were being sold off and judges and parts time judges' sitting days had been reduced. He had heard the backlog was over 39,000 Crown Court cases in March 2020. It must be expanding exponentially now that courts were not sitting. At least he supposed there would be work available for the Bar for years to come, pity the remuneration could not be returned to the levels of years ago!

He checked the news on his phone and noted that day the Lord Chief Justice, Lord Burnett announced that a limited number of jury trials would recommence on 18th May 2020.

"It is important that the administration of justice continues to function whenever it is possible in an environment which is consistent with the safety of all those involved."

It did not overly concern David. It was unlikely he would have to risk catching covid by attending court. Neither of his outstanding cases were likely to start soon. Both defendants were on bail and he imagined that priority would be given to cases where the defendants were in custody. It seemed to him that the Courts worried more about Custody Time Limits (CTLs) than about trials. It was important to ensure that a trial started within the Custody Time Limit, though in practice the limits were often extended. David also imagined that only short cases of a few days or so would start first. Cases potentially lasting over a week would probably not be started for some months yet.

He did not dare look at his credit card statements or his bank account.

He contemplated his increasing bulk, his gym had closed which meant no swimming and staying at home had meant he had been eating and drinking more, purely out of boredom. He might not have to worry about covid, diabetes would probably get him! He resolved he must change. He must do those jobs he put off and he must do more exercise, even a few laps around the garden and the odd solitary walk to the park would be better than nothing, that is if the Government allowed him to leave his home!

Periodically David phoned up chambers to discover whether there was any private work out there that he could do. A private motoring plea of guilty in the Magistrates Court often paid more than a 5 day trial in the Crown Court and would certainly assist him. Sadly, he was always met with the same type of response from John who was also 'working' from home.

"Sorry Sir, I've got you very much in mind and I have been trying to steer some private work your way but unfortunately the solicitors are either not willing to pay enough to make it worth your while or they are asking for Mr Wontner."

I bet, was all that David could think. As usual the clerks' room was protecting the Head of Chambers at the expenses of others and most concerningly, himself.

He thought of looking in the newspapers and online to see if there were any reasonably paid jobs that he could do in the short term, but he soon dismissed the idea as impractical. He did listen to horror stories from several junior members of his chambers who were threatening to leave the Bar altogether because they stated they were close to bankruptcy. One even told him they were considering a job fruit picking in Kent in the summer as the pay was better than that of a junior barrister!

At least David had two good cases which he knew would eventually be good payers and he had some Court of Appeal work that he could do via computer screens using the new system adapted by the courts called the Cloud Video Platform (CVP). It would allow him to appear in the Court of Appeal and various other courts through a computer based in his study. Consequently, he knew that things would change at some stage, the only question was when?

CHAPTER 11

THE RELUCTANT DEFENDANT

The months passed slowly for David and probably even more slowly for Wendy who had David home for most of the time. Unbeknown to him he had started muttering a lot about finances and bills and she had to speak to him about it frequently.

Apart from a little exercise David had not really left the house during the first lockdown. He did conduct a few cases by CVP, but nothing particularly remunerative and certainly no jury trials.

Finances were tight due to covid restrictions, but the fact that they had not been able to dine out or travel anywhere and Wendy had not been able to go, 'essential clothes shopping' had reduced their expenditure such that in July 2020, they were able to afford a week's holiday in a hotel in Studland Bay in Dorset.

The hotel had recently reopened after lockdown and Wendy had been one of the first to book a large room for them with bed, breakfast and an evening meal.

The holiday was much needed after the covid lockdown and all three of them had enjoyed the good weather and excellent scenery. Rose had been particularly popular with the waiters and waitresses in the hotel and the three of them really enjoyed themselves, David and Wendy regretting that they had not booked the hotel for longer even though it would have been pushing their finances to the limit.

It was Thursday 30th July 2020 and they only had two days left before they left the beautiful Studland Bay Area. They had visited most of the local sights such as Corfe castle, Durdle Door, Lulworth Cove, Brownsea Island. They had spent time on the beach with little Rose, who thoroughly enjoyed herself making sandcastles with her father. He had enjoyed putting work behind him and just concentrating on an enjoyable family holiday. They were a little sad that they were leaving so soon but generally, all three of them were in a good mood, until Wendy's phone rang.

David watched Wendy's demeanour immediately change as he listened to an increasingly worrying conversation.

"What?"

"You're kidding?"

"He did what?"

"A Bulgarian lorry driver?"

"Dover?"

"In custody?"

"Is there any chance of bail?"

"Of course, he's with me now, I will put him on."

Wendy passed the phone to a bemused David, who whispered to her, "Who is it?"

She whispered back, "It's Uncle Robert's solicitor."

That was one name David did not want to hear on his holiday. Quickly analysing the comments, he had just heard it soon dawned on him what this call was about!

David spoke slowly into the phone.

"Hello, David Brant here."

The voice on the line was the familiar one of Henry Granger, Uncle Robert's solicitor.

"Oh, Mr Brant, good to hear your voice. I am so sorry for disturbing your holiday, but it is a bit of an emergency."

"Oh yes, what's has Uncle Robert done now?"

He did not feel like extending the courtesy of calling him Nashad when whatever he had done had disturbed David's holiday.

"I had wanted to call you first, but Nashad asked me to call his niece, your partner first. I think the Covid lockdown got to Nashad."

David grunted, "I think it's got to us all. What has he done though?"

"He was caught at Dover trying to leave the country."

"What?"

"I'm afraid so. He somehow managed to get a dodgy passport and then he persuaded a Bulgarian lorry driver to try and smuggle him out of the country in the back of his lorry."

"That's crazy, they have heat scanners and all types of electronic equipment these days at the ports to detect people being smuggled into and out of the country."

"He thought they would only have equipment to check on people being smuggled into the country rather than out of the country."

"I'm still surprised a lorry driver would take the risk. They confiscate the lorries these days, impose massive fines and imprison the drivers."

"The lorry driver was quite a young one, he started working for a company quite recently and no doubt thought he would take the risk for the right award."

David thought for a moment, he supposed that made more sense than an experienced lorry driver getting involved in smuggling a single person out of the country.

"So, what happened to Uncle Robert?"

"Nashad got stopped at Dover on a routine check apparently. He was arrested for breaching his bail conditions and has been remanded in custody awaiting a bail application."

"He's got no chance of bail having tried to skip the country in the back of a lorry with false documentation."

Henry sighed at the other end of the line.

"We know that David and I have explained that to him, but he wants you to make a bail application on his behalf."

"I'm on holiday until Saturday and I won't be back home before then. I supposed if you put the necessary paperwork into court and you can persuade them to list the case, I could make the application on Monday."

Henry hesitated before answering.

"Nashad did ask if we could list it tomorrow as he is worried about staying in custody over the weekend."

It was fortunate that Henry could not see David's expression. David paused for a few seconds before answering politely.

"I suspect he will be in custody for a lot longer than the weekend!

I regret it is simply not possible for me to make the application tomorrow even if you could get the case listed. I am on holiday; I do not have access to any secure computer equipment here and I am not able to return home before Saturday. I regret that he will have to wait until Monday, unless Chambers can persuade Sara to make the application?"

"No, he is quite insistent that you make it."

"Very well, then can you try to get the application listed on Monday and meanwhile send me Uncle Robert's full instructions on; why he did this, how he obtained a passport, where was he intending to go and how did he think he would fend for himself as a fugitive from British justice?"

CHAPTER 12

THE BAIL APPLICATION

On 7th August 2020 at 09:55, David found himself staring into his computer screen situated in his study. He was waiting to connect to the CVP system for his bail application for Uncle Robert. He had not quite got used to conducting hearings through his computer's built in camera and would have much preferred to attend court in person. It was difficult to judge the feel of the court or have pre-hearing discussions with the prosecution and a client through a computer camera system. In court he could have asked the prosecutor in advance of the hearing what the prosecution's objections to bail were and what those objections were based on. He would then prepare a response. Through the CVP system this was not possible and he would first hear the detailed objections at the same time as the judge and have to respond to them immediately.

In this case it was obvious to him what the objections would be and that he had a very limited response to them. In addition, at least he did not have to go the expense and time of travelling to Salisbury before the hearing, a travel time of 5 hrs, door to door and back.

At 09:56 David was into the system. He checked that his microphone and camera worked and noted the other 'guests'. His solicitor, Henry Granger, had signed in from his office conference room. David could see some of his Army paintings on the wall, no doubt to attract Court Martial work from the local Barracks near Salisbury plain, the Army's training area. David's junior, Sara, had signed in from her bedroom, her décor was somewhat more austere, with a plain blanket draped across some piece of furniture behind her. The officer in charge of the case, DC Sonya Sharpe was there although her camera was off and the sound was muted. Finally, the judge, His Honour Judge Reginald Gold QC, a Circuit Judge in Salisbury Crown Court, came into view, clearly seated in his chambers with a stern expression on his face suggesting, 'why arc you wasting my time'. David knew he would have an uphill task ahead of him.

The prosecutor, Lawrence Winder, the junior barrister instructed for the prosecution, addressed the judge first.

"Your Honour, I appear for the prosecution, my learned friend, Mr David Brant, Queen's Counsel, appears for the applicant. It is my learned friend's application, so maybe you would like to hear from him first?'

The judge responded immediately and sharply, "No, this is a contested bail application, I should like the prosecution to outline the facts of the case, the anticipated trial date and what the objections to bail are."

Lawrence cleared his throat which seemed amplified through the computer audio.

"Yes, of course. The case is a serious allegation of manslaughter. The prosecution case is that the defendant was the managing director of a company that was supplying a so called slimming aid to the public through the internet. The product was in fact DNP, an industrial fertiliser and explosive that is poisonous to humans. The Defendant's company supplied a number of pills containing DNP, 2,4 Dinitrophenal to several people who ordered them on the internet. One person, a body builder, called Jensen Willmott, ordered several shipments and took the DNP as a form of body sculpting.

As a result of taking this poisonous substance supplied by the defendant he died. The prosecution's case is that the defendant was well aware what this substance was, or at the very least, ought to have known what it was and that it was not fit for human consumption. There is clear evidence in this case that false packaging was used to disguise what the real product was. Nevertheless, despite this fact, the defendant supplied this poison to vulnerable people like Jensen Willmott, not caring what happened to them after they had taken the substance and the prosecution say he is guilty of gross negligence manslaughter."

Lawrence could be seen on the computer screen looking down at his notes before he continued.

"The prosecution object to bail on the basis that there are substantial reasons for believing that because of the serious nature of the charge, the strength of the evidence, the likely sentence and the fact he has already tried to leave the country illegally, the defendant will abscond before trial.

The defendant has no previous convictions and although he has spent most of his life outside the jurisdiction, he was a granted bail on a number of conditions, namely; he must reside at an address in Milford, he should surrender his passport, he should not apply for any travel documents, he should cooperate with his solicitor and provide full instructions and finally, he should attend court when required to do so.

He has breached a number of those conditions, either fully, or in an anticipatory fashion."

The judge looked up and stared at his screen, "Anticipatory breach!"

He frowned as he continued, "Surely that is a concept for the civil courts dealing with contracts, it's not a criminal concept!"

Lawrence did not react at all to the implicit reprimand but merely replied, "I meant it in the sense that if he had applied for a false passport, he was hardly likely to surrender it to the authorities and as he was found in the back of a lorry on the way to Bulgaria, it was clear he would not be appearing in court when required to do so."

The judge simply stared at his screen still frowning, so Lawrence continued.

"The defendant was stopped at Dover in the back of a Bulgarian lorry, headed for Sofia in Bulgaria. He was found in possession of false travel documents. It is clear he had no intention of remaining in the country and no intention of returning to the country for his trial, hence it is believed he will abscond again if he is granted bail again. Those are the prosecution objections to bail unless I can assist your honour in any other way?"

The judge ignored him and asked, "Mr Brant what are your submissions?"

David nodded, he could not be bothered smiling as the judge was either in a bad mood or constantly moody.

"Thank you, your honour. The prosecution has conceded an important point in this case, namely that the defendant is a man of good character with no criminal, convictions recorded against him anywhere. That is an important factor when assessing whether there are substantial reasons for believing he would abscond before trial."

Lawrence could be heard on the computer contemptuously clearing his throat.

The judge immediately intervened, "Mr Winder, are you ill?"

Lawrence looked surprised, "No, your honour."

"Then kindly be quiet whilst Mr Brant, Queen's Counsel, addresses me."

Lawrence stuttered a reply, "Y.. yes, your honour."

The judge now nodded to Lawrence.

"Thank you, now Mr Brant, kindly proceed."

David did acknowledge the judge with a smile this time. Maybe there was some history between the judge and his opponent that he was unaware of? Whatever it was, the judge was at least listening to David. He knew many who would not after a client had absconded.

"Thank you, your honour. I was about to point out that the defendant is 74 years of age and it is therefore doubly important that he has no criminal convictions recorded against him anywhere in the world despite being an accomplished traveller who has lived in many countries under many legal jurisdictions, many of which are highly restrictive.

Of course, it is right he did try to abscond. This was during the covid epidemic and was more out of panic than trying to avoid a trial. He is an old man; he has little family in the United Kingdom and none where he lives. He had a date for his trial and was ready to attend and fight to establish his innocence. However, Covid struck, with all the fear that has for people of his generation. The date for his trial was moved and no new date was set and, regrettably, a date still hasn't been set. He began to feel depressed, wondering whether he would ever be able to establish his innocence before his own demise.

At the height of his depression, he met someone, purely by chance, in a Public House. After a few drinks he explained his predicament and this person put him in touch with someone who was able to obtain false papers for him.

Blinded by depression he took the foolish course of dealing with a human trafficker who, for an exorbitant fee, most of the defendant's life savings, arranged the false papers and the transport. If he had thought through what was on offer, he would have realised, in this age of universal communication, there would have been nowhere he could flee to. He realises that now. It has been a painful and expensive lesson and not one he will ever repeat.

At his age, if he is not granted bail now, he may well die before his trial is ever listed. Of course, the court will be mindful of his recent foolhardy behaviour so I am suggesting that he be granted bail albeit on strenuous terms. Having an electronic tag is an obvious condition that would mean his whereabouts are constantly known. If a condition of residence is attached as well with a curfew, it is almost guaranteed that he will not abscond again and will await his trial whenever that might be."

The judge asked the parties to wait for ten minutes before he gave his ruling. To David that was promising, particularly as he had believed that his application would be dismissed immediately.

Ten minutes passed and David signed onto the system again. He had to wait another five minutes before the judge appeared on the screen.

"Mr Brant, I have thought long and hard about your application. At first blush, the fact that your client has already obtained false travel documentation and attempted to flee the jurisdiction, few would think any court would be open to granting further bail. However, you have made some valid points on behalf of your client; his good character, his age, covid, the fact that no trial date has been fixed yet. Of course, though I must weigh the points for the prosecution. This is a serious case; I cannot forget that someone died because of your client supplying them with a substance that the prosecution refers to as a poison and an explosive. If convicted, there will be a lengthy sentence which your client may not be able to fully serve because of his age. Along with his lack of family ties, the fact that he has spent a considerable amount of time outside this country in various jurisdictions where he has no doubt made contacts, makes him a flight risk.

I have consulted with my list officer and we can accommodate this trial in November this year. That at least defeats your point that your client has no idea when his trial may be heard.

In the circumstances, I will not grant your application for bail on the basis there are substantial grounds for believing your client will abscond before trial. However, the case will be listed for trial in November this year on a date that I trust is suitable for all counsel. That is my ruling.

I thank both counsel for their assistance in this matter."

With that the screen went blank.

CHAPTER 13

ANOTHER CONFERENCE WITH THE CLIENT

"I am deeply disappointed David. Did you really do your best? I think I should have been granted bail, particularly at my age and as I have no criminal convictions recorded against me anywhere in the world!"

David listened to Nashad whilst trying to control his own annoyance and rising anger. It was Friday 14th August 2020 and a prison conference by CVP had been arranged with Nashad at Winchester prison, as the prisons were still not allowing legal visits in person. It made preparing a trial difficult, but at least David had not had to travel miles for the conference and he was able to conduct the conference in his study at home. Sara was also in her own home, also appearing on the screen, so now the two of them could only communicate by text message using their mobile phones. David was already penning a few choice words to her as Nashad was speaking.

David had no need for such a conference at this stage and as Wendy, Rose and he were going away to Corfu the next day for a two-week holiday, he could have done without it. He had only agreed to this conference as a matter of decency in order to speak with Nashad to discuss the bail application and the future progress of the trial.

David continued to listen for a few more minutes as Nashad continued his tirade. David watched the solicitor on the screen carefully to see if there was any reaction from him. He could discern nothing from the solicitor's poker face and so he listened until Nashad finished.

"Nashad ...,"

How he hated to use that name but in the circumstances he felt he had no choice.

"... if you believe that I did not do my best for you or that I did not advance every argument on your behalf, there is a simple choice. You can sack me and find another counsel to conduct your trial. I have plenty of other work that I can conduct if that is what you want."

Obviously at the time with covid drastically limiting court appearances, David meant that he had plenty of decorating work and other jobs around his home that he could get on with, not cases, but there was no need to spell that out to Nashad.

David could see Nashad's demeanour visibly change with his comments. Nashad clearly wanted to rant, to pass blame to someone else for his own behaviour, not to change counsel and potentially end up with one who might not be as good as David. At least he knew with David that David would be thinking of Wendy's reaction if he was convicted and he thought that David may go the extra distance to ensure that did not happen. He would not have that advantage with any other barrister.

David could see Nashad thinking and so he decided to press the matter.

"Indeed, if you feel that I have not represented your interests to the best of my ability, or put forward every possible argument, I am probably professionally embarrassed and must withdraw from the case myself."

With that David leaned forward to the computer as if to turn it off.

Nashad reacted quickly, "No, no, forgive me David, I am an old man getting on in years and do not fully understand the predicament I am in, or why I am in it!

I do not doubt for a moment that you did your best and advanced every argument you could. I just feel there has been a miscarriage of justice and quite frankly, I just do not know how I will cope being incarcerated for such a long time before trial."

David looked at him sternly but then seemed to mellow.

"I understand Nashad, it cannot be easy for someone who has led such an open life to have to deal with incarceration, particularly with the risks and disadvantages of covid to deal with.

However, I do have to make it plain; it was never likely that you would get bail from any judge with any advocate representing you. This is a very serious charge, only one less than murder.

Judges are reluctant to grant bail in the first place in case someone does abscond and the newspapers blame the judge for releasing them on bail. In your case, you had absconded and you obtained a false passport. In addition to manslaughter, you have been charged with breach of bail and an offence under section 4 of the Identity Documents Act 2010. The latter case has a maximum sentence of ten years and almost always carries a sentence of imprisonment on conviction."

Nashad tried to say something, but David stopped him.

"Please, let me continue. I understand what you say about the reasons why you absconded; the panic, the fear, the difficulty of being on your own in what to you, must seem like a foreign country. However, although it is perhaps understandable why you felt the need to run, it made it almost impossible for any judge to take a chance and grant you bail. The only good thing that has come out of this is that we have an early date for a trial. We could have been waiting until mid-2021 otherwise."

"But at least I would have been on bail!"

"Yes, if you had not absconded, you would be and you would have had to wait a lot longer before this case was resolved. Now I know you will want this case to be over with as soon as possible."

Nashad was silent for a few seconds before adding, "Yes David, but with the right result. I never killed anyone. I never intended anyone to die. All I wanted was for people to benefit from a substance that I thought was a safe slimming aid."

David put as much compassion in his voice as possible when he replied, "Yes Nashad, I know what your defence is to this charge and we will seek to persuade the jury that you are not guilty of this very serious charge.

Now let's get on with the conference, there are several issues we need to deal with. The first one is your breach of bail and the passport offence. We need to get rid of them as soon as possible. You have no defence to those charges and you should plead guilty as soon as possible to get the maximum credit, potentially up to one third credit. I am going to suggest that the case be listed as soon as possible for you to enter a plea of guilty to those two offences. Don't worry, you won't be sentenced straight away, the judge will wait until the end of the trial before sentencing you.

I must tell you the sentencing guidelines suggest a sentence of 12-18 months for the passport offence. With an early plea we might be able to get that down to 8-12 months of which you will do half.

Nashad looked horror stricken.

"Is there no technical defence we can mount."

He thought for a moment, "For example, I was temporarily insane?"

David's mind wandered for a moment as he contemplated the word, 'temporary', but no, putting aside his own view of the sanity of Nashad he replied, "There are no technical defences available for you Nashad. Your only option is to plead guilty and to do it as soon as possible."

CHAPTER 14

A WELCOME BREAK

David picked up his Corfu beer, sipped from the bottle, rearranged himself in his hammock and looked at his phone. It was Sunday 23rd August 2020 and Wendy; Rose and he had already spent a lovely week in Corfu. Restrictions had been lifted in England and they had been able to obtain flights to Corfu without too much hassle and they had also obtained a villa at a very reasonable cost, probably because fewer people were travelling abroad because of covid. At least that was one advantage of this appalling epidemic.

Corfu had been idyllic after suffering what seemed an interminable lockdown in England. The island had not suffered many covid cases to date and certainly not many deaths and even though shop and restaurant staff all wore masks, many of the locals he met seemed a little blasé about it all. One local man joined Wendy, Rose and he at dinner, uninvited, and subjected them to a diatribe stating that he had not heard of anyone dying from covid and did not believe it was that serious. David tried to correct him, pointing out the number of deaths in Great Britain but he had not changed his annoying stance and had then flirted with Wendy when David got up to settle the bill calling her 'angel eyes.'

Funny, thought David to himself, that's the first time I have met a local in Corfu that I do not like!

They had not seen much in Corfu. As usual they were staying in the Arillas area in northwest Corfu. Trips to see the Roman site of Butrint or the mineral lakes in Albania were not available and indeed there was very little else available to see which had at least limited their expenditure to meals and drinks which were considerably cheaper than the same would be in the United Kingdom.

Despite being considerably cheaper than normal, Corfu had stretched the family finances with the limited court work at the moment and therefore the sparse amount of money coming into the family finances, but David had decided that the family's mental, as well as their physical wellbeing, needed a break and Wendy had also contributed the majority finance to the vacation by using money that a maternal Aunt had given her, apparently worried that she might succumb to covid and the tax man might take most of her money in inheritance tax. He was so glad they had all decided to go on this holiday and was rather unhappy that within a few more days it would all come to an end and he would probably return to a self-imposed lockdown.

Uncle Robert had for the most part been put out of his mind. Wendy had raised the case quite a few times, mainly trying to see what the latest position was and what David thought about the trial and Uncle Robert's chances. However, David had refused to be drawn on detail, not for reasons of confidentiality but simply because he wanted to put the case and in particular, Uncle Robert, out of his mind. Fortunately, Wendy finally got the message.

As far as he was concerned Uncle Robert did not exist on this holiday. He had never liked the man and representing him had not changed that position. Of course, when the time came, he would do his best for him, David was after all a professional, but that time was not now. It therefore came as a bit of a shock as he read a news story on his phone that referred to DNP poisoning.

This was his holiday, he was not sure when his next one would be and he deeply wanted to ignore the article, but he could not.

As he delved deeper into the story, his demeanour changed. He was no longer relaxed and the Corfu beer no longer had that pleasant taste and relaxing feeling.

The article was by a news reporter, Romy Greer, reporting on a recent case in the United Kingdom of another young man, Nicholas Hurst, who had taken DNP. It had photographs of him and his family, taken before he took DNP and then a photograph of his gravestone surrounded by his grieving family with a heading, "Who's next?"

Nicholas was only 23 but had been obese since childhood. He had been subjected to both verbal and physical attacks from other children throughout his schooling and his young adult life and had decided to do something about it. He had come across a 'miracle slimming aid' and had lost many pounds within a short time of taking it. However, he, like Jensen Willmott, had taken a large amount and within days had died of DNP poisoning as his organs had failed. The article stated that the DNP was obtained through the internet, through a man called Brian Butler, situated in Bristol, and that he stated he obtained his supplies through a Chinese salesman who originated from Hong Kong.

With some difficulty, David negotiated his way out of his hammock and went to sit by a table near the villa's pool. He left his beer behind. All semblance of relaxation had gone, he was now interested in this article and its author, Romy Greer.

He noted that the article had been syndicated to a few National newspapers and therefore a wide number of people from around the United Kingdom might have read it. Uncle Robert's case was less than three months away so potential jurors may have also read the article and may remember it when they tried him. Also, the Chinese connection could well be Lee Han Ong. It was not clear from the article whether Nicholas Hurst died before or after Jensen Willmott, either way, if Lee Han Ong was involved in this case it meant that he had probably carried on with his business after knowing someone had died from taking his product. David would need someone to investigate this in case it might show Uncle Robert was just an innocent dupe as he claimed.

Wendy came out of the villa and at first headed towards the hammock with a tray of selected fruit. She stopped when she saw David had moved and looked at him. She could see he was no longer the relaxed individual she had seen over the last few days. He was clearly concentrating on something important.

She knew David well. The only matter that was likely to get him out of that hammock was probably something to do with one of his cases. As far as she was aware, the only case he had on now was Uncle Robert's. It had to be something to do with that. She smiled to herself as she sidled over to the table. A few choice questions and no doubt all would be revealed!

CHAPTER 15

RESEARCH

"It is quite interesting, David," said Sara in a scholarly fashion. It does appear that Lee Han Ong has been behind several DNP companies. He is always a silent partner and when his partner is arrested either under the Food and Drugs Legislation, or for something more serious, like manslaughter, he disappears and creates another company with another director to front it."

David returned from his holiday two weeks earlier and had immediately contacted both Sara and Henry Granger and asked them to find out what they could about Nicholas Hurst's case in Bristol. Both had made enquiries and now all three of them were together in David's room in chambers discussing their research.

Henry butted in, "Sara is right, it could blow this case wide open."

David smiled, in forty years at the Bar he had never seen a case, 'blown wide open' by defence evidence, though he had seen cases where it made a difference, sadly a difference in both ways and usually in favour of the prosecution! Nevertheless, maybe this was one of those rare cases where it might make a difference to Nashad's defence case?

Henry continued to speak without reading or even being aware of David's thoughts.

"It's clear that this Lee Han Ong is heavily involved in this business and sets up company after company and then gets innocent dupes, like Nashad, to run it for him."

David thought that was going a little too far in Nashad's case, but he said nothing as Henry continued.

"It appears that he got a chap in Bristol called Brian Butler to front a company like Nashad's which supplied DNP to people who wanted to slim. Lee Han Ong took most of the profits but left Butler to be prosecuted. Butler claimed that he had no idea what the product was but believed it was a slimming aid. Do you think we should take a witness statement from him?"

David paused before replying, reading a note that Sara had made.

"I note here that Brian Butler was convicted of manslaughter. That does make a difference to the case. A jury did not believe his, 'innocent dupe' story then and our jury are not going to believe it now Butler has been convicted.

Despite the obvious logic in these comments, Henry was not going to let go of what he saw was a good point.

"No, but if they had known of Nashad's case, the verdict might have been different!"

David shook his head, "We cannot establish that as a fact and the trial judge would not let

Butler's case be tried at the same time. At the moment all we have is a man was convicted of manslaughter as a result of supplying DNP as a slimming aid. On its own, that fact helps the prosecution in Nashad's case."

He could see the crestfallen look on Henry's face. He could also see that Sara looked a little disappointed so he quickly added, "However, as Sara says, it is interesting that Lee Han Ong was involved and it shows that he was heavily involved in supplying DNP and continued to do so after he was aware people were dying from taking it. That is a good point we can make in Nashad's defence and that fact may well assist his case."

David turned to another subject. "I have been contacted by the prosecution Silk in Nashad's case. He has said there is some more evidence on the way that makes interesting reading and could make a considerable difference to Nashad. However, he wouldn't be drawn on what it says but told me we can expect it any day. Do either of you have any idea what it is?"

He could see from the blank expressions from both Sara and Henry that neither had any idea before they both verbally confirmed this was the case. They would have to wait until the Crown Prosecution Service uploaded the material to see what it was and whether it would make, a 'considerable difference' to the defence case.

CHAPTER 16

NEW DEVELOPMENTS

They did not have to wait long before they discovered the extent of the new evidence. The Crown Prosecution Service uploaded a further tranche of evidence to the system. On 9th September 2020, David received a notification on the system that there was further material available, the notification system did not always work so he was lucky this time. He poured himself a large cup of filter coffee made from a machine that Wendy bought him as a Christmas present and settled down to read them. Within an hour he had finished reading all the statements and the exhibits referred to in them. There was no doubt, the evidence raised his concerns about Nashad's defence.

Early in the case police sent Nashad's company computer off for interrogation by a computer expert, Dr Clark Roberts. Due to his heavy backlog of work, it had taken months before a report was prepared. There was then a further delay whilst the Crown Prosecution Service considered the report before then sending it to prosecution counsel for their consideration and then finally uploading it to the system.

Within two days of receiving the report, Sara, with her usual efficiency, created a document that referred to all the emails in date order, with a column linking the emails to other evidence in their case and then with a further column with her detailed comments. As usual, David found her work very useful and it saved him a great deal of reading, searching and noting the evidence himself.

On 18th September 2020, David had another conference by CVP with Nashad at Winchester Prison. As usual there was a wait until the computers connected and until David could see a small image of Nashad on a screen in a booth surrounded by smaller images of Sara, Henry Granger and himself.

After the usual attempted pleasantries, immediately followed by Nashad complaining about being, 'incarcerated with common criminals', David began the conference. He dealt with all aspects of the previously served evidence that he had noted after the last conference, before moving onto the email evidence.

"Nashad, you know that further evidence has been served relating to a search of your computer."

Nashad quickly interrupted, "It's not my computer David."

David looked at him, hiding a slight degree of annoyance.

"It does not matter whose computer it is, Nashad, the evidence relates to the emails found on that computer and those emails relate to you and Lee Han Ong."

Nashad shook his head vigorously, "I know nothing about any emails. I am being set up David, you must protect me."

David looked at the video image of Henry Granger, "Nashad has been sent the latest evidence, hasn't he?"

Henry nodded, "Oh yes, and I provided a covering note detailing the important emails."

David turned back towards the image of Nashad.

"Nashad, the emails are clearly between you and Lee Han Ong. They refer to the business and obtaining supplies of the 'slimming products'; they refer to the source of the product, how to use a device to place the powder in capsules, how you should disguise them when you supply them and more importantly in two of those emails, Lee Han Ong refers to the product as DNP!"

Nashad put his head in his hands, "David, I swear I have never heard of DNP. These emails must be fake. The prosecution has clearly fabricated them to make their case stronger against me!"

David tried to keep his poker face but was finding it more difficult with the absurd stance that Nashad was taking.

"Nashad, it is abundantly obvious these emails are genuine and have not been fabricated. The prosecution's expert has viewed them in detail and has checked the background data relating to them."

Nashad looked alarmed, "Perhaps he is part of the attempt to frame me, David?"

David immediately responded, "Dr Clark Roberts is a respected expert who deals with thousands of cases for both the prosecution and defence. He is not going to jeopardise his career by fabricating emails in a case against you."

Nashad shook his head, "You never know David, he may have done it before?"

David frowned, "Nashad, if we are to have any chance of securing an acquittal in this case we do not want to embark on a hopeless defence or fanciful arguments. Yes, people have been framed in the past; yes, evidence has been fabricated, no doubt some experts have exaggerated evidence and no doubt a few have lied, but this is not one of those cases. If we suggest that the prosecution and their expert has fabricated evidence against you, the jury will reject that out of hand and will assume you are lying and that nothing else you say can be trusted. The result will be a conviction for manslaughter and you will spend a large number, if not all, of your remaining years behind bars.

I want you to be realistic in your responses. Look at the messages closely. Did you read them at the time, did you fully understand them, did you even care what was in them?"

Nashad hesitated before answering. "I am sorry David, Sara, Henry. I panicked. The truth is all these emails are genuine. The truth, and I hope you believe me, is that I was only interested in receiving a good return on my investment. I believed this was a miracle slimming aid. The letters, 'DNP' meant nothing to me. I had never heard of it, nor did I have any idea what it was, nor did I check. I followed the instructions about putting the powder into capsules, measuring it carefully using an industrial machine that filled several hundred capsules at a time. I followed the instructions about the false labelling because I thought there would be less hassle and no problems about red tape. Not once did I believe this was a munition, an explosive powder or heaven forbid, a poison. At all times I thought it was a genuine slimming aid. I thought I was helping people, not killing them.

David nodded and after dealing with a few other matters he ended the conference. Just as he was about to leave Nashad put his hand on David's arm.

"Are you alright David?"

David muttered, "Fine, thanks."

"It's just I have noticed that your neck seems swollen on the left side, the veins appear to stand out. I have heard that is a sign of high blood pressure, 'a silent killer'. You may want to get your health checked out."

David thanked him and involuntarily touched the left side of his neck. He did not notice anything but, nevertheless, he did start to worry a little as he noticed Sara and Henry staring at the left side of his neck.

CHAPTER 17

MORE HEALTH CONCERNS

Although David felt fine, he decided that a trip to the doctors might be worthwhile. The earliest he could obtain an appointment was at 9:15am on Thursday 8th October 2020 and he decided to couple it with a trip to chambers as he had not been in to see his clerks for a very long time.

He was not able to see his favourite doctor, Dr Rachel Best, he was instead given an appointment with his least favourite, Dr Thornton. He took the appointment because although he did not like to admit it, Nashad's comments had got to him.

He attended the surgery fully masked. He was concerned that someone with covid might appear there and he did not want to take any chances.

He took a seat near to Doctor Thornton's room and looked around at the other patients who were there. Some looked distinctly ill, others looked well. He uncharitably thought they probably wanted another certificate so they could miss work until he remembered that he looked well and was only there for a routine check-up.

As he waited, he looked at his phone and started typing in 'high blood pressure' onto his search engine just to see what it came up with. He was concerned to see that Nashad's description of it as a 'silent killer' was correct. He read that it puts extra strain on your blood vessels, heart, brain, kidneys and eyes and that persistent blood pressure could increase the risks of heart attacks or strokes.

He quickly looked at ways of reducing high blood pressure and was reading through a list when after a fifteen minute wait he was called into Dr Thornton's room.

He entered the room and smiled at the doctor and was about to say hello when Dr Thornton said, in a bored matter of fact way, "What's the problem?"

David was not taken aback at the abruptness of this question, he was used to Dr Thornton.

"Well, I am slightly worried that I might have high blood pressure."

If it was possible to look more bored, Dr Thornton achieved it as she replied, "Very well, let's test you then. You do know that you can buy your own very good blood pressure monitors, don't you?"

David nodded a response as Dr Thornton applied a cuff to David's left arm and then used an electric machine to inflate it.

She did this twice before announcing, "This is not good, this is not good at all. Your readings were 164/85 and 159/84. They should be 120/80 or less."

She thought for a moment before asking, "Are you particularly stressed at the moment?"

David replied jokingly, "Only being here!"

Dr Thornton looked right through him. "I will write up a prescription for twenty eight, five mg tabs of Amiodipine. You must take one a day to reduce your blood pressure."

David nodded and asked, "How long for?"

She looked at him with surprise that he had asked such a stupid question.

"Forever."

David paused for a few seconds.

"Is there an alternative, a change in lifestyle for example? Before coming here, I read that reducing salt intake, reducing alcohol intake, increasing exercise, increasing the amount of potassium you have and drinking beetroot juice might help?"

Dr Thornton frowned at him.

"There is no alternative. You have come here for my medical opinion, you have received it. I have sent your prescription direct to your local pharmacy that is recorded on my system so you can collect it today and start taking the pills today. Gooday."

David felt summarily dismissed as if he was some schoolchild. He left the surgery distinctly feeling that Dr Thornton was either married to one of the heads of a pharmaceutical company or had a large number of shares in such an industry and that she had taken a PHD in poor bedside manners.

He decided that he would obtain the prescription, just in case he needed it, but he was determined to try out everything he had read about first and he was going to buy his own blood pressure monitor so he could check his own levels every day and see whether he did need the pills. He did not want to visit Dr Thornton again in a hurry.

As he had planned, he then made his way to chambers thinking as he went that the clerks better not get on his wrong side today.

CHAPTER 18

A NAME FROM THE PAST

David left the doctor's surgery and made one of his very few forays into his chambers. There seemed little point these days. If there was any work available for him, he would usually receive a phone call and be able to download the papers securely from the internet. He wondered why criminal barristers were paying exorbitant rents for their rooms in the Temple or one of the other Inns when, in reality, they did not need them.

In the past rooms were needed because they contained chamber's library and research could be conducted or conferences with clients could be organised. If chambers did not have a legal publication that the barrister needed, the Temple law libraries were nearby and they were almost certain to have a copy. There was also the sociable element. Barristers could meet up after a stressful day and have a drink or two, boring each other silly with details of their difficult day in court and the difficult judges they had to deal with. Now though; with almost all criminal cases being put on the Court digital system and easily downloaded, large numbers of conferences taking place on CVP or actually in a prison, or, if the client was on bail, in a solicitor's office, virtually all chambers subscribing to a digital library with up to date publications and the advent of covid reducing the ability and interest to socialise, he could see little point in paying rent for spacious rooms in chambers. If the barristers needed to meet personally to discuss anything important, such as sacking dishonest clerks, (often a barrister's favourite subject), they could always hire a large office space for a day.

Nevertheless, he was paying a large percentage of his income to chambers and he decided to attend them today, mainly because his original reason was that he wanted to get out of his home. His place seemed to get smaller with covid and he almost felt like the walls were moving closer together. He had an added reason now; he was in a bad mood after seeing Dr Thornton and he wanted to think about it before returning to Wendy and Rose.

He arrived in chambers at 11:30am and saw the usual hive of activity in the clerks' room. He wanted to ask what they were all doing, but knowing there would be no sensible or credible answer, he restrained himself.

He gave a friendly wave to the clerks, noticing that John Winston was on the phone with a stern look on his face. He seemed to brighten his expression when David walked in and returned his wave. David walked away from the clerks' room and made his way to his room. Chambers seemed empty of barristers now and so he did not have to share his room with anyone, which was a blessing considering his present mood.

He had not seated himself for more than a couple of minutes before John appeared with a beaming smile. David was immediately concerned, if John was smiling it was not usually good news for David. He did not have time to ask why his clerk looked so happy before John volunteered the answer.

"Good to see you Mr Brant. I've got some good news for you."

David looked cautiously at him but did not speak. In fact, he was not given the chance as John quickly blurted out.

"You remember Jimmy Short. He was a good client of ours and provided us with a lot of good quality, well paid work."

David frowned a little, he remembered the odious little man too well. John pretended to ignore David's grimace and continued.

"Anyway, Jimmy Short finds himself in a bit of a trouble. He's being investigated by the SRA. A completely false allegation!"

David's expression changed so, finally Jimmy Short was being investigated by the Solicitors Regulation Authority. It was about time.

"That is good news," replied David.

It was John's turn to frown.

"That's not the good news, sir!"

David looked surprised, "So what is?"

"Jimmy remembers all the hard work you carried out for his clients and the many acquittals you got for him. He has asked if you can represent him. He says he's been charged by the Authority with improperly withdrawing, or allowing to be withdrawn, money from his firm's client account. He says the allegations are false and completely outrageous and if any money was taken by accident, it has been, or will be, repaid.

He said he's been fitted up by others in the firm who want rid of him and he needs a good advocate to represent him."

David did not answer but looked stunned as John continued.

"He won't be able to pay you, but he says that if you succeed in getting the charges dismissed, you will never have to look for another brief. Every murder, every large-scale fraud, every decent private case, will be sent your way. It will be good for you and good for chambers."

David continued to look stunned as John waited for a response. He did not have to wait for long.

"John, this is a great opportunity for chambers."

He paused before continuing, noticing John's appreciative smile.

"We can now get rid of that odious little creep and will never have to work for him again! As far as I am concerned Jimmy Short should have been before a Solicitor's Disciplinary Tribunal years ago and struck off. He is a horrible little man and in my experience, he cannot be trusted about anything. Whenever I have had to work for him, I have felt deeply concerned about his conduct. Whenever I have met him, I have always felt the need to have an immediate and lengthy hot shower.

However, little work I might have in the future, there are no circumstances I ever want to work for him again. It follows that there are absolutely no circumstances in which I would represent him before a regulatory tribunal, indeed, if asked, I would willingly give evidence against him!"

It was John's turn to look surprised. In his opinion, yes, Jimmy Short was an acquired taste, but he had come across a lot worse in his career as a criminal clerk. He wondered whether to try and argue with David but he could see from the latter's expression that would be pointless.

Eventually after thinking for a few seconds, John asked, "I suppose that means you wouldn't like to write a letter on his behalf about his good character?"

CHAPTER 19

A TRIP TO SALISBURY

The train was eerily quiet. David was the only passenger in his carriage and he felt strangely alone as if on some ghost train in a 'B' horror movie. It was Sunday 8th November 2020 and he was on his way by train to Salisbury to conduct Uncle Robert's trial which was due to start the following day. There had been one other hearing in the case on 25th September 2020 when Nashad had pleaded guilty to breach of bail. Sara had covered that hearing and David had stayed at home as both of them were not required for a simple plea to be entered.

On 31st October 2020, a second national lockdown had been announced by the Prime Minister, Boris Johnson, to prevent a 'medical and moral disaster', for the National Health Service. The only people excluded from this lockdown were 'key workers', which of course mainly referred to hospital staff but which included barristers conducting trials. The trains were still running a service but few people were using them now which was why he was all alone on the two and a half hour journey between his home and Salisbury.

At just after 5pm he arrived at Salisbury station and hailed a taxi to his hotel, the Royal Grange Hotel situated in the High Street. He was happily surprised there were any taxis there in a lockdown, but in fact there were several of them.

Presumably the taxi drivers were hoping for customers, rather than expecting them.

The journey took him from the station and passed some of the famous and some of the recently infamous sites of Salisbury. The Cathedral looked splendid in the distance, but the restaurants and pubs involved in the Skripal poisoning, less so. The poisoning of the Russian defector and his daughter was still a raw subject in Salisbury and the taxi driver grimly pointed out the various sites affected by it during the journey. David made a mental note not to dine or drink in any of these places if they did open for service during the trial.

The taxi soon arrived at the hotel and David disembarked out of the taxi and watched it promptly drive away. He was then a little perplexed to note there were no lights on in the hotel and he could not see anyone manning the reception through the glass doors. He approached the door and tried to push it open. The door would not move and he began to wonder if he had the right hotel or worse, the hotel owner had changed their mind and decided not to accept guests.

He put his suitcase down and walked around the outside of the hotel looking for any signs of life. He peered through windows, hopeful that he would not frighten any guests. Eventually he saw an A4 sign outside the hotel, with a painting of a massive Manor House which did not resemble the building at all. Underneath in bold writing were the words, "The Royal Grange."

At least this is the right place he thought. He approached the doors again and this time saw a small note, with very small writing, which had been sellotaped to the inside of the glass door. He peered at it and used the torchlight on his phone to read it. He noted it gave a mobile number and a request to call this number if a guest wanted to enter the hotel. He did so and got through to a manager who said she would be with him in a few minutes.

After five minutes a large, heavy set, red-faced lady appeared on the other side of the reception door breathing heavily. She had clearly been running so he immediately told her to rest, there was no hurry. She thanked him and then opened the reception door.

"Good evening, I'm Mrs Barry, the owner of the 'Royal Grange', you must be Mr Brant?"

David returned her greeting and asked, 'Yes I am, how did you know?"

Mrs Barry looked serious for a moment, "I am afraid you are our only guest and will be so for the foreseeable future. I really don't know how we are going to survive yet another lockdown."

David looked sufficiently concerned for her even though he was desperate to get into his room and use the facilities.

Mrs Barry ushered him in and then explained everything to him.

"As you are our only guest, we won't be manning reception, so if you want to get into or out of the hotel, you will need to call my mobile, the number you just called. Also, I am sorry to say that because of lockdown the kitchens are not open so there are no evening meals, but if you wish, I can provide a breakfast for £5. It will consist of cereal, milk, coffee, fruit juice, two slices of toast, butter and marmalade. Would you like that?"

Not sure where he was going to get food for the next two weeks, David readily agreed.

"I have got some good news, as you are our only guest, we have upgraded you to our best room, it's a double room overlooking the courtyard."

It sounded delightful and David looked forward to the opulence it offered. However, he was somewhat disappointed to find that the room was quite small and the courtyard was even smaller. When he looked out of the window, he was staring at a brick wall, barely 6 feet away from his bedroom window and over a 'courtyard' that consisted of two or three paving stones and some dying plants.

He immediately asked, "Is this your best room?"

Mrs Barry looked at him sweetly. "Oh yes, it is, you should see some of the other rooms, they are so small I am sometimes embarrassed to let them out. I am so glad we were able to upgrade you for your stay with us."

Leaving David with a bemused expression she immediately left his room and he settled down to what promised to be a long night.

CHAPTER 20

NASHAD'S TRIAL

"You will do your best for me, won't you David?"

David, Nashad and Sara were seated in one of the smallest cells David had ever been in. There were three small seats and a table that was no more than two feet across. Sara and David were cramped on one side of the table and Nashad was on the other. So much for social distancing, thought David, hoping no one had covid.

"Of course, we will do our best for you Nashad. We are professionals and it is our duty to do our best for every client, whatever they are charged with, rest assured that we will."

Nashad did not look his usual self. He was beginning to have a 'prison pallor'. Months of incarceration particularly during covid were clearly taking their toll. He looked older and more tired than David had ever seen him before and it was noticeable that he coughed a little. In view of covid, David involuntarily tried to move further away but it was impossible in this small cell to move back further than a couple of inches.

David had to ask the question.

"Nashad, have you had a recent covid test?"

Nashad looked surprised at the question. "David I am lucky to get anything approaching edible in prison, never mind have 'luxuries' like covid tests!"

David nodded, it was probably too late to worry about covid.

"Nashad, we are going to start today. The jury will be picked first. You are told you have a right to object to any of them but that is only for what's called 'cause'. In other words, we must have a good reason to object to a juror. As we are not told anything about the panel of jurors and are not allowed to ask them any questions, it is almost impossible to object to any of them unless you know one of them. So please do not object to anyone unless you recognise them. Otherwise, we will have a disgruntled juror trying your case who feels some resentment towards you because you unsuccessfully challenged them!

Nashad nodded, and added, "Do not worry David, I am willing to be guided by you on these matters."

David smiled, Nashad seemed to be a lot more helpful that usual. Probably his incarceration had mellowed him.

"Nashad, there are a few matters I want to deal with. Firstly, the trial will commence by the prosecutor 'opening' the case. That just means that he will address the jury, introduce the parties and then tell the jury what the prosecution case is referring to the evidence he will call before them.

He will then start calling the evidence. He will call the witnesses and then ask them questions and then I will get an opportunity to ask the witnesses any questions I have."

Nashad gave David a puzzled look.

"What about your opening speech David? You have not mentioned that. I think it essential that you tell the jury as soon as possible what my defence to this appalling charge is."

David nodded, "I tend to agree with you. In complex cases I believe the defence should be able to address the jury at the start of a trial and tell them what the defence is so they know what to look for as they hear the evidence. Sadly though, that is not the case in England and Wales unlike in the United States. If you have ever watched court dramas from the United States on television, you often see defence counsel making defence opening speeches in those programmes. We are not allowed to make such speeches in this country, save in exceptional circumstances, such as cases that are going to last for months. Your case does not fall into that bracket and I will not be allowed to make an opening speech."

Nashad looked crestfallen. He pondered what David had said, thought for a few seconds and then commented.

"David, it seems to me that I cannot have a fair trial. I fear the jury will simply convict me because someone died, even though that had nothing to do with me."

CHAPTER 21

THE TRIAL COMMENCES

At 10:45am all the parties were in court when the trial judge, Mrs Justice Laura Monteith QC came through the judges' entrance followed by her clerk, Joanne Lewis. Noticeably both wore covid masks.

Joanne carried the judge's computer into court and set it up and then moved the judge's chair for the judge and then pushed it in when the judge sat down. It was a ceremony that she had become used to over the last three months since she took up her role as a judge's clerk.

Her ambition was to be a practicing civil barrister and although she had passed all her examinations, she was still trying to obtain an elusive pupillage to train as a barrister in a set of civil chambers. She knew how difficult it was to find pupillage in civil sets unless you had a family connection and she had hoped that taking on this role would introduce her to the right people. However, so far, she had mainly seen Mrs Justice Monteith QC either doing paperwork, telephone injunctions or criminal cases and she had not met any civil practitioners.

Once the judge and Joanne had taken their seats, they both removed their masks.

The court staff would normally have used the resident judge for a trial but he was currently sitting on a murder case and they had decided to obtain the services of a High Court judge for Nashad's case because of its importance and the fact that the case had attracted a lot of press attention and they did not want any mistakes.

The Court was fitted out for covid and felt a very strange environment to David. Firstly, it was a relatively cramped court at the best of times but now it was made even smaller by the installation of Perspex on the desks between each of Counsel's positions and the fact that the jury box, which normally seated twelve, would now only seat six with Perspex sheets between each juror's seat. Three other jurors would be seated to the side of the jury box all separated by Perspex and three others would sit behind David, Sara and the prosecution team, Gerard Smedley QC and his junior Lawrence Winder.

The jurors behind David were also separated from Nashad by a small walkway and a large glass sheet that stretched from chair level to the ceiling in the dock. They then had further Perspex sheets separating them from each other and from David and Sara.

David was immediately concerned that it would be impossible to take instructions during the trial without one of the jurors hearing! He had no choice but to raise the issue at the start of the trial before the jurors came into court.

"My Lady, I have not visited this court before and I was unaware of the covid preparations that have been undertaken. Obviously in these difficult times everyone must be careful and I perfectly understand why all the jurors cannot be crammed into a jury box. However, I am concerned that Ms Petford-Williams and myself will have three jurors sitting behind us and in between us and our client. It will be impossible to take instructions during the trial when we are in court without the jurors overhearing. I wonder if the jurors could be moved or if there is any other court available with better arrangements?"

The judge looked at David over the top of her reading glasses.

"Mr Brant, we do live in difficult times as you acknowledge. Indeed, they are extraordinary times with the country being locked down once more. Covid is a serious virus that has caused something like 60,000 deaths in this country and hundreds of thousands in the world to date and still rising. Obviously, it affects everyone and the government has ordered this lockdown to hopefully deal with its spread.

However, it is also importance that justice be carried out and we have all been enjoined to keep the courts working so that defendants, particularly those in custody like your client, have their trial as soon as possible. I accept that the arrangements in this court are not ideal, but I am informed by the court staff that they are the best we can do with the available facilities.

There are no other courts available to us and we cannot rearrange the seating in this one. However, I am keen that your client should be able to give instructions when he needs to. What I suggest is that if he needs to give instructions to you, he should contact the dock officer, who will then contact my usher and then we will adjourn for you to take instructions in the cells.

I hasten to add that I trust that such interruptions will not be too many. With the new arrangements in place, it will take more time and prove far more difficult to get the jury in and out of court."

David thanked her and was about to sit down when the judge spoke to him.

"Mr Brant, I have been advised of the occupations of the jury panel and I note that one is a practicing criminal barrister on the Western circuit, which of course includes this court and one is a civilian worker for the Crown Prosecution Service. They rightly brought this to the attention of the court staff and I made further enquiries. I understand that neither has had any prior involvement in this case. Do you have any objections to either of them being on this panel?"

David wished that he did as the civilian worker for the Crown Prosecution Service might feel some friendly bias towards a case brought by his or her employees and a criminal barrister would probably know all the tricks of the trade and might be a little too cynical towards the defence. However, any challenge he made to a potential juror had to be for cause and the mere fact that one was a civilian employee of the Crown Prosecution Service and the other a criminal barrister was not a good enough reason to object, unless he, Sara or his client knew them. As neither Sara nor David regularly practiced on the Western circuit, it was unlikely they had met either of them and as Nashad did not know anyone in the area it was extremely unlikely he knew either of them.

"No, my Lady, unless my client or my junior, Ms Petford-Williams, or I recognise either of them we have no objection based simply on their occupations."

The judge smiled at him, "Thank you Mr Brant, I thought that might be the case.'

The jury panel of fifteen was brought in and within a short time a jury of twelve was selected. David did not recognise any of the jurors and had no idea whether the either of the two jurors mentioned by the judge had been selected but by the law of averages the chances were that both had been selected.

Once the rest of the panel was dismissed the jury were told by the clerk of the court that Nashad was charged with manslaughter. He then read out the particulars of the charge.

"Nashad Pritchard on 28th September 2019, unlawfully killed Jensen Willmott in that:

I.   He placed on the market and distributed for consumption by humans a product containing DNP;

II.   The product was unfit for human consumption, injurious to health and potentially lethal;

III.   He owed a duty of care to consumers at large not to place the product on the market for the purpose of human consumption;

IV.   In gross breach of that duty of care he:

    a) placed the product on the market,

    b) in particular with the intention or reasonable expectation that it be consumed by those who might wish to use the product as a slimming agent,

    c) advertised and encouraged the product to be so consumed by humans and in particular as a slimming agent,

    d) knowing that the product was unfit for human consumption, injurious to health and potentially lethal,

V.   Jensen Willmott so consumed the product and in particular the DNP which caused his death.

David looked at the nine faces he could see to his left. There were a few raised eyebrows when they heard the charge. Jurors never knew what type of case they would try until they were in the courtroom and two older, rather large ladies looked shocked when they heard the word, 'manslaughter' and frowned when they heard the particulars read out. Three or four of the nine he could see looked towards Nashad in the dock with stony faces. David could already sense, without looking behind him at the remaining three member of the jury, that this was going to be an emotive and difficult trial.

CHAPTER 22

THE PROSECUTION OPENING

After the charge was read out the judge addressed the jury.

"Members of the jury, in a few moments Mr Smedley QC will address you on behalf of the prosecution, telling you what this case is about. Before that takes place, I should give you a few directions.

You have just taken an oath to try this case on the evidence. What Mr Smedley says to you or whatever any counsel in this case says to you, is not evidence, it is counsel commenting on the evidence that you will hear or have heard in the case. You should only rely upon the evidence that you hear in this case and not on anything else. You should not, for example, carry out any research yourself, for example through looking on the internet to look up people or places or by visiting any place that is mentioned in this case. I must give you this serious warning. Parliament has now enacted that any juror who breaches this rule commits a serious offence and could and likely would, face a prison sentence."

A few jurors looked surprised at the suggestion that they could be imprisoned for doing their own research. The looks were not lost on the judge and satisfied that her stark warning had got across, she indicated to Gerard that he could now open the case to the jury.

Gerard Smedley QC rose to his feet, scanned the faces of the twelve jurors, because he could see them all from his position and addressed them. He started by introducing the defendant and the advocates and then commenced by telling the jurors the facts of the case from the prosecution's point of view.

"On 28th September 2019 a vulnerable and deeply troubled young man, Jensen Willmott, aged 25 years, suffered a most distressing death having bought on the internet and consumed, a highly toxic chemical, effectively a poison, called 2.4 Dinitrophenol, 'DNP' for short. That toxic chemical was sold to him by this defendant who falsely advertised that it was a slimming product.

Let me deal with DNP first.

There is a long history to the use of DNP and you will discover its history during the course of this trial. Because of its potentially explosive qualities it was first used as a base material for munitions in the First World War. It was during that period that it was discovered that many of the workers who worked with DNP lost weight.

It was found that DNP would stimulate the human metabolism and eat away calories and in the 1930s it was actually used as a slimming product. However, it caused a number of deaths and was banned in the USA and was not heard about again, until relatively recently.

It started to be sold worldwide through the internet, often with devastating consequences to those who purchased and used it.

The defendant and another man, Mr Lee Han Ong, who has not been arrested but is wanted by the police, created a company called Slimming, Limitless Inspiration and Motivation UK Ltd (SLIM UK for short) clearly demonstrating that they wanted people to believe that they were selling a slimming product.

Mr Lee Han Ong appears to have been mainly a sleeping partner in the company and the day-to-day running was carried out by this defendant, Nashad Pritchard.

The defendant obtained premises in the Salisbury area at 10 Coventry Street, Salisbury, barely a mile away from this courtroom, and the business was operated from there. They bought the DNP from an industrial chemical factory in China. It was supplied in large 10kg or 25kg drums that were shipped to this country. An empty 10 kg drum was found at the defendant's home address. A half empty 25kg drum and a full 25kg drum were found at the defendant's business address. All these drums it appears were originally delivered to the defendant's business address.

DNP is a yellow powder and the defendant used specialized equipment to take the powder from the drums and place it in small blue and yellow capsules that were then sold on the internet.

The potential profits were huge. A 25kg drum of DNP could be purchased and shipped to the United Kingdom from China for around £400-£500 and once placed in capsules it could realise a profit of in excess of £100,000."

He paused for a few seconds for those figures to sink in.

"The defendant operated the company solely on the internet. It was not a high street business where people could walk in and purchase capsules. Buyers would come across SLIM UK's website and send orders and the defendant would accept the order, make up the capsules and supply them by post.

Mr Pritchard went to great lengths to disguise the product he was supplying by labelling and misdescribing it in such a way as to deceive customs and other authorities in the UK and elsewhere. Upon entering the country, the chemical drums of DNP were accompanied by documentation describing them as a fertiliser and referring to them as DNP. However, the defendant changed that description when he sold the capsules.

A package was found at the defendant's business address, labelled, 'Food Colouring Pigment.' A similar package was found at Jensen Willmott's home with the same description. The contents of both packages were analysed and found to contain the toxic DNP which has no use whatsoever as a food colouring pigment."

Again, he paused before continuing.

"Let me move onto Jensen Willmott and his death.

Sadly, during his life Jensen had an undiagnosed condition called body dysmorphia. We will look at his psychological and emotional condition in some detail later during the trial. For now, I can summarise it.

Body dysmorphic disorder (BDD), or body dysmorphia, is a mental health condition where an individual will worry about what they see as flaws in their appearance. These flaws may exist or they may not and if they do, they are often unnoticeable to others but to the person suffering from this condition they are major flaws.

Body dysmorphia can affect anyone of any sex and age group although it is more prevalent amongst teenagers and young adults like Jensen.

A person who has this condition is not vain or self-obsessed. It is a recognised psychiatric state and can have a major effect on someone's life.

It is not known what causes body dysmorphia in a person but it is thought it might result from genetics. If a relative has body dysmorphia it is more likely that you will have it. It may result from a chemical imbalance in the brain or due to a mental health condition. It can arise as a result of a traumatic experience in a person's past, such as bullying at school or abuse when a person was a child. Jensen's diaries do, sadly, refer to abuse that he suffered as a child from a close relative.

Whatever the specific reason, it seems clear from Jensen's diaries and emails to friends that he suffered from body dysmorphia. He made frequent references in his diary to what he thought was his excessive weight and how repulsive he thought his body looked in the mirror often describing it as looking like a 'barrel' and having the physique of an unfit seventy year-old.

In fact, there was nothing wrong with his body; he was not overweight nor did he look like a barrel, yet that is the way he thought he looked. He was so concerned about his weight and what he thought he looked like that he desperately searched the internet for slimming products.

Having tried several different products, he finally came across the defendant's website, offering a miracle slimming product.

Jensen's diaries state that he contacted the defendant and made some enquiries about the slimming product. It is clear that the defendant falsely claimed that the product was a miracle slimming product. The defendant claimed the recipe for this slimming pill was only recently discovered by accident by his colleague Lee Han Ong, a Chinese collector of ancient manuscripts. He claimed that Lee had purchased a very old manuscript in a Hong Kong market and found that it revealed an ancient formula for a slimming aid. A formula that had been lost for centuries.

The fact the Defendant was purchasing DNP in 25kg industrial chemical drums from a Chinese factory was hardly in keeping with his claim to Jensen that this was a miracle slimming product created from a centuries' old formula!

As a result of these false claims Jensen started to buy 2,4 dinitrophenol (DNP) from the defendant. His first purchase was on 8th September 2019. Over a very short period of time, he became at the very least psychologically addicted to and dependent on the chemical.

You will readily appreciate that the material available to the prosecution and the defence teams in this case consists of thousands of pages of material. Fortunately, you do not need to see everything that was recovered because large amounts of material are not relevant to your task and a large amount of this case will be reduced to a document that you will receive, headed, "Agreed Facts". These will be facts agreed by both prosecution and defence and which therefore do not need to be laboriously proven before you.

Doubtless some of the material you will see may appear complicated, but we have no doubt that by the end of the trial you will have mastered it all with our assistance.

We have reduced the vast amount of material recovered in this case to three lever arch files of papers for you, coloured red, white and blue and containing, in all, about seven hundred pages of material. They contain in the first file; company documents including sales and banking documents, in the second file, a medical history of Jensen Willmott taken from his personal medical records and his diaries, and in the third file, documents dealing solely with the defendant, containing photographs, emails and bank statements.

I will take you through some of those papers now in opening the case and later you will be taken through the remaining pages in greater detail when the evidence is presented before you. These files are yours to use as you wish during this trial. You can make notes on them that no one else will be allowed to look at.

Few witnesses will be called before you as most of the material is agreed. You will hear from a Trading Standards Officer who fully investigated the matter. You will hear from an expert on DNP, Professor James Bulling. You will also hear from a forensic psychiatrist Dr Charles Langdon, who did not see Jensen Willmott during his life, but has used medical documents and Jensen's diary, papers and emails to determine just how vulnerable Jensen Willmott was to someone like the defendant who was selling this substance.

Let me ask you briefly to look at the first jury bundle, the red one labelled, "Jury Bundle No 1, Indictment, Trial Documents and Company Documents".

The first few pages contain essential trial documents, including the indictment (the charge sheet) that has already been read out to you by the clerk of the court. You will see the one charge, 'Manslaughter' and the particulars of that charge.

On the next page you will see a photograph of Jensen Willmott and following that a photograph of Nashad Pritchard."

David noted that as usual the prosecution had chosen the best photograph they could find of Jensen Willmott making him look happy, young and full of life and a rather sinister looking photograph of Nashad, frowning, as his mugshot was taken when he was in police custody.

Gerard swiftly moved on to explain the timeline document which gave a chronology of events. He highlighted particular dates.

"Members of the jury, I will not take you through every date on that timeline now, just a few important ones.

On Tuesday 4th April 2019, the company, 'Slimming Inspiration UK Ltd' was registered at Companies House. The Managing Director was one Lee Han Ong.

On Friday 3rd May 2019 the company changed its name to 'Slimming, Limitless Inspiration and Motivation UK Ltd (SLIM UK)'. In interview Nashad Pritchard stated it was his idea to change the name and he conceived the new name. As you will see at this time, before the company had sold anything, Lee Han Ong resigned as Managing Director of the company and Mr Pritchard took over the company in that role.

On 8th June 2019 the first shipment of DNP arrived in this country. By that stage SLIM UK had its own website up and running and was advertising slimming pills for sale.

The first orders to the company were made in early June 2019 and then there was a steady flow of DNP, falsely labelled as, 'Food Colouring Pigment', from the defendant's business address.

At Pages 156-280 of the first bundle, the red bundle, we have banking records for the company. We will see that the first few months have mainly outgoings but by September 2019 the company is turning over a large profit of approximately £20,000 a month. You do not need to look now but when we look at Jury Bundle 3, 'The Defendant's Finances', you will see that he was taking 25% of the profit that was regularly flowing into his bank account. The rest was transferred to bank accounts based in Hong Kong no doubt controlled by Lee Han Ong and possibly others.

On 8th September 2019, Jensen Willmott ordered the 'slimming pills'.

From Jensen's diary we see that on 12th September 2019, he received his first dose of DNP from the defendant. He noted that the DNP was labelled 'Food Colouring Pigment.' According to his diary he was concerned about this and he phoned the defendant who reassured him that the product he received was the 'miracle slimming drug.'

The Defendant's website advised that people should not take more than one capsule a day for fear of unpleasant side effects. You will hear evidence that in fact there is no safe amount to take. One capsule of this toxic chemical could kill you!

Jensen Willmott did not know this. He consumed the first batch, probably taking two capsules a day, according to his diary. He then ordered more of the product.

On Friday 27th September 2019, the day of his death, Jensen received his final batch of DNP sold by the defendant.

You will hear that Jensen had recently met a young lady called Zoe Slater and they had arranged to meet that night for a date. She phoned Jensen at 6pm to make sure their evening was still going ahead but was surprised that he never answered any of her calls. She went around to his flat as arranged at 7pm. She had a key to the flat given to her by Jensen just a few days earlier. As she received no answer from ringing the bell, she used the key to open the flat door and she peered inside.

What she saw terrified her!

Jensen was spread out on the sofa. He looked asleep but was very pale with a yellowish pallor to his skin and he was breathing heavily, making what she describes as, 'a throttling or choking sound'. She saw that he had vomited and she could see that there were some blue and yellow capsules in the vomit.

She believed he had taken an overdose and she quickly rang emergency services. They arrived and tried to resuscitate him. They could not do so they took him to hospital where the medical staff worked on him trying to save his life.

Sadly, they could not and at 1:55am on 28th September 2019, the doctors certified that Jensen had deceased.

You will hear from a pathologist, Dr Andrew Worthington, that he carried out a postmortem on 30th September 2019 and then certified that Jensen's death was due to DNP poisoning.

We, the prosecution, will call a number of other witnesses before you. You will hear from Harvey David from the local Trading Standards whose job it was to discover who was behind the sale of the DNP that killed Jensen Willmott. He will describe what steps they took to discover the source of the DNP.

You will hear that the trail soon led to this defendant. He was arrested by police on 4th November 2019 at his home address and taken to the police station. At the same time his business address was searched. You will find photographs from those searches at pages 300-340 of Jury Bundle 1.

There he was interviewed on 4th and 5th November. He had the benefit of a solicitor who had a private consultation with him before the interview. During the interview he denied having ever heard of DNP keeping up with his false claim that he was supplying a miracle slimming aid. He was then shown photographs of the drums that had been recovered from his business premises which showed that the drums labelled as 'Fertiliser' and DNP and then he was shown packages of blue and white pills labelled 'Food Colouring Pigment'. He admitted that these were all false descriptions, claiming they had been used because they had not had time to have their, 'miracle slimming drug' licensed and authorised yet and there was no intentional dishonesty, they were simply trying to avoid unnecessary paperwork.

The business's computers were taken away by police but due to financial limitations and difficulties with getting experts to do the work, those computers were not examined at the time of the arrest. They were examined months later. In Volume 1 of the Jury Bundle, you will see copies of many emails extracted from those computers.

We are going to look at some messages simply to give you an idea of how the business was set up and by whom; how advice was given on how to package the DNP and how the name DNP was frequently referred to. We suggest it will be obvious from those emails that Nashad Pritchard knew all along that DNP was being supplied and knew all along that it was a dangerous poisonous substance but that he nevertheless supplied it to people like Jensen Willmott, simply to obtain a vast profit, regardless of the danger it posed to Jensen Willmott and others.

At page 287 of the first jury bundle, you will see an email from this defendant to Lee Han Ong that clearly demonstrates that the defendant knew how dangerous this chemical was. He knew that because he had been affected by it.

On 9th August 2019, this defendant wrote in that email,

"Dear Lee,

I have had to stop filling the capsules for the last few days. On Tuesday this week I inhaled some of the powder and felt very nauseous and very ill. I was really concerned for my health and decided to stop producing the capsules until I feel better and when I will take better steps to prevent myself actually inhaling the powder.

Yours,

Nashad."

The prosecution case is that when Nashad Pritchard supplied this toxic substance to Jensen Willmott, he was solely motivated by making a profit and had a callous disregard for the safety of those who might take it, including Jensen Willmott. He knew how dangerous this substance was but did not care whether anyone he supplied it to might be taken ill, have serious organ damage, or even die from taking DNP.

In those circumstances we say having listened to the evidence, you will be sure he is guilty of manslaughter.

CHAPTER 23

THE FIRST WITNESS, THE DNP EXPERT

As Gerard sat down, David scanned the jurors he could see without turning around to face those behind him. He could only see the six in the original jury box and the three to the side but that proved to be enough to glean the impression that Gerard's speech had upon them. Clearly, they appeared horrified that a young, apparently healthy man, could lose his life from taking a poison disguised as a slimming product. Gerard had made a good opening that certainly made David's task a difficult one.

Gerard finished his opening shortly before lunch at 12:50 and the judge agreed that the first witness need not be called until 2pm.

At 2:05pm Professor James Bulling entered the court room. David had come across him before in a poisoning case and had a good deal of respect for this witness. Some experts came across as dogmatic, arrogant and unnecessarily superior. David recalled that this witness was none of those things. He came across as friendly, trying to be helpful and slightly self-deprecating. It was far more effective with juries than the arrogant, dogmatic approach.

The witness took the oath and then at Gerard's request started to reel off his qualifications.

"I am a Consultant Physician in General Medicine and Clinical Pharmacology and Therapeutics at the Birmingham General NHS Foundation Trust and a Consultant Clinical Toxicologist in the Birmingham General Hospitals Clinical Toxicology Service.

In those roles I am responsible for the management of patients presenting with drug overdoses and other forms of poisoning. This would include several hundred adult patients presenting with drug overdose or other forms of toxicity each year. I am also Professor of Clinical Pharmacology and Therapeutics at Birmingham University, and a past Chair of the Clinical Standards Group of the National Poisons.

I have expertise in clinical toxicology and the management of poisoning and have published several academic papers in this subject. My academic qualifications are BSc (biochemistry), MBBS, FRCP (London), FRCP (Edinburgh) and MD. I am accredited in General Internal Medicine and Clinical Pharmacology and Therapeutics. I am a Fellow of the European Association of Clinical Toxicologists and Poisons Centres and the American Academy of Clinical Toxicology.

I am also ..."

Gerard interrupted him, "I suspect that is enough Professor."

He turned towards David, "I doubt anyone will suggest that you are not an expert in this field."

David gently shook his head, it would be foolish to challenge his expertise in view of his already impressive listed qualifications.

Gerard thanked David and then continued, "Professor, you are here to give evidence about DNP. Can you assist us at to what experience you have had dealing with DNP.

"Yes, certainly. Sadly, I have a great deal of experience with DNP or 2.4 dinitrophenol to give it its full name. I have been involved in several cases of DNP poisoning, many of which sadly resulted in death. I have been involved in investigatory work involving DNP and studied literature from many countries where DNP has been used."

"Yes, thank you. Have you brought any DNP into court for the jury to see?"

"Yes, I have."

The witness reached down to pick up his bag and then produced a large heavy metal case from which he carefully took out a labelled test tube containing a bright yellow powder.

He held the test tube up so the jury could see it.

"This is what DNP looks like."

"Thank you, professor." Gerard turned to the judge, "Might this be exhibit 1 in the case?"

Before the judge answered, Professor Bulling intervened, "I am not sure that is good idea!"

Gerard looked surprised, "Why not professor?"

"As I am about to explain, DNP has explosive qualities. Even a small amount like that in this test tube can cause a small explosion that could injure someone. That is why I have kept it in a solid metal case. I am aware that because of its explosive qualities, Salisbury Council refused to store the drums discovered at the defendant's premises for fear that they might explode or self-combust."

Gerard nodded, "I see, very well I won't ask that this be exhibited. Professor would you carefully return the test tube to the metal case you have brought with you."

David looked at Gerard without a noticeable expression, but he felt that this whole incident almost looked scripted as if Gerard wanted to get across the dangers of this substance in a graphic way.

Gerard carried on without looking at David, "So, Professor, what is DNP?"

Professor Bulling turned toward the jury,

"2.4 Dinitrophenol ('DNP') is a chemical. It is a synthetic benzene. Benzene is a chemical that is a colourless or a light yellow liquid at room temperature. It has a sweet odour and is highly flammable. Benzene evaporates into the air very quickly. Its vapor is heavier than air and may sink into low-lying areas. Benzene dissolves only slightly in water and will float on top of water.

The substance we are dealing with is a powdered form of Benzene. It was originally used in the manufacturing of explosives and then dyes, wood preservatives, photographic developers, and insecticides. If I were to set fire to this yellow powder it would burn brightly like gunpowder and leave a black residue. In a confined area, such as a barrel, a spark could turn it into a bomb."

Gerard waited for a few seconds for the jury to take that in and then asked.

"Professor, can you tell us what effect this chemical has on the human body of it is ingested?"

"Yes, certainly. It is a highly toxic substance when ingested, inhaled, or absorbed through the skin and is not designed for human consumption. However, despite the fact it is toxic, it has been used as a 'fat burning' and weight reducing product.

It does have this effect on the body because the chemical blocks the way energy is stored in the body. It consumes or burns off fat and carbohydrates. That in turn, causes energy to be converted into heat. The result is that the person's body temperature and metabolic rate, all increase ...."

He paused before adding the word, "dangerously."

He continued, "The release of heat from the body is uncontrollable and can result in a very high fever, and in many cases, multi-organ failure and death.

Once ingested a person can feel an initial agitation, followed by flushing and hyperthermia."

Gerard intervened and asked, "Can you tell us what hyperthermia is?"

"Yes of course. Hyperthermia is an abnormally high body temperature caused by a failure of the heat-regulating mechanisms of the body to deal with the heat coming from the environment. It is often accompanied by sweating, abdominal pain, nausea, vomiting and diarrhoea. This progresses to worsening hyperthermia or a very high fever, accompanied by rapid breathing and a rapid heart rate. That is followed by dehydration, thirst, muscle rigidity and then muscle breakdown (called rhabdomyolysis), acid in the blood (acidosis) and other chemical disturbances of the blood (for example high potassium or blood glucose).

The organs will then start to fail, so kidney failure, liver failure, heart failure, circulatory shock, coma, convulsions and cardiac arrest can then occur in more severe cases.

This is essentially what happened to Jensen Willmott in this case."

Gerard nodded and looked at his notes before asking,

"Has DNP undergone any development or clinical tests which one would expect for a pharmaceutical or medicinal drug?"

"No, not at all. Despite what appears on websites and internet forums there have been no clinical tests into this substance. This lack of research means that no 'safe' dose has been established and there is no reliable evidence on which to base dosing recommendations. A single capsule of this powder can result in someone's death."

Gerard looked towards the jury to see the effect of this evidence. Satisfied by the juror's reactions he asked, "You have mentioned death, how many times has this substance resulted in death?"

"It has been associated with deaths for over one hundred years now. At first the deaths were in munitions factories where there was inadequate ventilation or protective clothing offered to workers. Thirty-six workers died in munitions factory in Paris during World War 1 for these reasons.

Although it has never been approved as a drug product, it was used for weight reduction in the United States in the 1930s.

Maurice Tainter at Stanford University in 1933 discovered that the human consumption of DNP led to significant weight loss and soon DNP was popularised as a weight loss drug. While consumption of DNP was shown at that time to produce weight reduction, unfortunately this was too often associated with uncontrolled release of heat resulting in high fever that in some cases lead to multiorgan failure and death. It was discovered that the risk of death increased with higher doses of DNP or long-term use. It was also associated with other side effects including the formation of cataracts. Consequently, in the United States DNP was labelled as 'extremely dangerous and not fit for human consumption' by the Federal Food, Drug and Cosmetic Act of 1938.

Sixty-two deaths were recorded from DNP poisoning in the 20th century, but most of those were pre-1938. Only two of those deaths occurred after 1938 and both of those were in the 1950s.

However, between 2000 and 2010, twelve deaths were recorded. These all resulted from ingesting DNP as a supposed weight loss treatment. There is an overlap in the statistics reported, but statistics for the United Kingdom between 2007-2017 refer to ninety-eight reported cases of DNP poisoning. Of those fourteen resulted in death. There were six deaths in a single year, namely, 2015.

It follows that any human use of DNP may therefore be considered as extremely dangerous."

"Are there any groups who would be particularly vulnerable to this substance?"

"Yes, weight plays an important part. The less you weigh the more lethal this substance will be. It follows that it is particularly dangerous to those who suffer from anorexia and other eating disorders where their weight is so reduced as a consequence of the condition.

A single capsule of 250mg of DNP could be a lethal dose. Each time you take one you are dicing with death. Clearly, the more you take, the more lethal they become.

Jensen Willmott appears to have consumed two such pills a day for a few weeks and then consumed some four capsules the evening before he died.

Sadly, it was almost inevitable that he would succumb to the toxic effect of these pills."

CHAPTER 24

CROSS-EXAMINING THE EXPERT

As David rose to cross-examine, he could hear coughing behind him coming from the dock. He waited until Nashad stopped before asking his first question.

"Professor, effectively your evidence is that DNP is a poison that should never be ingested by human beings?"

"Well, I think I said a little bit more than that but yes, that is essentially the point I make. It is a deadly poison never intended to be ingested by humans and has caused numerous deaths."

"Your evidence is that any dosage of DNP is potentially deadly?"

"Yes."

"Now in this case there is no suggestion that Mr Willmott was aware that he was taking DNP?"

"That appears correct. He seems to believe he was taking a 'miracle slimming cure', not a poison."

"One of the issues that the jury will have to determine in this case is the defendant's knowledge of whether this was DNP or a miracle slimming drug. Your expertise cannot help on that topic, can it?"

"No, it would be simply comment on my part and not based upon expertise."

David nodded, "Thank you, Professor. Now let me deal with the issue of toxicity of DNP. As you have told us, it was originally a munition, also a fertiliser and in the past was tried as a slimming aid?"

"Yes, that's right, although it was never licensed to be used for human consumption."

There was further coughing from the back of the court, but David ignored it and continued.

"Professor, I would like to deal with licenced medicines for a moment. Clearly if too many prescribed drugs are taken, this can result in death?"

"Of course. A significant amount of hospital time is taken dealing with overdoses from prescription drugs."

"The same applies with non-prescription drugs such as paracetamol?"

"Absolutely, there are frequent admissions to hospital for people who have overdosed on paracetamol."

"Paracetamol is something that you can buy over the counter in a chemist, or indeed, these days in a supermarket?"

"Yes, certainly."

"It can be a useful drug for pain relief or cold symptoms?"

"Yes."

"But if too many paracetamol tablets are taken it can result in liver damage and in some cases death?"

"Yes."

"Do you know how many deaths there are annually in England and Wales from people taking paracetamol?"

"I cannot give you exact figures, but I believe that it amounts to over two hundred every year."

David picked up some statistics that Sara had provided from her research.

"If I were to say, 219 in 2016, 218 in 2017, 210 in 2018 and 211 in 2019, would that accord with your knowledge?"

"Yes, as I said, about 200 a year."

"In the past there were many more deaths weren't there?"

"I believe so but the management of cases of paracetamol poisoning has improved."

"If I were to suggest around 500-600 death a year in England and Wales in the 1990s would that accord with your recollection?"

"Yes, I believe it is something around that number."

"Now of course large numbers of people take paracetamol as opposed to DNP, but clearly there were and are far more deaths from paracetamol poisoning than DNP poisoning?"

"Yes, but as you have pointed out, far more people take paracetamol, millions of people in England and Wales, whereas only a handful take DNP."

"Well, is it a handful?"

Professor Bulling hesitated before answering, "Well I cannot be precise because there are limited records and it is supplied through the internet, but I would doubt that there are more than a few hundred users in the country and hopefully, less."

There was a loud spate of coughing from Nashad and David turned round to look at him. Nashad held a handkerchief to his mouth and waved David to continue.

"Professor, you cannot say whether hundreds or even thousands take DNP can you?"

"No, but I doubt it runs into millions like users of paracetamol."

"We know that DNP was used as a slimming aid in the 1930s but was banned in the United States of America as a result of side effects and deaths?"

"That is correct."

"It was still used as a slimming aid in the United States after that period?"

"I regret I do not know the answer to that question."

David looked surprised.

"You are an expert in this field, aren't you?"

The Professor prickled a little at the possible insult.

"I like to think so."

"You must have heard of Dr Bachynsky then?"

Professor Bulling paused and then nodded as the name struck a chord in his memory.

"Yes, I have. A discredited doctor in the United States who was struck off. I trust you are not relying on him as an expert!"

Professor Bulling could not help himself smile at his own answer. David's expression did not change and he immediately responded.

"No Professor, we are not, but I do want to ask you some questions about him. Are you aware that he was born in Russia and first became aware of DNP when he was translating some Russian medical journals for the American Government in the 1960s?"

"I believe that is right."

"Those journals referred to the Russians using DNP for their soldiers to keep them warm in winter with the main side effect being weight loss?"

"Again, that accords with my recollection."

"As a result, in 1981 Dr Bachynsky processed industrial DNP into tablets which he marketed and dispensed under the trade name 'Mitcal' through his private weight loss clinic?"

"Yes."

"He advertised that weight loss occurred using 'Mitcal' through a mechanism he called intracellular hyperthermia therapy?"

"Yes, in my opinion a highly discredited therapy."

"I accept that Professor, however what I want to ask you about is the numbers he treated. Proceedings were brought against him and it was alleged that he treated over 14,000. Were you aware of that?"

"I do not have the exact details in front of me but that does sound like the figures I have read."

David thanked him and continued.

"Now it is right and it is only fair that the jury are aware of this that people being treated by Dr Bachynsky started reporting adverse effects, such as fever, shortness of breath and sweating?"

"Yes, I recall that."

"And there was one fatality recorded?"

"I believe so."

"Out of 14,000 users?"

"Yes, but many suffered serious health problems. DNP was never meant for human ingestion."

"I do not disagree with you Professor, but I just wanted to ask you this. You state one dose of this chemical could kill you but it appears 14,000 people took it in the 1980s, at least 14,000 doses and yet there was only one fatality?"

"I do not know the full details of that case, but in my opinion there have been many deaths using this chemical. There are horrendous side effects from taking it and it should never be or taken by anyone. As I said earlier, it is like playing Russian Roulette. You might not die from the first dose, but it will eventually affect you seriously in some way and may lead to death."

David paused before asking, "May it be that this death occurred because too much DNP was taken?"

Professor Bulling looked straight at the jury, "There is no doubt too many capsules were taken in this case, but in my opinion one capsule could be enough to kill and it should never be marketed or sold and definitely never ingested for any reason, let alone slimming."

There was a sudden spate of coughing from the back of the court and after a few seconds Gladys Rogers, the dock officer who had sat bored throughout these proceedings, raised her voice and spoke loudly to the judge from the dock.

"Excuse me, your honour, I think Mr Pritchard might have covid, he's developed a permanent cough and he seems clammy and is sweating profusely!"

CHAPTER 25

COVID?

The jury were sent out whilst the judge addressed David.

"Mr Brant, would you and your junior like to take instructions from your client?"

David answered immediately, "My Lady, bearing in mind the dangers of catching and spreading covid, neither my junior, nor myself, have any intention of going down to the cells and taking instructions from Mr Pritchard. An experienced dock officer has suggested that in her opinion Mr Pritchard may have covid. In the circumstances we suggest the appropriate course is not for us to go to the cells and risk catching and spreading the disease, but that Mr Pritchard should be taken back to the prison in isolation, then isolated in a cell whilst a covid test is administered. I am sure that can be arranged quickly in prison, at least I hope so and hopefully the results will be very quick as well. If he does not have covid, we can continue, if he has covid then the jury will have to be discharged."

The judge paused for a few seconds before turning to Gerard and asking him.

"Mr Smedley, what do you say?"

Gerard slowly rose to his feet and stood for a few seconds before replying, obviously thinking of a suitable response.

"My Lady, I can understand why my learned friends are reluctant to go to the cells and take instructions. Many people are dying from covid in this country and we do not want to help its spread with all the risks to life that entails. In their position I would not want to go to the cells.

We have only just started this trial and we could abandon it and start again with a new jury once we discover that the defendant is free of covid. However, we know that Professor Bulling is a very busy expert witness and it may be some time until we can secure his attendance at court again.

The judge thought for a few moments before replying.

"Yes, I agree defence counsel should not be expected to go to the cells just in case Mr Pritchard does have covid. We do not want to be responsible for spreading this awful, indeed, deadly virus.

I will send the jury home and ask them to come back tomorrow by which time, hopefully, Mr Pritchard will have had a covid test and we shall have the results. I will ask the jury to come back at 2pm. We shall reconvene at 10am. If we have the result all well and good and we shall continue at 2pm with the jury. If we do not have a result, it will give us time to warn the jury not to attend in the afternoon."

CHAPTER 26

THE TRIAL RECOMMENCES

David spent the next few days in his hotel staring at the courtyard, wondering when he would get out of this place. Sara was staying at a different hotel, they were not supposed to socialise due to covid, despite sitting close together in court but, in any event, there was nowhere to go to, no restaurants, pubs or other places were open, just the odd takeaway. They had returned to court on Tuesday morning but the prison staff then stated that it would be three days before they received a response to the covid test.

The judge had asked them to expedite matters and had ordered the case to be listed every day at 10am for an update. Each day they had all gone into court only to be told that the test results had not been returned yet. It had meant that David and Sara were able to claim their daily refresher fee, but David would rather have got on with the trial than face even longer staying in Salisbury than was strictly necessary.

Finally on Friday, 13th November 2020, they reconvened the court with a full complement of jurors and with Nashad. The test results had come in the previous afternoon confirming that Nashad did not have covid and that the trial could recommence.

In the morning David went to the cells with Sara and once more they were placed in the small cell just feet away from Nashad. David waited until Nashad was seated before addressing him.

"Nashad, how are you feeling?"

Nashad shook his head whilst replying, "I am not feeling well David. I am not convinced about the prison tests and I fear I may have covid. I wonder if the test results are wrong. Is there any way we can discharge this jury and start again in the near future when I am well?"

Neither David nor Sara had anticipated this. They thought that he would be overjoyed to obtain a negative result and be declared healthy. It now crossed David's mind that Nashad's suspected covid and illness was related to the evidence that he heard on Monday that week, rather than any genuine medical condition.

"Nashad, you have been given the all clear from covid, the test results are unlikely to be wrong when we have taken so long to obtain the results. You have also been seen by a prison doctor today and they said you were fit to attend court and be tried."

"Phhh."

Nashad almost spat out a response.

"David, I am sure the results of the covid test are wrong, I will become very ill if this trial continues. It must surely come to an end now and I should be retried when I am well and fit enough to endure this enormous stress!"

"If you are really ill, of course I will apply to the Judge to discharge the jury so you can have time to recover, but at the moment there is insufficient medical evidence to make such an application. The covid test states you do not have covid and as I said, the prison doctor stated today that you are fit for trial."

"Phhh, the prison doctor certifies everyone as well! His job is to ensure defendants are fit to attend court, not to see if anyone is actually ill!"

David thought there might be an element of truth in this but he also thought Nashad was probably trying to avoid the trial.

"Nashad, it is Friday, we do not have many witnesses today and then you will have the weekend to rest and recuperate. As we do not possess any sufficient medical evidence to adjourn this case, I suggest you try to soldier on for now, otherwise the judge might think you are trying to avoid the trial and won't listen to us if we subsequently make an application to adjourn when you are really ill."

"David I am really ill."

"Alright, I can make an application to adjourn if you want but the judge will probably not believe you are ill and may hold it against you later when we might need her to believe you."

Nashad, thought for a few moments before replying, "Very well, David as it is Friday I will struggle on. I just hope than I can make it to the end of the day without collapsing.

Twenty minutes later David and Sara were in court with Nashad seated behind them in the dock, when the judge came in.

Everyone waited until she was seated and then she addressed them all.

"I am glad to see that Mr Pritchard does not have covid and is well enough to continue."

There was a slight grunt from behind David which David hoped the judge did not hear. It appeared that she did not as she continued.

"I am sorry to say that the clerk of the court has only just been informed that one of our jurors is ill today. It is apparently not covid so they expect to return to court on Monday. As we are at an early stage of the trial, I do not propose to discharge that juror but to simply adjourn the case until Monday when hopefully that juror will be well enough to attend court. If they are not, we will consider the matter then."

There was an audible, "yes" from the back of the court. Everyone ignored it.

CHAPTER 27

THE GIRLFRIEND

Monday 16th November 2023 arrived and David made his way to court walking along Castle Street, past Zizzi's where the Skripals had dined before they collapsed due to the Novichok poisoning. He assumed he was following part of their route as he took a right and strolled over Market Walk, then turned left walking along the Maltings past the Bishop's Mill pub and then across the Maltings bridge into Bridge Street.

Salisbury was still dead as far as he was concerned. Nothing was open and it was like walking through a ghost town as he made his way to court.

Eventually he arrived at the court doors and he was waved through by security. So few people were using the court that security did not even pretend to check his court pass, never mind check his belongings.

At 9:30am Sara and he went to see Nashad who complained about, 'not feeling well' and asking if the case could be aborted because of his ill health. David told him he would need to have some kind of medical certificate to support any application and as he had been checked by the prison doctor that morning and certified as fit to attend, that was not likely. He reassured Nashad that the case would not take a great deal of time once they got started and he would surely want it to come to an end as soon as possible. He left the cells with Sara shortly afterwards.

At 10:30am the court convened and a few minutes later, the prosecution's first witness of the day walked into the witness box. It was Zoe Slater, the deceased's girlfriend. David had not asked for her to be called as a live witness, happy to agree her evidence, but Gerard thought it would have far more impact if she gave her evidence from the witness box rather than he read her witness statement out.

Zoe was affirmed and gave her name and then Gerard began asking her a few questions.

"Ms Slater, we have heard that you knew the deceased in this case, Jensen Willmott?"

Zoe nodded and took a handkerchief out of her handbag to dab at her eyes.

"I'm sorry Ms Slater, everything has to be recorded in court and your nodding is of course not picked up by the system."

Zoe straightened up and clutching the handkerchief in her right hand she replied.

"Yes, I knew Jensen."

"How long had you known him?"

Zoe stifled a sob as she answered.

"It was only a short time, less than a month. We met on Saturday, 31st August 2019 at a friend's party. I wasn't even going to go but at the last minute I decided to go for a few hours. Jennie, my friend introduced me to Jensen saying we might have something in common because we both liked photography. We started chatting and carried on chatting all night. We arranged to meet again on the following Tuesday and then we met two or three times a week until ..."

At this stage Zoe burst into tears and David could see some of the jurors looking sympathetically towards her and could sense the ones behind him were feeling the same way. Gerard's calling her live was beginning to pay off for the prosecution.

Gerard looked at Zoe sympathetically, "Take your time Ms Slater, we all know this must be an ordeal but it is important you give your evidence clearly, there will not be many more questions."

Zoe dabbed at her eyes again and then nodded. Gerard gave her a comforting smile and continued.

"What was Jensen like?"

David wondered whether to object, what Jensen was like could not be relevant to any issue that the jury had to try, but he did not want to be seen by the jury as trying to hide anything so he stayed silent.

"He was a wonderful man. He had dreamy eyes, a fantastic physique. He looked like a body builder to me but he always complained that he was fat and he needed to go on a strict diet. I told him he was being silly but he never listened. I thought him a little down, a little depressed, but he seemed to be cheerful in my company and so I didn't think too much off it."

"Did you know that he was taking any so-called slimming products?"

"No, he never mentioned any to me. I thought his worries about his weight were a silly phase and that he would soon get over it. I never knew he was going to take anything to lose weight."

Gerard looked down at his notes and then gave a sympathetic look towards Zoe.

"I am truly sorry that I have to ask this but I need to ask you about the night he died."

Zoe nodded and quietly said, "Yes."

"Hopefully we can take this shortly. You had arranged to meet up on Friday 27th September 2019?"

Zoe quietly whispered, "Yes".

Gerard responded quickly but with sympathy, "I am very sorry Ms Slater but I barely heard that and I am much nearer to you than the jury. Could you please repeat what you said?"

"Yes, we did arrange to meet on the Friday, 27th September 2019 at about 7pm."

"Did you go to his flat?"

"Yes, I did."

"Did you have any contact with him first?"

"I tried to phone him at about 6pm but I got no reply."

"Did you know why that was?"

"Not at the time, I was just hoping that he wanted to see me but I rang just in case he was going to cancel."

"Did you go to his flat?"

"Yes, I went at about 7pm."

"What did you do?"

"I rang his doorbell a few times but there was no answer, so I opened the door with a key Jensen had given me."

"What did you see?"

Again, Zoe dabbed at her eyes and stifled a few sobs.

"It was horrible. Jensen was on a sofa. He looked asleep but he also looked terribly ill. His face was all yellow. He was breathing heavily making a sort of constant choking sound as if he could not get his breath. He was so hot to the touch."

"Did you notice anything about the room?"

"Yes, there was a terrible smell and I could see that Jensen had vomited. There was a pile of vomit by the side of the sofa with a couple of blue and yellow capsules in it. There was a bag of them nearby in a metallic looking bag that was inside a ripped brown bag."

Gerard produced the bag that the police had found in the flat when they searched it after Jensen's death.

"Is this the bag and the capsules you saw? Do not worry, the capsules have been emptied."

Zoe took the exhibit and studied it.

"It looks like the bag and the capsules."

"What did you do?"

"I called 999 and asked for an ambulance. I thought he had taken an overdose."

Gerard turned to the judge, "With your Ladyship's leave I will now play that 999 call."

Gerard asked his junior, Lawrence to play the audio.

The audio was very loud and almost made David wince in the small court room. They heard Zoe sobbing loudly as she asked for an ambulance for her boyfriend who had taken an overdose. The 999 operator had been calm and had given instructions on how to seat Jensen and explained that the ambulance would be there quickly.

Gerard waited until the audio was finished before asking his next question.

"We know that the call was made by you at 7:05pm and the ambulance arrived at 7:25pm. How long were the paramedics there?"

"I don't know, it seemed a long time, possible an hour."

Gerard looked down at his notes, "This isn't a memory test, in fact they were there 30 minutes before they made their way to the hospital. It undoubtedly seemed longer to you."

"I thought it was about an hour but I wasn't looking at my watch or a clock."

Gerard nodded, "Of course not. I believe that you went in the ambulance with Mr Willmott and the paramedics and went to the hospital with him?"

"Yes, I did."

"We will hear that the doctors worked on him all night to bring him round and save his life but were unable to and he was pronounced as deceased at 1:55am?"

Zoe sobbed again as she answered, "Yes."

"Thank you, Ms Slater, I have no further questions, Mr Brant on behalf of the defendant Mr Pritchard may have some."

With that he sat down and David stood to say, "We have no questions thank you".

He immediately sat down but the judge looked at him quizzically.

"Mr Brant, if you had no questions, why was this witness asked to attend court and endure what was clearly an upsetting experience for her?"

David stood to his feet glad for the opportunity to make an address in front of the jury.

"I do not know My Lady. We did not request that this witness attend court, we were happy for her statement to be read so that she could be spared the ordeal of giving evidence. It was the prosecution who requested that she attend in person, not the defence."

CHAPTER 28

THE MEDICAL EVIDENCE

Gerard did not react to the judge's scathing frown. As far as he was concerned, this was his case and he was going to conduct it in the best way possible for the prosecution. Ignoring the judge, he announced to the jury that he was going to call the medical evidence in the case. He stated that neither the paramedics nor the hospital doctors who certified death were required to be called by the defence and he was now going to read their evidence to the jury.

The judge gave the jury a direction that the evidence they would hear was going to be read to them by agreement because both the prosecution and the defence did not require the witness to attend court and the evidence was not challenged. She directed them that it was nevertheless important evidence in the case and they should treat it as if it came from the witness box with the added benefit that as it was not challenged, they would be able to accept it as accurate.

She also asked, "Do you mind Mr Smedley reading the statements whilst the court's cleaner comes in and cleans the witness box before another witness enters it? As you know, but the jury probably do not, in these covid times we have to clean the witness box after every witness."

Gerard gave his politest smile to the judge.

"May I suggest that the cleaning takes place now and then I read the statements. I would not want the jury to be unnecessarily distracted when important evidence is given."

The judge frowned slightly, "Very well then, I was only hoping to save some time."

The cleaner came into court wearing a covid mask, rubber gloves an apron and carrying an industrial size cleaning spray. He looked like something from a chemical warfare factory as he sprayed the witness box and then vigorously rubbed it down as everyone in court watched.

After the cleaner finished, Gerard read the two statements from the paramedics who had attended Jensen Willmott after Zoe Slater had phoned the emergency services. They covered; when they arrived at Jensen's property, what they saw there, the steps they took at the address to stabilise Jensen and the journey to the hospital. He then read a statement from Dr Robert Finnegan who certified that Jensen was pronounced dead at 1:55am on 28th September 2019.

Once he finished reading, Gerard looked at the jury and announced that next he was going to call, Dr Andrew Worthington, a forensic pathologist.

Five minutes later Dr Worthington entered the court carrying a folder full of papers. David recognised him from a previous case some years ago. He was surprised he was still practicing as he was probably in his mid to late seventies now. David recalled that he was very precise in giving his evidence. A traditionalist with a no-nonsense approach to evidence.

Dr Worthington was sworn and then gave his name and an impressive list of qualifications.

"I am a Bachelor of Medicine, a Bachelor of Surgery, a Fellow of the Royal College of Pathologists, and I hold the Diploma in Medical Jurisprudence (Forensic Pathology). My name appears on the current Home Office Register of Forensic Pathologists; I have provided forensic pathology expertise to police and coroners since 1985. I have published papers on the pathology of injury, and on coroners' investigation of deaths in England and Wales."

Gerard thanked him for providing his credentials and then asked, "Dr Worthington you carried out a post-mortem on Jensen Willmott on Monday 30th September 2019, can you provide us with your findings?"

"Of course, I examined the body of Jensen Willmott on 30th September 2019 between 14:00-16:05. I then sent blood and other samples off for a full toxicological analysis which I received two weeks later on 15th October 2019.

I checked the body of Jensen Willmott. He was a well-nourished male with a good physique. He had tattoos on his shoulders and legs and some evidence of old scars on both arms and both legs. He had some small bruises on his right lower leg.

I found no other evidence of injuries to the head, arms, legs, or body. There was no evidence of haemorrhage, in other words no bleeding from a ruptured blood vessel, nor was there any infarction, in other words, no evidence of tissue death due to inadequate blood supply. There were no contusions or bruises.

I then investigated his internal organs. The anatomy was normal. There were no enlarged glands, the heart, liver, kidneys, pancreas and testis were all normal.

The lungs did contain serous effusions (approximately 100 ml each side) and there was oedema fluid present. Both conditions means that there was watery fluid within the lungs. Oedema is a build-up of fluid in the body which causes the affected tissue to become swollen. Effusion is an abnormal collection of fluid in hollow spaces or between tissues of the body.

In respect of bony structures within the body there was no evidence of any bony injury, no fractures were detected anywhere.

I received the toxicology reports on the blood and tissue samples that had been sent off for toxicology. Toxicology revealed low concentrations of paracetamol, citalopram, ibuprofen, caffeine and diazepam in postmortem blood. These were in keeping with therapeutic use, probably administered in hospital, rather than an example of excessive use of these drugs.

2,4-Dinitrophenol (DNP) was also detected in his blood.

There was no evidence of significant natural disease that may have caused or contributed to his death."

Gerard thanked him and then asked, "Where you able to ascertain why he died?"

"Yes, in my opinion it is likely that the DNP caused death due to toxic side effects. I certified the cause of death to be: 2,4-Dinitrophenol Toxicity."

"Are you able to assist as to whether there is a safe dose of DNP for humans and whether that was exceeded in this case?"

"DNP is a synthetic chemical used historically in the manufacture of explosives, dyes, herbicides and fungicides, but more recently it has become popular for its use as an unlicensed diet aid. It is known commercially by names including 'Suifo Black' and 'Nitro Kleenup'. However, it is known to cause severe systemic poisoning with symptoms including an increased heart and respiration rate, highly elevated body temperature, a lack of energy and hypotension. Deaths have been solely attributed to DNP poisoning.

There is little to no data regarding blood or plasma concentrations of DNP, both from asymptomatic exposed persons and those taking the compound for weight loss purposes. However, three deaths owing to dinitrophenol poisoning as a weight loss product were found with ante-mortem blood DNP concentrations of 28, 36 and 99 mg/L. In this case the concentration was in the order of 21 mg/L.

Although it is not possible to determine a fatal DNP blood concentration, it is very likely to have resulted in very serious toxic effects."

David had not intended to ask the pathologist any questions but he decided he had one or two matters to cover.

"Dr Worthington, I understand from your report that DNP is not addictive like for example, heroin or cocaine?"

"That is right, there is no suggestion that once a person has embarked on taking it that they become dependent upon it, unless they have some underlying psychological disorder."

"Thank you. It's right isn't it that some of the literature you have referred to in your report does refer to death being caused by 'overdosing on DNP'?"

"It does although I consider that is mistaken. The expert evidence out there states that any dose of DNP can kill, so it is wrong to talk of 'overdosing'."

"But nevertheless, some of the literature does state that?"

"It does, but wrongly in my opinion."

"Generally, your findings were that the deceased was formally a fit male?"

"Yes, physically he was in a fine condition except for his lungs."

"I wanted to ask you about that, you have referred to oedema fluid, the fluid found in his lungs. Would I be right in thinking that in most cases of oedema it is as the result of heart problems?"

"Yes, in the majority of cases pulmonary oedema is often caused by congestive heart failure."

David nodded and continued, "As I understand it, that is when the heart is not able to pump efficiently. Blood backs up into the veins that take it through the lungs. As the pressure in these blood vessels increases, fluid is pushed into the air spaces, the alveoli, in the lungs."

David paused before asking, "Could that be a possibility in this case, namely that the deceased had a weak heart?"

Dr Worthington thought for a few seconds before answering.

"It is always difficult to rule anything out in medicine, but, in this case, I found nothing to indicate that the heart was not functioning properly. Indeed, it looked very healthy. Fluid can collect in the lungs for other reasons. These include pneumonia, contact with medications, trauma to the chest wall, traveling to or exercising at high elevations, or as I believe the case to be here, contact with certain toxins."

David nodded and then added, "But you cannot rule out that there was some other cause of death and that is why you stated, 'it is likely that the DNP caused death due to toxic side effects'?"

"That is right, I cannot rule out some other unknown possibility which is why I said, 'likely', however, I was satisfied that it was DNP that caused his death which is why I certified that the death was caused by DNP toxicity."

"Nevertheless, you understand from your experience that we do not deal with 'likelihoods' in criminal cases, we deal with, 'beyond a reasonable doubt'?"

"I appreciate that, but I am satisfied to that standard that DNP toxicity was the cause of this man's death."

"Even though you only used the word, 'likely' in your report?"

"Yes, absolutely."

CHAPTER 29

THE NEW HEAD OF TRADING STANDARDS

The medical evidence finished at 3:45pm and Gerard announced that he had no more evidence for the day. The judge agreed to adjourn the case but she made the acerbic comment that they would rise early today but that she hoped there would be more witnesses available tomorrow in order to properly utilise court time.

On Tuesday morning at 10:35am, Harvey David, the new Head of Trading Standards in Salisbury, strolled into the witness box, bristling slightly at the strong smell of the cleaning products used to clean the witness box. The witness box had received a thorough clean overnight and the smell permeated the courtroom.

Harvey was in his element. He was feeling very confident. He had played the game well at work and allied himself to virtually everyone in the office except for Roger Lovesay and his acolyte, Deborah Shaw. It had only been a few months before Roger found it intolerable and had been moved on to something in the Department of Parks and Gardens and Harvey had taken over in the top job. He had soon persuaded Deborah to move as well and she had taken some obscure post somewhere. He could not remember what it was, nor did he care.

Harvey was sworn and gave his name and then Gerard began to ask questions.

"Mr David, can you assist as to what your role is in this case?"

"Yes, I am employed as a Senior Environmental Health Officer with Salisbury Council. I currently work within the Commercial Safety Team. I hold a BSC Honours Degree in Environmental Health and I am a Chartered Environmental Health Practitioner. I have been qualified for 25 years. I am authorised by Salisbury Council under the Food Safety 1990, the Food Safety and Hygiene Regulations (England) 2013 and the Food Information Regulations 2013, the Health and Safety at Work etc. Act 1974 and allied regulations."

"Thank you, now can you assist as to what investigation you carried out in this case?"

"Yes, on 15th October 2019 I attended a meeting at Salisbury Council Offices to discuss a potential joint food safety operation. The meeting was called by the then head of the department, Roger Lovesay."

It was noticeable to David that Harvey smiled at this stage. He assumed there must have been some office politics at play here.

Gerard had also noticed the smile but ignored it.

"Can you tell us what the investigation was about?"

"Yes, at the meeting, I was provided with information from the local NHS and a police report suggesting that we look into any potential Trading standards offences relating to the death of a young bodybuilder, a twenty-five year-old male who died from DNP toxicity (the toxic effects of consumption of an alleged weight loss capsule known as DNP which stands for 2,4-dinitrophenol)."

"Had you ever heard of DNP before?"

Harvey hesitated a little, "I believe I had heard of the substance, but I had never been directly involved in a case concerning its use."

David noticed that Harvey was sweating a little. So did Gerard, but again he ignored it and he asked, "What information were you given?"

Harvey looked more confident as he replied, "A member of my staff, Deborah Shaw had carried out extensive enquiries and had established that the deceased, Jensen Willmott, had purchased DNP from a company called 'Slimming, Limitless Inspiration and Motivation UK Ltd (SLIM UK)'. In her research Deborah discovered that the defendant in this case, Nashad Pritchard, was the company director of that organisation.

I put together a team from my offices to fully investigate the matter, namely, Kerry Williams, Peter Wilson and Jenny Seaton."

Gerard paused before asking, "You mentioned that a Ms Shaw had carried out a lot of investigative work prior to you being asked to take over this investigation. Was she a member of your team?"

It was Harvey's turn to pause.

"No, I believed that she would have been an excellent addition to the team but she was involved in a number of important projects and could not be spared for this investigation."

Again, it was noticeable that Harvey was sweating profusely. This time Gerard made a comment.

"Are you alright Mr David?"

Harvey paused and took a sip of water before answering.

"Yes, sorry, I had covid four weeks ago and although I am covid free now, I am still a little weak."

The judge quickly intervened.

"Mr David, would you like to give your evidence seated? No one will object."

"No thank you, your honour, I prefer to stand."

The judge ignored that she had been wrongly addressed by the witness, in her experience most witnesses got the address to a High Court Judge wrong.

Gerard however, made the point for her, "Thank you, My Lady. Mr David can you tell us what your investigation revealed?"

"Yes, certainly. A co-ordinated investigation was carried out with Salisbury Council to follow the link with Mr Pritchard and the company SLIM UK. Checks were carried out by Salisbury Council and they identified that Mr Pritchard was associated with two addresses. His home address at 6A Ashton Street, Milford and a business address at 10 Coventry Street, Salisbury.

On 2nd November 2019 I applied for a Warrant of Entry at Salisbury Magistrates' Court to enter both addresses, so they could be searched simultaneously, this was authorised the same day.

I then arranged with the police to carry out the searches and to arrest Mr Pritchard.

On 4th November 2019 at approximately 6:20am I attended Mr Pritchard's home address with police officers and members of my staff, Kerry Williams and Peter Wilson. Simultaneously Jenny Seaton and other police officers attended the business address.

Police officers asked Mr Pritchard to open the door of his home but as he failed to do so and made no response to their request, they were forced to break down the door using a police battering ram.

I was present during his arrest when he was arrested for the manslaughter of Jensen Willmott. He was cautioned and made no reply. He was then handcuffed and taken away by police whilst we searched his premises.

Together with the police officers we made a thorough search of Mr Pritchard's address moving from room to room and bagging the evidence. Photographs were taken on entering each room. We worked systematically as a team searching all the rooms for evidence and placing all the evidence we found on a dining table in the kitchen.

That evidence was then taken to our offices so we could consider it in detail."

"What type of items did you take away?"

"There was a great deal of correspondence, many examples of Asian artefacts, £9,000 in cash, as well as phones and a Chan Lai series 11 laptop computer. There was also an almost empty 10kg drum that had traces of yellow powder in it. The drum was later checked and the traces of powder were found to contain 92% DNP."

"Was there any other DNP on the premises?"

"No, this was his home address, which was of course separate to his business address. We did not find any other evidence of DNP except for the small trace amounts of powder in the drum."

What did you do with the phones and the laptop computer?"

"They were sent to a forensic laboratory to be analysed."

Gerard nodded, "Yes, we will hear about their findings later.

What was in the documentation that you found?"

"We spent a great deal of time sifting through it. A lot was personal documentation that was irrelevant to our investigation and which we put aside in order to return it to Mr Pritchard.

There was a large amount of bank correspondence including bank statements for SLIM UK LTD as well as Mr Pritchard's personal banking accounts. We sent all those documents to our Financial Investigation Department to deal with, headed by Peter Wilson who was with me during the search."

He did not add that apart from a seventeen-year old school leaver, Terry Finnegan, who had recently joined the organisation, Peter Wilson was the 'Financial Investigation Department.'

Gerard interrupted again, "Yes, we will hear from Mr Wilson later in the case."

"What did you do with the Asian artifacts you seized?"

"Those were placed into storage pending the result of this case."

From the back of the court there was a semi-audible, "They have nothing to do with this case."

The judge looked up and asked, "Mr Brant is your client trying to communicate something?"

David looked round at the dock and saw the bemused faces of two jurors between him and his client, before he saw Nashad shaking his head.

"No, My Lady I don't believe so."

The judge looked sternly at Nashad who started to fidget, then she turned to Gerard.

"Continue Mr Smedley."

Gerard gave her a polite smile before stating, "Thank you, but in fact I had finished my examination in chief."

The judge looked slightly surprised but then she turned to look at David, "Mr Brant, do you have any questions of this witness?"

David responded, "Thank you, My Lady, I do have a few."

CHAPTER 30

CROSS-EXAMINING TRADING STANDARDS

David slowly turned towards Harvey and paused for a few seconds as he was in no rush. He then asked his first question, "Mr David, when you first began this investigation, you were not Head of Trading Standards, Mr Roger Lovesay was?"

"That's correct."

"When did you take over the investigation from Mr Lovesay?"

"I was involved in the investigation from the very beginning and put the investigation team together. Mr Lovesay had given me the task of investigating the matter but he took no part in the investigation himself, so I never, 'took over' the investigation from him, as such."

"Thank you, I suppose that explains why there is no statement from Mr Lovesay in the papers."

"Yes, that's right."

David consulted his own papers for a few seconds before asking, "So as the Head of Trading Standards and as the head of this investigation, I presume you have had access to all the papers in this case as well as photographs, emails, videos and police bodycams?"

Harvey hesitated before replying, "I have had access to all that material but I have not had the time to consider it all. As head of the investigation, I have had an overarching approach to the material and have considered the reports generated by others, but I have not looked at every document that was seized, there simply wouldn't be the time."

David nodded as if he understood.

"You told us that you had heard of DNP before but had never been involved in a case concerning its use?"

"That's correct."

"What had you heard before about DNP?"

Harvey hesitated and was visibly sweating again.

"I had heard of its existence. I had heard that some people had used it as a slimming aid and I had heard that it was dangerous. Nothing more than that."

"And was that knowledge as a result of your then position in Trading Standards?"

"Yes, I believe so."

"So, it wasn't as a result of general knowledge or general reading?"

Harvey looked quizzically at David.

"I'm sorry I don't understand what you mean."

"What I am suggesting is that your limited knowledge about DNP is as a result of the nature of your work and not as a result of knowledge gained as being simply a member of the general public?

"I suppose that must be right."

"Because generally the public has not heard of DNP?"

"No, it not been very well publicised. It should be so that we can avoid more deaths like the one in this case."

Harvey was particularly pleased with that answer. David just ignored it and carried on.

"So, a general member of the public would not know what DNP was?"

"Probably not unless they were a body builder or an anorexic and had been looking for a slimming aid."

Harvey was building in confidence now.

"They would not know what it looked like?"

"No."

"Nor what legitimate uses it had?"

"No, I doubt it."

"Nor whether it was poisonous or not?"

"I suppose not."

"So, if someone was selling DNP which they had been told was a miracle slimming drug, their general knowledge would not have alerted them to the fact it was a poison?"

Before Harvey could answer, Gerard was on his feet.

"I do object to that question My Lady, it is asking the witness, who is not an expert, to speculate about the knowledge that some wholly unknown person might have. It is asking for speculation and guesswork and is entirely hypothetical."

The judge turned to David, "That must be right Mr Brant. You are not really asking a question but asking the witness to make a comment that he is probably not qualified to make?"

David hesitated, he knew he was on shaky ground, but it did not matter, hopefully the jury would get the point that Nashad had no reason to know he was selling a poison, without obtaining a specific answer from the witness.

"Very well My Lady, it is the defendant's case that he was unaware of what he was selling believing it to be a slimming aid, but I will not ask this witness anymore about it and I will see if there is another witness who can deal with this point. I shall move on now."

The judge looked at him over her spectacles, clearly annoyed that he had not simply desisted from asking the question rather than make a short speech about his client's case, but she decided to say no more.

David turned back to the witness.

"You have told us that you obtained a warrant and went with the police to execute it at Mr Pritchard's home address?"

"Yes, that's right."

"You have made a witness statement about that visit but not exhibited any notes you took at the time. Did you take any notes?"

"Yes, I would have jotted some down and then used them to make my witness statement later."

"Do you still have those notes?"

Harvey hesitated and thought for a moment, "I don't believe so. As soon as I made the witness statement, I would have shredded the notes."

"Is that standard practice?"

Harvey looked a little uncomfortable.

"I don't know if it is a standard practice, but it is mine."

David looked at Harvey's witness statement in front of him.

"So, the notes you relied upon to make this statement are no longer in existence?"

"That's right."

"So, we cannot check the accuracy of your witness statement against those notes?

"No, you can't but I would have done at the time I made the statement."

David paused before asking his next question.

"You have told us that you went to the address and because Mr Pritchard did not open the door quickly enough, the police smashed the door down?"

"Yes, that's right."

"How long did they wait before smashing the door down?"

Harvey exhaled loudly, "I don't know."

"Was it seconds or minutes?"

"I don't think it was minutes."

"I suggest that Mr Pritchard replied when the police announced their presence and said something like, 'I'm coming'?"

"I didn't hear that."

"There was only one external door and it was quite thin?"

Harvey hesitated a little but then replied, "I believe so, it's a few months ago now."

"I suggest that the police officers almost immediately smashed the door down as soon as announcing their presence?"

"I think a few seconds passed and there was no sign that Mr Pritchard was going to open the door."

"The battering ram was used to smash the door down and after the first hit on the door, Mr Pritchard shouted something like, 'Stop, I'm coming'?"

"I never heard that."

"But the officer smashed the door down anyway?"

Harvey shook his head and then smiled as he said, "The police did use the battering ram but they were obviously concerned that Mr Pritchard might try and dispose of items before they gained access."

He was quite happy with that answer. David was not.

"Are you seriously suggesting he could get rid of a 10kg drum that contained traces of DNP in the few seconds it took to break down the door? He could hardly put it down the toilet!"

Harvey wiped the sweat off his forehead, it was feeling very warm in this courtroom.

"Obviously not, but he could have got rid of documentation."

"Large amounts of documentation were seized as well as a laptop computer containing thousands of documents and emails?"

"Yes."

"He could not have got rid of those."

Harvey asked the judge if he could sit down as he was not feeling very well. The effects of covid were weakening him. The judge agreed and Harvey sat down in the witness box before David carried on.

"When you gained access to the flat, the police immediately arrested Mr Pritchard on suspicion of causing the manslaughter of Jensen Willmott?"

"Yes, that's right."

"They cautioned him?"

"Yes, they did."

"It would have been obvious to you that Mr Pritchard was in a state of shock?"

"I don't believe so.

"Really?"

"I believe he was quite calm. He almost looked like he was expecting us."

Harvey was happy with that answer, take that Mr Queen's Counsel!

David did not change his pace, "Mr Pritchard replied to the caution with the question, What?"

Harvey tried to remember what he had said earlier.

"I don't think he replied to the caution."

"Is it that you cannot remember whether he did or not?"

"I believe he did not reply to caution."

"That's what you said in your witness statement."

Harvey smiled, "Yes, I recall now he didn't say anything after he was cautioned."

"Are you sure?"

"Yes, positive."

David made a quiet comment to Sara, who pressed a few buttons on her computer. He then turned to Harvey.

"As head of this investigation you have had access to all the bodycam videos taken by the arresting officers?"

Harvey suddenly realised where this was going and he wiped his forehead furiously. He felt he was drenched in sweat.

"As I said, I had access, but I didn't watch them."

David smiled at him, "Let's watch one together then."

He turned to Sara who now pressed play on her computer. It was linked to the televisions in the courtroom. The video started up and was taken from an officer's bodycam. It showed the other officers obtaining access to the premises within seconds of asking Nashad to open the door. A muffled voice could be heard from the flat saying something like 'I'm coming.' The police officer smashed at the door with the battering ram and again a muffled comment could be heard saying 'Stop' but the officer with the battering ram kept hitting the door until it came off its hinges and collapsed inside the flat. Nashad's face could be seen on the video. He looked in a complete state of shock and when told he was being arrested, he said, 'What?'

David turned to the witness, "Does that bring back any memories now?"

Harvey did not reply.

CHAPTER 31

THE SENIOR ENVIRONMENTAL HEALTH OFFICER

After lunch Gerard announced that his next witness was Jenny Seaton of Salisbury Trading Standards.

After a few minutes, Jenny walked into court. She was dressed in a dark blue trouser suit with a blouse with a lacy collar. She wore dark rimmed glasses and was heavily made up. David thought she was probably in her forties. She looked as though she was an efficient no-nonsense type of person.

Jenny took an affirmation and then gave her full name and her qualifications.

"I hold a BSC (Hons) Degree in Environmental Health and I am a qualified Environmental Health Officer registered with the Environmental Health Registration Board. I hold Chartered Membership of the Chartered Institute of Environmental Health. My current position is as a Senior Environmental Health Officer with Trading Standards. I have been working in that position in Salisbury for the last twelve years.

Gerard began questioning straight away.

"Ms Seaton, I understand that on 15th October 2019 you first attended a meeting about this case in your offices in Salisbury?"

"Yes, that's right."

"At the time the Head of Trading standards was Roger Lovesay and I believe he mentioned that he was looking into a case of DNP poisoning?"

"Yes, that's right."

"Had you heard of DNP before that meeting?"

"No, I don't believe any of us had."

Gerard looked up from his papers hoping she was not going to contradict Harvey David. He continued cautiously.

"I believe Mr David took over from Mr Lovesay, I understand he had heard of DNP before?"

Jenny raised her eyebrows slightly and hesitated a little, "I don't know, I suppose he may have done. I certainly had not."

"So, you had never been involved in any cases involving DNP before that date?"

"No, I had not."

"We have heard that Mr David was tasked with putting a team together to investigate the death of Jensen Willmott and you were part of that team?"

"That's right."

"After initial investigations, Mr David obtained warrants to search the home and business premises associated with Nashad Pritchard, the defendant in this case?"

"That's right."

"On 4th November 2019 you together with police officers searched Mr Pritchard's business address at 10 Coventry Street, Salisbury. Can you tell us what happened that day?"

"Yes, certainly. There was no one at the premises and the police officers had to gain access by breaking the door using a police issued battering ram. The police entered first and then when they announced it was safe, I followed."

"What did you find?"

"The premises were quite small. We entered a large room at the front, there was one 'office' at the back of the premises next to a kitchenette. The large room had clearly been set up to produce capsules. There was plastic dust sheeting covering the floor, protecting the carpet and a small desk that contained a large bag of capsules. Some were blue in colour and some were yellow. There were several boxes of items and two large 25kg drums with labels on them that was written in what appeared to be Chinese. On examination one was found to be full of DNP and the other was half full of DNP. The later analysis stated that the contents were each approximately 92% DNP."

David looked at Jenny, she was clearly a positive individual, she had not referred to the drum as being 'half empty'!

Jenny continued without noticing or caring that David was looking at her.

"On a table towards the back of the main room were two plastic tubs with small amounts of yellow powder and an encapsulating piece of equipment that appeared to have been used to place yellow powder in the blue and yellow capsules."

"Was that yellow powder later analysed?"

"Yes, it also contained approximately 92% DNP."

"What happened to the powder?"

"We had to dispose of it quickly and safely. We were informed by Government chemists that it is extremely dangerous and in large containers it could explode so we decided against storing it for this trial."

"What else did you find in the premises?"

"On the floor near the table there were further bags of blue and yellow capsules, a measuring jug that was covered in a yellow powder, some plastic packaging and next to them was another stainless steel piece of equipment."

"Did you take any photographs of the search and what was found?"

"Yes, I did."

Gerard asked the jury to turn to Jury Bundle 1.

"At pages 300-340 of Jury Bundle 1, we have a number of photographs taken on 4th November 2019. The first fifteen were taken at Mr Pritchard's home address, the next twenty-five were taken by you at the business address. Can you just confirm that you took those photographs."

Jenney opened the bundle and looked through it carefully until she came across the photographs she had taken. She then looked at each one of the photographs carefully.

"Yes, pages 316-340 of that bundle are the photographs I took at 10 Coventry Street, Salisbury."

"Did you find anything else in the premises?"

Yes, there was a set of cupboards on the side of the room. In the central cupboard I found a box of syringes, some cardboard boxes with vials and different chemicals in jars and bottles."

"What type of chemicals?"

"They appear in the photos but there was a great deal of Amino acids and you can see in photograph 327 something called, Caffeine Anhydrous Pharma-Grade."

"Did you search any other areas?"

"Yes, we searched the office and found items of correspondence which we put into exhibit bags. We also searched the small kitchenette. Behind one kitchen cupboard door there was a large autoclave. The type seen in laboratories and used to sterilise equipment. I recall that it was very large and very heavy. One of the police officers struggled a bit removing it from the cupboard.

"How would you describe the premises?"

"Throughout the room there was a fine layer of yellow dust. It covered every surface and all the equipment. It was all over the plastic that protected the carpet and in parts where the plastic did not cover the carpet, the carpet was stained yellow."

"Were you wearing masks during the search?"

"When we entered the premises, we weren't but after seeing the yellow powder everywhere we all put masks on for the search."

"How were you when you left?"

"I did feel very hot and nauseous. I was fine before I entered the premises so I put it down to exposure to the yellow dust before I put my mask on."

CHAPTER 32

MAKING HEADWAY?

Gerard thanked the witness and sat down. David rose slowly to his feet. In reality there was little he could ask the witness. Unlike her boss, she had given her evidence factually without nuance and she seemed more intelligent and so was unlikely to make any mistakes. A different approach was needed.

"Ms Seaton, when you first gave evidence today, it sounded like you believed that when you had your first meeting about this case on 15th October 2019, that no one in your office save for Mr Lovesay and Ms Shaw had heard of DNP?"

Jenny looked a little uncomfortable.

"I didn't think anyone had heard of it before but obviously I didn't know. Someone may have heard of it."

"What about Mr David?"

Jenny hesitated.

"I didn't think he had heard of it before, but I don't know."

"Why did you think he had not heard of DNP before?"

Jenny looked uncomfortable but she had taken an oath.

"I thought that because I discussed the case with him after the meeting and I thought he told me he had never heard of DNP before ..."

She quickly added, "... but, of course I could be wrong."

David could not resist, "Oh, I doubt that."

The judge peered at him over her glasses. David decided it was time to move on quickly.

"As you have told us, on 4th November 2019 you and several police officers searched Mr Pritchard's business premises at 10 Coventry Street, Salisbury?"

"Yes."

"That property was in a residential area, it was not an industrialised area?"

"No, it was in a row of residential houses."

"From your description, the place sounds like it was chaotic?"

"I'm not sure I'd use the term chaotic, but it was in a bit of a mess."

"You referred to entering the property and then you said, 'The large room had clearly been set up for the production of capsules'?"

"Yes, that's right."

"It was very amateurish though wasn't it."

She looked at him aporetically.

"I don't know what you mean."

"This was not a standard factory, was it?"

"No."

"It was not in an industrialised area?"

"No."

"There were few if any safety precautions for anyone dealing with DNP?"

"No."

"As you have told us, there were dust sheets around but these did not even fully cover the carpet?"

"No."

"There was yellow dust everywhere?"

"Yes."

"There were no air filters in place?"

"No."

"No proper cleanup of the material?"

"No."

"The equipment was all over the place and not all neatly stacked in one place?"

"No."

"Clearly there was potential contamination everywhere?"

"Yes."

"You did not see any protective clothing or masks?"

"No."

"The place was chaotic."

"I suppose it was."

David paused so the jury could take this exchange in.

"You have told us you were in the premises for a short time and yet you fell ill, probably because of the DNP in the air?"

"I was in the premises for four hours in all."

"But only a short period without a mask?"

Yes, I believe so."

"Anyone working in that place for a number of hours would clearly have been exposed to DNP?"

"Definitely ..."

She quickly added, "... in my opinion."

"If the person placing the DNP into the capsules knew it was DNP and how toxic it was, you would expect them to take precautions, such as install air filters, wear body suits, wear masks or some form of head covering?"

Gerard was on his feet again.

"My Lady, I do object, Mr Brant is asking this witness to speculate."

David frowned as he addressed the judge.

"With respect, the question is perfectly permissible, my learned friend has taken this witness through her qualifications and her job description as a Senior Environmental Health Officer with Trading Standards and through a detailed questioning of what she found in the premises and its uses. I am entitled in the circumstances to ask for her assistance in this regard."

The judge thought for a few seconds, "I will allow the witness to answer the question, but please Mr Brant do not take this subject any further than you have to."

David thanked the judge, "Ms Seaton, can you answer my question?"

"I suppose it depends on the individual concerned but I would be surprised if someone who knew the risks, would work in that environment for any appreciable length of time."

David smiled at her and thanked her for her evidence before sitting down.

CHAPTER 33

THE LAPTOP EXPERT

After Jenny had given her evidence, the judge adjourned the case to the following day. On Wednesday morning Gerard announced that his next witness was Harry Dowse, a computer expert.

Harry came into court carrying a large file of papers. David knew from the papers that he was the prosecution's computer expert. He had not come across him before and so he observed him as he set up in the witness box. Harry wore spectacles and was dressed casually in jeans and a chequered long sleeve shirt without a jacket. The days of experts wearing suits to court were clearly coming to an end. He was probably mid-thirties and looked like someone who spent most of his time bent over a computer screen.

Harry affirmed that he was going to tell the truth and then gave his name and his qualifications.

"I am a Digital Forensic Investigator at Rogers and Dowse Forensic Computer Consultants, specialising in the forensic examination of computers. I have a Master of Engineering (Computer Science) and I am a Member of the British Computer Society. In March 2021, I successfully completed the X-Ways Forensics Course. I have written reports in several hundred cases and I have given evidence in over two dozen cases."

Gerard thanked him and then moved on, "Mr Dowse, I understand that you examined a Chan Lai series 11 laptop computer in this case that was seized from Mr Pritchard's home address at 6A Ashton Street, Milford?"

"That is correct."

"Can you tell us what your findings were?"

"Yes, certainly, a forensic copy was made of the computer's hard drive onto an evidence disc to avoid any possible corruption of the computer during the investigation. That evidence disk was given the number NP171181924.

The first information was that the registered owner was Nashad Pritchard. The last recorded use of the computer prior to our investigation was on 17th November 2019 at 4:17pm.

Several photographs were discovered on the computer disk which clearly were of Nashad Pritchard and I assume members of his family and friends.

The laptop contains personal information such as a Curriculum Vitae and shows the author was Nashad Pritchard.

I continued to examine the material captured on the evidence disk and discovered reference to the company, 'Slimming Inspiration UK Ltd' being registered at Companies House on 4th April 2019. The Director then was one Lee Han Ong.

Further documentation indicated that on 3rd May 2019 the company changed its name to 'Slimming, Limitless Inspiration and Motivation UK Ltd (SLIM UK)'.

I found documents relating to the purchase of laboratory equipment on 13th May 2019 and on the same day documents relating to orders for DNP to be purchased and shipped from a Chinese company."

Gerard interrupted the witness.

"Is there a description of the equipment on the computer?"

"Yes, it was called a single punch tablet machine, the same type as those used to the pharmaceutical industry. There was a pdf file on the computer which was an instruction manual for this piece of equipment."

"Can you assist what 'a single punch tablet machine' is?"

Harry looked at his notes.

"Yes, the manual described it as a Pharmaceutical Tablet Press, also known as tablet punching machine and a tablet compression machine. Apparently, it is a mechanical device that compresses powders or granules into tablets which are all uniform size shape and weight and which all contain approximately the same quantity of a powder."

"So presumably a device to fill the blue and yellow capsules in this case?"

"Yes."

"What else did the computer reveal?"

Harry again looked at his notes.

"The computer also revealed that on 13th May 2019, 10,000 foil bags labelled, 'Food Colouring Pigment' were also ordered.

Further records on the computer showed that the first shipment of DNP arrived in this country on 8th June 2019 and that was followed by a large number of internet orders for DNP.

Of note there was an email on 9th August 2019, where Mr Pritchard wrote an email to Lee Han Ong saying he had to stop filling the capsules for a few days because he had inhaled some of the powder and felt nauseous and very ill as a result.

I was asked to concentrate on orders by and shipment to a person called Jensen Willmott. He first ordered the produce on 9th September 2019. He ordered 10 pills on that occasion, a further ten pills on 15th September 2019, a further ten pills on 18th September 2019 and a final order of 30 pills on 23rd September 2019."

Gerard interrupted, "So, a total of 60 pills in 15 days?"

"Yes."

"Four a day on average?"

"Yes."

"At a total cost of £165."

"Yes."

"Just help us with this, did you ever find a note on the computer system recommending how many pills should be consumed?"

Harry looked through his notes, "Yes, I found a document that was to be printed out and presumably placed within each package that said no more than one pill should be consumed in a 24 hour period."

"And yet an average of 4 pills a day were being sold by Mr Pritchard to Mr Willmott."

"Yes."

Gerard looked at the jury to see if they had got the point, satisfied that they had, he thanked the witness and asked him to remain there as there might be some more questions.

CHAPTER 34

A QUESTION OF MATHS

David did not waste any time but immediately dealt with the last issue raised by Gerard.

"Mr Dowse you have told us about the orders made for this slimming product by Mr Willmott?"

"Yes."

"But of course, the company received thousands of orders, didn't it?"

"Yes, I was asked to concentrate on Mr Willmott, but there were thousands of other orders."

The company was making something like £20,000 a month profit after the price of purchasing the product, the equipment, rent and all other costs were considered?"

"I don't know the exact figures but I believe I have seen something like that figure in the papers."

"Well, it was a figure given by Mr Smedley in opening this case for the prosecution, so I'm going to assume that it is accurate."

Harry looked a little uncomfortable as he replied, "I'm sure it is."

"If a package of 10 pills cost £30 and a packet of 30 pills cost £75, there must have been thousands of packages being sold each month?"

Harry did the mental maths.

"Yes, depending on how many of each package was sold, it would be between hundreds and thousands to make that type of profit."

"If there was only one person in the office; taking the orders, taking the payments, keeping a record of those transaction, pressing the powder into capsules, packaging it into the foil packages and posting the orders, they would be very busy, wouldn't they?"

"I would think so."

"Probably working seven days a week?"

"Possibly"

"They would not have had the time to check how many orders were made from an individual customer. They would have been concentrating on fulfilling the orders for hundreds if not thousands of customers."

Harry nodded, "I think that's fair."

"You were asked about the number of pills that Mr Willmott ordered."

"Yes, that was the area I was asked to concentrate upon."

David looked at his note.

"It was put to you that Mr Willmott ordered sixty pills in a fifteen-day period, namely, four pills a day."

"Yes, it was."

"But clearly Mr Willmott did not consume sixty pills in fifteen days?"

Harry looked confused.

"I have no idea how many he consumed."

"Precisely. You can only assist us with how many he ordered. You don't, as an example, know if he gave any away to other body builders?"

"No, of course not."

"Or whether he planned to store any, for when he felt he needed them?"

"No, of course not."

"I suggest that a supplier would have been in the same position and would have no idea how many pills a purchaser consumed in any time period?"

"I suppose that must be right."

"In any event, the dates of orders were not the dates when the pills arrived at Mr Willmott's home address?"

"No, obviously it would take some time for them to be sent through the post."

David nodded and pointed to Jury Bundle 1.

"We know, from documents supplied by the prosecution, that Mr Willmott kept a diary. We have copies of it in the Jury Bundle 2 at pages 110-207."

Harry looked concerned, "I haven't seen that diary, I was only asked to look at the computer."

David nodded, "I understand that, but let me ask you to look at it now. Could we all turn to page 195."

Everyone turned to the Jury Bundle including Harry who had now been supplied with a copy.

"If we look at that page, we see that Jensen Willmott wrote in his diary on 12th September 2019 that the first batch of the slimming pills arrived?"

"Yes, I see that."

"At page 201 he wrote on 18th September 2019 that he received another ten pills. At page 204 he wrote that he received another ten pills on 22nd September 2019. At page 207 he wrote that he received the final batch of thirty pills on 27th September 2019."

"I see that."

"So, he received thirty pills in a period from 12th September to 26th September 2019 and the final batch on 27th September 2019?"

"Yes, I see that."

"We know he did not consume all of the final batch. Twenty-six pills were found in the bag when the police searched his flat?"

"I wasn't aware of that."

"No, I'm sure you were not, but it is an agreed fact in this case. It means that at most Mr Willmott consumed 34 pills from the date of receiving them on 12th September 2019 until 27th September 2019?"

"Yes."

"A period of 16 days. An average of just over 2 pills a day?"

"Yes."

"In other words, 2 pills a day until 27th September when he took 4 pills?"

"Yes, I assume so from the figures you have given me."

CHAPTER 35

THE FINANCIAL EVIDENCE

In the afternoon Gerard called his next witness, Peter Wilson. Peter was sworn on the bible and then gave his name. Gerard bowed slightly to the judge and then turned to Peter.

"Mr Wilson, I understand that you are the Head of the Financial Investigation Department at the Salisbury Trading Standards Offices."

Peter gave a broad smile as he answered, "I suppose you could call it that!"

Gerard looked a little surprised, that was how Peter's witness statement was headed. He tried again.

"You are the Head of the Financial Investigation Department?"

"Technically, yes. However, there is only me who works there regularly and we currently have seventeen-year-old school leaver, Terry Finnegan, helping me out, so I suppose that makes me the head!"

Gerard was not enjoying this and he decided to move on rapidly.

"Mr Wilson, I understand that you were given a number of documents seized from both the defendant's home and business addresses and were given access to documents found on his laptop. Is that correct?"

"Yes, that's right."

"Did you have access to any other documents that might assist you?"

"I made some searches on-line and checked the SLIM UK LTD website, but I found very little other than the documents that you have mentioned."

Gerard looked at his jury bundles.

"Can you take Jury Bundle 1 please and open it at page 156?"

The witness and the jury did so and Gerard carried on.

"Do we see here a selection of documents relating to the company's finances?"

"Yes, we do."

"Now if you turn to jury bundle 3, pages 110 onwards. Do we have documents relating to the defendant's personal finances?"

The witness swopped jury bundles and then replied.

"Yes, we do."

"You have analysed these documents?"

"I have."

"And what have you discovered?"

"Starting with the company. There were clearly a lot of 'start up costs'. There was the renting of premises to conduct the operation from; costs of machinery and items useful in the operation itself, the costs of importing the DNP, the cost of setting up a website, the costs of obtaining a laptop and phone line for the business and other ancillary costs."

"Were there any profits in the first few months?"

"No, the business started off slowly and the overheads were quite expensive, but within about three months the business was established and making about £20,000 profit a month."

"How were the pills supplied?"

"At first it was a relatively small amount with people purchasing a packet of ten pills to try. Usually within a very short time they were ordering packages of thirty pills and some were ordering the largest size packages of 100 pills."

"How much did the packages cost the customer?"

"The ten pill packet cost £30, the thirty pill packet cost £75 and the hundred pill packet cost £150."

"So, there was a large bulk price saving?"

"Yes."

"Were the pills ever sold in larger sizes?"

"No, the one hundred package was the largest."

"Were you able to estimate how many pills were sold in the business during its operation?"

"It's not easy to work this out as there were thousands of separate orders of different sizes. By the time the £20,000 a month profit was being made I estimate approximately 10,000 pills a month were being sold."

"We know the defendant started selling pills in June and started making £20,000 a month profit by September. Until the defendant was arrested on 4th November 2019, how many pills do you believe were sold.

"I have tried to follow all the orders, I believe something like 40,000-50,000 pills were sold by the defendant in a mixture of 10, 30 and 100 pill foil packets. Most of the sales were for 30 pill foil packets."

Gerard looked towards the jury to see that figures were being taken in and that the jury would realise that Nashad sold 40,000-50,000 potentially lethal doses of poison to the public. He was happy to see four or five jurors were jotting this figure down. He turned back to the witness.

"Now let us deal with the defendant's finances. You had an opportunity of looking through his bank statements that appear in Jury Bundle 3?"

"Yes, I did."

"What were your findings?"

"The defendant entered into an agreement with one Lee Han Ong. A copy of the contract was found on the laptop. Once overheads were considered, the defendant was to take 25% of the profit. The rest was to be sent to Lee Han Ong who would keep 25% for himself and pass on 50% to someone referred to only as, 'the main investor.'

"Was there any clue as to who that person was?"

"No, the document trail ends with the transfers to Lee Han Ong."

"So, what would be Mr Pritchard's profit in this case up to the time of his arrest on 4th November 2019?"

"There were documents suggesting that he made an initial outlay of £4,000. That was paid back to him by the end of August 2019. Thereafter he made approximately £4,000 a month profit."

"So, a profit of approximately £8,000 up to 4th November 2019, that means, that after August 2019, he received his investment back every month selling these pills to the public?"

"Yes, approximately."

CHAPTER 36

FINANCIAL HEADWAY

Gerard had sat down with a flourish hoping to have created the impression that Nashad was a greedy businessman pedalling death at a great profit to himself.

David rose to his feet thinking that impression had been firmly made and wondered now how he was going to dispel the notion!

"Mr Wilson, you are the Head of the Financial Investigation Department?"

"Yes."

"You have told us that the department consists of you and a school leaver, Terry Finnegan. I take it you delegate some of your work to Terry?"

Peter hesitated before replying, "Yes."

"How much of the detailed examination that you have given us, was work done by Terry?"

"None, I did it all myself."

"So, you never delegated any of the work in this case to Terry?"

"To be quite frank, Terry is still learning the ropes and if I set him a task, I often find I have to spend more time than if I did the task myself.

I invariably end up carrying out the task myself as well as checking the work Terry carried out!"

"So, we can assume that your analysis of the documents and bank accounts is an accurate one?"

"I'd like to think so."

"It is obvious from your findings that Mr Pritchard was just one of the persons making a profit from this organisation and was clearly not the main profit maker?"

"Yes, as I've said, he was making 25%, Mr Lee Han Ong was making 25% and an unknown person was making 50%, the rest of the profit."

"Yet it appears that Mr Pritchard was doing most of the work. Ordering the product from Hong Kong, taking the orders, filling the capsules, putting them into foil bags and posting them to purchasers?"

"Yes, there was no financial evidence of anyone else working from the business premises."

"Mr Pritchard appears to have been more of a 'dogsbody' in the company than a passive investor?"

"I'm not sure I would use the word 'dogsbody' but he was certainly completing a lot of tasks in the business. His signature was on most of the documentation."

"You have told us that there is evidence that he invested £4,000 into the company that was utilised to purchase equipment or the product?"

"Yes."

"Were you able to discern from the documentation just how much was invested by Mr Lee Han Ong and the mystery investor?"

"From checking the setup details, much more significant sums were invested than the £4,000. Most of the money appears to have come from Lee Han Ong. It is difficult to be precise because they were not keeping tax records, but it appears about £25,000 was invested by Lee Han Ong."

"You say they weren't keeping tax records but of course this was a new business. They would not need to file tax records for over a year?"

"That's true, but no tax software had been set up."

"Equally, although the payments of about £25,000 came from Lee Han Ong, you do not know whether this was all his money or some, or all of it, came from the so called, 'main investor'.

"Again, that's true."

"In all the documentation you saw, did it seem clear that setting up this business was the idea of Lee Han Ong or maybe, the 'main investor' and not Mr Pritchard?"

"Yes, I discovered documents about the start-up of the company and it is clear that Mr Pritchard was not behind the creation and startup of the business but was asked to join later and run it."

"And in all that documentation that you saw, is it fair to say there was no mention of starting up a business to sell DNP as a slimming product."

Peter looked confused.

"I'm sorry, I don't understand?"

"No, I'm sorry Mr Wilson, let me put the question in a different way. There is no reference in any of the startup documents to asking Mr Pritchard to sell DNP?"

"No, there's no reference to selling DNP."

"All the documentation sent to Mr Pritchard was to the effect that they were setting up a business that would sell a new miracle slimming aid?"

"Yes, that's right."

CHAPTER 37

THE PSYCHIATRIST

There was a delay starting on Thursday morning as the next witness was a psychiatrist, Dr Charles Langdon and he was travelling some distance and could not be at court until 11am. Gerard had also indicated to the court that prosecution Counsel wanted to discuss some of his evidence with him when he arrived.

Shortly after 11:30am the case was called on and Dr Langdon went into the witness box, affirmed and then gave a list of his qualifications.

"I am a Consultant Forensic Psychiatrist to the Manchester Forensic Service, in Hyde Mental Health NHS Trust. My qualifications are MBBS MRCPSYCH MSC. I have completed higher training in psychiatry at the Manchester Hyde hospital and the Institute of Psychiatry in London. In the NHS I work with many peers in a specialist services directorate, that is a national provider of tertiary eating disorder inpatient hospital services.

My personal area of specialist practice is that of mentally disordered offenders I have clinical experience in a wide variety of other psychiatric specialties, including the assessment and treatment of people with eating and personality disorders, cared for both in the community and in hospital. I regularly see body builders referred with the full range of mental health conditions, including disorders of eating and body image. I have treated athletes from across the world of sport and provided consultation to sporting bodies. I have published peer reviewed research in these areas and have provided psychiatric trainees for examination through the Royal College of Psychiatrists."

Gerard thanked him and looking at David, commented, "Dr Langdon, I doubt anyone doubts your expertise."

David smiled and shook his head. The experts that the prosecution were calling in this case were clearly of high quality and no doubt expense.

Gerard continued.

"I understand that you have relied on Jensen Willmott's medical records and his diaries to perform what is effectively, a postmortem diagnosis on his mental health?"

"That's right."

"You never met him in person?"

"No, I only became aware of his case once he had deceased."

"Can you tell us your findings?"

"Yes, obviously there are limitations in determining someone's mental health after they have died and that must be taken into account when making an assessment. However, I have reviewed all the material available and in particular, I have gleaned a great deal from his diary notes. He was a prolific diary writer."

"Can you tell us something about his background?"

"Yes, he was one of two children. He had an elder sister who was two years older than him. They shared the same mother but had different fathers. It appears that he did not see much of his birth father over the years and a major influence on his life was his uncle, his mother's brother.

When Jensen was eight, he claimed to his mother that her brother had, 'touched his willy' several times. It appears that she did not believe him and it was only when he repeated the allegation to a teacher that social services became involved. His uncle denied that any such thing had happened but in order to protect Jensen, the uncle was banned from having any unsupervised access to Jensen.

Jensen had an unhappy time at school and was subject to bullying. He was moved by his mother several times to several different schools which probably increased the problem as Jensen was unable to make any stable friendships or relationships.

When he was twelve years of age he saw a doctor about nocturnal enuresis, bed wetting. He was doing this three to four times a week. He was sent for renal scanning by his general Practitioner but no physical issues or concerns were discovered. It was believed by his general practitioner that the bedwetting was a result of instability, emotional or developmental problems in childhood. He seems to have stopped this behaviour when he reached late teens.

His diaries demonstrate that in his late teens, he disliked his body, believing he was morbidly obese, in bad physical shape and with the body of an unfit sixty to seventy-year old. He did attend his General Practitioner for help, but the General Practitioner always told him there was nothing wrong with him and in the notes the General Practitioner has stated that he told Mr Willmott that he had an 'enviable' physique.

It was in Mr Willmott's late teens that he started attending a gym, 'his Temple' as he referred to it in his diaries. Despite attending virtually every day, he never felt that he achieved anything and he believed he was still morbidly obese. His diaries refer to taking steroids, some which he obtained from other body builders at the gym and they also refer to illicit drug taking. He took cannabis and cocaine quite regularly in his late teens. He also dabbled with alcohol, sometimes to extreme, when he was particularly depressed.

His mental health was referred to by his general practitioner, Initially the general practitioner was concerned that he had mood swings and was depressive and had a depressive order, but he was not referred to a psychiatrist.

Because he believed he was morbidly obese, he took a number of slimming aids, mainly pills and diet and protein shakes. None of these seemed to satisfy him and he continued looking for new remedies, which is why he came across the defendant's 'diet pills'."

Gerard thanked him and asked, "From these medical notes and diaries are you able to make any diagnosis?"

"Yes, although I have indicated, it is difficulty to make a diagnosis without being able to examine the patient in person, I believe it is possible to make a diagnosis in this case. I believe that Jensen Willmott suffered from body dysmorphic disorder, BDD, or body dysmorphia as it is sometimes known."

"What is body dysmorphia?"

"It is a mental health condition where a person spends a lot of time worrying about their appearance."

"Is it the same as being vain?"

"Absolutely not, it is a recognised serious mental illness."

"What are the symptoms of such a condition?"

"There are numerous, but basically a person fixates on their body having a completely negative view of their appearance. So, they either refuse to have mirrors in a house or avoid mirrors or conversely, they are constantly checking themselves in mirrors. They try to hide parts of their body with baggy clothes, hats, scarves or in the cases of women, makeup. They constantly exercise or groom themselves. They will constantly ask others how they look or compare themselves with others. They tend to avoid social activities.

In extreme cases they will have unnecessary plastic surgeries, feel depressed, ashamed and even contemplate suicide."

"Is there any evidence that Mr Willmott contemplated suicide?"

"No, although he was depressed at times, there is no suggestion that he ever contemplated taking his own life."

"We know that he started taking the defendant's DNP. You have examined all of Mr Willmott's medical records and diaries, is there any evidence that Mr Willmott had become psychologically dependent on the DNP he was taking?

Dr Langdon thought for a few seconds. He had answered this question in his report, but he wanted to think for a second having recently reviewed his notes.

"There are many studies out there on the syndrome of dependence and there is a wide body of agreement. It is recognised that psychological dependence can develop in relation to any behaviour. This includes those behaviours that involve the ingestion of a substance, so long as the rewards are perceived. There are a number of factors associated with substance abuse:

(a) a sense of compulsion to take a substance,

(b) difficulties in controlling substance-taking behaviour in terms of levels of use,

(c)   evidence of tolerance, so that increased doses of the substance are required to achieve the effects originally produced by a lower dose,

(d)   persisting with substance use despite clear evidence of overtly harmful consequences.

In this case Mr Willmott's diaries declare how bad he felt using the DNP, but nevertheless he continued to take it, eventually as we have seen in an increased dose.

"So, you would say that Mr Willmott had become psychologically dependent on the DNP he was taking?"

"In essence, yes."

"What is the likely effect of Mr Willmott's mental health on his perception of any dangers associated with taking the DNP?"

"There is an accepted framework for considering a person's ability to perceive risks and dangers in making choices and it is addressed in part 1, section 3 of the Mental Capacity Act 2005. Thus, a person is generally considered unable to make a decision for themselves if they are unable:

(a) to understand relevant information to the decision,

(b) to retain that information,

(c) to weigh that information as part of the process of making the decision,

or

(d) to communicate their decision by any means,

In this case Mr Willmott does not appear to have been aware he was taking DNP as he thought he was taking a legitimate slimming pill so he did not have any, 'relevant information' to use or retain or weigh as part of his decision making process to use it.

He was aware that the pills were causing him health issues when he took them but he believed these were a natural consequence of the slimming process and his diaries state that he contacted the defendant, who reassured him that these symptoms were normal.

However, he did take more pills than were recommended and this leads me to the opinion that he had been told the risks of taking excessive amounts but nevertheless continued to take those amounts and that does show a psychological dependence on the DNP.

"We know that in reality there is no safe dose of DNP but Mr Willmott was told one pill a day was safe. Would you say he had a choice when he first took twice the recommended dose and then finally four times the recommended dose?"

Dr Langdon paused for a few seconds and looked at his notes.

"I am aware of the test expressed in the case of R v Kennedy in 2007, namely, whether Mr Willmott was;

i) less than fully responsible for his actions by virtue either of vulnerability or

ii) otherwise having been unable to make, a voluntary and informed decision to act in [one] way rather than another'.

I consider because of the diagnosis of body dysmorphia that I have made, after first taking the pills and experiencing the effects, Mr Willmott had a psychological dependence on the pills and was unable to make a voluntary informed decision when it came to taking two or four times the recommended amount."

CHAPTER 38

CHALLENGING THE PSYCHIATRIC EVIDENCE

David had a copy of Dr Langdon's report in front of him. Dr Langdon had not changed his stance at all from that report and not raised any doubts about his findings.

One of the major issues in the case was Jensen's Willmott's mental health because David wanted to rely on the fact that whatever the realities about safe dosages, Jensen Willmott had taken four times the dose recommended by Nashad. The Psychiatrists evidence was clearly that he had no choice because he was effectively compelled to take this amount.

Sara had written an advice to extend legal aid to cover obtaining a report from a defence expert and they had received their own report. Unfortunately for Nashad, the defence psychiatrist had agreed with the prosecution one, so they had not relied upon it. Under the rules they were perfectly free to ignore it but as a result they had no psychiatric evidence to rely upon and David felt there was little headway he could make against Dr Langdon's evidence. Nevertheless, he would try to make a few points.

"Dr Langdon, how many patients do you think you have seen in your career?"

"Gosh, I have never been asked that question before, I have no idea, it must run into the thousands."

"Is it important in your line of work to see a patient several times and obtain a full profile from them, a full background and ask a large number of investigative questions before making any diagnosis?"

"Absolutely, it is necessary to have as much information as possible before making any diagnosis."

"I take it you would be loath to make a diagnosis after just one hour of speaking to a patient?"

"It does depend on the patient and their symptoms, but certainly in complex cases, ideally I would see them a number of times before making any diagnosis."

"Would you say that 'body dysmorphia' is a complex condition?"

"Yes, there are usually early signs in a session that point to such a condition, but ideally I would not make such a diagnosis until I had seen a patient a number of times."

"How often have you made a diagnosis of body dysmorphia without seeing a client?"

Dr Langdon hesitated.

"Never."

"Well, that's not quite right, you have made such a diagnosis in this case!"

Dr Langdon looked uncomfortable.

"Yes, I did. Obviously in this case I could not see the client because he had died, but I had seen the prosecution witness statements and exhibits including many years of medical history and of course Mr Willmott's diaries which were particularly helpful to me so that I could reach a conclusion."

"But you accept that none of that replaces your actually seeing the client in person over many sessions so that you could make a proper reasoned diagnosis?"

"I do consider that my diagnosis in this case is both, 'proper' and 'reasoned'. However, of course it would have been better if I could have seen Mr Willmott in person and asked him directly a number of pertinent questions."

"Is there a general rule in your profession that you should not make a diagnosis unless you have seen the patient in person?"

"Yes, but there are exceptions, where, as in this case the patient has died and cannot be seen in person."

"It is quite feasible that if you had seen him over a number of sessions your opinion might be different?"

"I would say it was unlikely. A lot of what Mr Willmott put in his diary is consistent with a diagnosis of body dysmorphia."

"It is quite possible that your diagnosis would be different if you had seen Mr Willmott in person?"

"Possible, but unlikely."

"The second area you have given evidence about was his ability to make a voluntary and informed decision to act in one way rather than another'?"

"Yes."

"Again, in order to make such an assessment, you are hampered by not having seen Mr Willmott in person and asking him a series of questions over a number of sessions?"

"I agree, but I still feel able to make the assessment I have, based on all the available material I was given."

"Do you accept that there is a need for extreme caution when providing opinions on functional ability such as mental capacity?

"Yes, I agree, but I felt I had sufficient material allowing me to make an assessment."

"Do you further accept that the Mental Capacity Act 2005, that you referred to, does not provide any assistance on retrospective assessment, that is in this case, an assessment after the patient's death?"

"I do."

"In all the circumstances, would you concede that it is possible you would have made a different decision if you had seen him in person?"

"I accept that is possible but that was simply not possible in this case and I did the best I possibly could with the material available."

"Would you accept that there is a difference between an inability to make a decision and making an unwise decision?"

"Yes."

"In other words, people may know all the risks but still make a conscious unwise decision such as taking four times the recommended dose of a substance?"

"Yes, I do."

"Is it possible in this case that Mr Willmott, knew it was risky taking four times the recommended dose of these slimming pills, but nevertheless had the capacity to make that unwise choice?"

"It is possible, but I still consider that because of his body dysmorphia, he was unable to make a voluntary informed decision about taking this substance."

"But you cannot know what was actually in his mind when he took four times the recommended dose?"

"No, I have made a calculated assessment."

"Which could be wrong?"

"It could, but I doubt it. I think it clear he suffered from body dysmorphia and that rendered his decision making involuntary. He was simply unable to make a voluntary informed decision when it came to taking four times the recommended amount."

CHAPTER 39

ONE LAST PIECE OF PROSECUTION EVIDENCE

The psychiatric evidence finished just before lunch and Gerard informed the court that they had no more witnesses available for that day. He told the jury that there was a great deal of evidence that had been put into a document headed 'Agreed facts' and the prosecution were hoping to finalise that document that day with the defence so that it would be ready the following morning and then he would call the police officer in charge of the case to deal with any outstanding matters.

The judge readily agreed to this course as happy as everyone else to have an early day and she sent the jury away until Friday morning.

On Friday morning Gerard presented the jurors with a document that was 31 pages long and dealt with all the agreed evidence. He told the jury that his junior, Lawrence Winder would read out the agreed facts.

As Gerard sat down and started to prepare potential cross examination notes for Nashad. Lawrence stood up and looked toward the jurors.

"Members of the Jury, I will be reading this document to you and during the course of that, I will be referring you to pages in the three jury bundles you have in front of you. It is likely that it will take something like two hours or so and I might ask for a break halfway through before you get too bored of listening to me."

Lawrence started reading out the document which contained all the agreed facts between the parties, referring to evidence that was not challenged by the defence and which the prosecution were not required to prove by calling formal evidence.

As he referred to the three bundles and read out various documents in those bundles to the jury, the whole exercise took close to two hours with a twenty-minute break to rest his voice in the middles of his narration.

Lawrence managed to finish at 12:30 and once he sat down Gerard addressed the judge.

"My Lady before we call the officer in charge of the case to give evidence there is a short matter of law that which counsel require your assistance on. We anticipate that it will probably take until lunchtime so you might wish to send the jury away until 2pm?"

The judge nodded, "Well members of the jury you heard that. As I told you at the start of the case matters of law are for to determine so I will deal with that. It means you will get a slightly longer lunch than normal."

With that she sent them away until 2:05pm. After the jury had left, she asked, "Well what is this matter of law that arises at this late stage of the case and which we couldn't have dealt with before the jury sat this morning?"

"My Lady, I apologise for that, I had asked the officer in the case to make some final checks and we only received the answer after the jury sat. In fact, there are no new matters to put before you and the matter I wish to deal with can be seen on the DCS, the Digital Case System at pages I 125-155."

"Let me look at those page references."

Everyone in court who had access to those pages now looked at them and waited for the judge to read them. Having skim read them the judge turned to Gerard.

"I see that this evidence refers to the defendant trying to leave the country in the back of a lorry and obtaining a false passport to do so. What application do you have in relation to that material, at this stage."

Gerard looked at David, "My Lady, my learned friend Mr Brant asked me not to open that material before the jury arguing that it was bad character and therefore should not be dealt with until the jury had sufficient evidence before them to assess the weight of the evidence. As your ladyship is aware bad character evidence should not be relied upon in a weak case so we agreed with that course even though we made it plain that we do not think that this is bad character evidence.

Mr Brant also argued that the evidence is inadmissible as he says it is not relevant to any issue in the case. The prosecution case is that this is not bad character evidence as it has to do with the facts of the case and not propensity or anything like that. The prosecution submit that the attempted escape, trying to flee the country and obtaining a false passport in order to do so, is highly relevant to the defendant's guilt. It is relevant to his mindset. He knew he was guilty of the offence and was trying to flee justice and the jury can take that into account when considering his guilt."

The judge turned to David, "Mr Brant?"

"My Lady, Mr Pritchard has pleaded guilty to breach of bail and a passport offence, those pleas we suggest amount to bad character and none of the gateways are available to make the facts of those pleas admissible in this case. As is conceded by the prosecution they do not amount to propensity evidence, similar fact evidence or any other possible gateway.

If the evidence does not amount to bad character, then before it can be considered admissible, it must be relevant to an issue in the case and must be more probative of that issue than prejudicial to Mr Pritchard's case. This evidence is prejudicial for the very reason the prosecution identify. Namely, the jury might consider he is guilty because months after the incident he tried to flee the jurisdiction.

We submit that in reality if he had tried to flee the jurisdiction immediately he heard Jensen Willmott had died, there may be something in that point, but the fact it was months later is more consistent with panic or the effects of lockdown and accordingly the evidence should not be put before the jury.

The judge thought for a few moments.

"Mr Brant I will allow this evidence to be admitted and will give a full ruling later. For now, it suffices to say that in my judgment this evidence is not bad character evidence but evidence that deals with the facts of the case. It is evidence of the defendant's mindset and the jury can assess it. You will of course be allowed to put that it is not evidence of guilt but evidence of panic or anything else you might suggest, but it will be for the jury to hear both sides and test the competing arguments."

CHAPTER 40

THE OFFICER IN THE CASE

After lunch Gerard announced to the jury that the prosecution were now going to call their final witness, the officer in charge of the case DC Sonya Sharpe, the police officer who had interviewed Nashad. Gerard also told the jurors that his junior Lawrence Winder would deal with the officer's evidence.

DC Sharpe came into court armed with freshly photocopied versions of Nashad's lengthy interviews. After she was sworn and given her name, the interview documents were handed out to the jury and the judge and Lawrence advised them to place the documents at the end of Jury Bundle 3.

Lawrence then told the jury they would read the interview out. The officer would take her role and he would give the defendant's answers in order to break the monotony of the jury listening to one voice for some time.

After an hour they finished reading out all the interviews and Lawrence then said there was one other issue that he wanted to raise.

"Is it right officer that Mr Pritchard was charged with manslaughter and then bailed to appear at this court?"

"That's right, sir."

"What happened to Mr Pritchard during that period?"

Mr Pritchard tried to escape justice by fleeing from the country."

David had agreed this evidence could come from the officer rather than from calling a number of witnesses as he felt it might be less prejudicial that way.

Lawrence continued, "When was this?"

"On Wednesday 29th July 2019 at 11am, Mr Pritchard was found in the back of a lorry at Dover after a routine stop by Customs officials. The lorry was driven by a young Bulgarian lorry driver, Marko Dimov and was headed to a town known as Arbanasi, in Bulgaria."

"Was Mr Pritchard arrested?"

"He was sir."

"Was anything found on him?"

"Yes sir, he was in possession of a forged passport in the name of Peter Lovesay."

"Was he interviewed?"

"He was sir; he was asked how he came into the possession of the forged passport, what was he doing in the back of a lorry on the way to Bulgaria and how had he arranged these things."

"Did he answer any questions?"

"No sir, he had a solicitor who advised him to make no comment and he refused to answer any questions as to why he was trying to flee the country."

Lawrence sat down in order for David to cross examine the officer.

David thanked Lawrence and started to question the officer.

"Officer, is this the first time you have dealt with a case of DNP poisoning?"

"Yes, sir."

"Had you ever heard of DNP poisoning before this case?"

"I don't believe so."

"I want to ask you a few questions about Nashad Pritchard. It's right isn't it that prior to pleading guilty to charges associated with his attempt to flee the country, he had no criminal convictions, cautions or police reprimands recorded against him?"

"That's right, sir."

"He was a man of good character."

"Yes sir."

"You have watched the police video from the bodycam at the time of his arrest and you can confirm he did say, 'What' when arrested and cautioned?"

"Yes, sir."

"And he appeared shocked."

She was loathed to admit that, but she knew the jury had seen the video and he did look shocked. She would be as neutral as she could be.

"Yes, sir, that's how he appeared."

"Mr Pritchard was taken to the police station where he was allowed to see a solicitor who came to advise him?"

"That's right sir."

"It soon became clear that the solicitor had advised him to make no comment to questions?"

"I'm sorry sir, I wasn't present when his solicitor advised him."

"I'm not suggesting you were in the private consultation, but you were present in the interview when the solicitor told him that there had been inadequate disclosure by the police and he should make no comment."

Sonya bristled slightly, "Yes sir, I recall that. However, we did give him as much disclosure information as we could."

"Well, let's not get into disclosure arguments now, the solicitor advised him to make no comment because of what he said was inadequate disclosure but Nashad Pritchard clearly wanted to answer your questions. He stated he had nothing to hide."

"I recall that, sir."

"On this occasion Mr Pritchard clearly ignored his solicitor's advice and answered your questions."

"He did, sir."

"He also provided you with some information that you were not aware of?"

"I'm not sure I understand sir."

"He told you that his last contact with Lee Han Ong was when Mr Ong was catching a flight to Hong Kong from Heathrow?"

"Oh yes, he did say that."

"And you were able to obtain flight information and discovered that Lee Han Ong did catch a flight at Heathrow Airport on 28th October 2019 at 17:00 heading to Hong Kong?"

"Yes, that's right sir.

"By the time you questioned Mr Pritchard, you had not managed to sift through all the evidence you had gathered, had you?"

"No that's right. We had carried out some investigation ourselves before we arrested him and searched through some records, but we had not had time to look through everything by the time of the interview."

"Thank you. Mr Pritchard also told you there was a 'sleeping partner' in the case who was taking 50% of the profit?"

"He did, sir."

"You were not aware of that at the time?"

"I believe we were not."

"Generally, throughout the interview, he was quite cooperative, wasn't he?"

She hesitated a fraction of a second before answering, "He was, sir."

"And throughout, Mr Pritchard denied knowing he was supplying DNP, didn't he?"

"He did, sir."

David took some papers from his bundle.

"Now officer, I want to deal with Mr Pritchard being stopped at Dover. He was bailed to stay at his address in Milford?"

Yes sir."

"He was alone there, throughout covid?"

"I believe so, sir."

"It was after spending months alone, with covid around, waiting for his trial that he foolishly tried to leave the country?"

"It appears so, sir."

"Now I want to ask you a few questions about Lee Han Ong. We know he fled the country before Mr Pritchard's arrest?"

"Yes, sir."

"You have no doubt searched for him and put out an international arrest warrant?"

"We have sir, but it has not been executed."

"Did you ask the authorities in Hong Kong to search for him?"

"We did make enquiries of the Hong Kong police because that was the last place we knew where he had gone when he flew from Heathrow."

"But they have been unable to discover where he went?"

"No, they have drawn a blank. They have evidence he entered Hong Kong when he flew there but since then he has disappeared."

"In your investigation have you tried to find out who the 'mysterious investor' was in this business?"

"We have tried sir, but we have again drawn a blank. There appears to be no trace of him or her."

"Have you ever considered that the so-called, 'mysterious investor' may have been Lee Han Ong?"

"We did consider that possibility but have been unable to conclude whether he is or not."

"If he was, he would presumably have been taking 75% of the profit in this company for himself?"

"Yes, subject to any other costs he might have."

"In your investigations you have discovered that Mr Pritchard has never been involved in any fraudulent or criminal activity before this case?"

"That is right sir."

"He has never been involved in selling 'miracle slimming aids' before?"

"No sir."

"But you have discovered that Lee Han Ong has been involved in selling 'miracle slimming aids' before?"

Sonya looked towards Gerard for guidance but as he ignored her, she answered the question.

"Yes sir, we discovered that he has been involved in similar schemes in the past."

"We probably do not need any great details but did you discover that Lee Han Ong has played a similar role in a number of companies and has left the country when anyone has died, usually leaving someone behind to take the blame?"

"Yes sir, our research indicated that he has set up three such companies before this."

"All selling DNP as a miracle slimming aid?"

"Yes sir."

"And Mr Pritchard was not involved in any of them?"

"No sir."

"Though I think on two of those occasions someone has died and Lee Han Ong almost immediately left the country?"

"Yes sir."

"Leaving others behind to face charges of manslaughter?"

David knew it was a slightly risky question as he knew Brian Butler had been found guilty of manslaughter, he was hoping the officer would not mention that.

"Yes sir, that's correct."

David thanked the officer and immediately sat down.

CHAPTER 41

THE DEFENCE CASE BEGINS

The prosecution case finished at 3:50pm on Friday afternoon and David announced to the court he would be calling Nashad to call evidence but would prefer to start his evidence on Monday morning so it could be dealt with in hopefully one session. As the judge wanted to get away shortly after 4pm in any event, she readily agreed to this course.

On Monday morning Nashad walked from the dock to the witness box. It was only ten yards or so but he walked slowly and it felt to him like he had entered a marathon. He began to feel pains in his chest and his breathing became laboured. He thought to himself, why did no one believe he was ill and had been throughout this trial. He tried to remember all the breathing exercises he had learnt under Guru Darsana in India, but he could not remember any. He slowly moved into the witness box wondering if he should ask for a short adjournment, but he decided against it. He wanted this to be over as soon as possible. He did ask the judge if he could be seated for his evidence and the judge agreed.

Nashad was sworn and gave his name and waited for David's first question. He did not have to wait long.

"Mr Pritchard, I want to ask you some background questions first. When were you born?"

"I was born on 20th September 1946 in Sheffield, Yorkshire."

"Was Nashad your Christian name?"

"No, Nashad is not a Christian name. My Christian name was Robert, but I only answer to Nashad now as it is my chosen name."

"What does Nashad mean?"

"It is an Urdu name originating in Arabia and it means 'unhappy' or 'morose'."

"Why did you adopt such a name?"

"In 1966 when I was aged twenty, I became disheartened with the Western world. I wanted to visit the East and discover what it had to offer me. My father had died when I was nineteen and left me a small inheritance. I decided to use it to travel to Kochi in South-West India.

I travelled extensively throughout India but eventually settled in Kochi and came under the spiritual guidance of the late, great, Guru, Darsana.

Darsana taught me many skills and suggested I take a chosen name. I took the name, 'Nashad' because I felt I had been morose and unhappy in the West and I only became enlightened when I was in the East. I kept the name just to remind me how I had been and how far I had come from those dark days."

David had not wanted to go into the background of Nashad's name and his attack on the West, but Nashad had insisted that he wanted the jury to know all about his background. David had finally relented thinking it would be better coming out early in Nashad's evidence, rather than have the prosecutor drag it out slowly in cross examination later.

"How long did you stay in Kochi, in India?"

"I did visit other areas including Thailand and Burma as it was known, Myanmar now, but most of my time was spent in Kochi at the feet of the Guru Darsana."

"What did you learn when you were in Asia?"

"I learnt many things. I studied zen philosophy but also I studied shiatsu and some ayurvedic medicine."

"Just in case some people in court do not understand these words, can you assist us, firstly, what is 'zen philosophy'?"

"It is difficult to explain it in simply a phrase or two. I suppose you could say that' zen philosophy' is a form of meditation based Buddhism that does not rely on scriptures or doctrine but is passed on from master to disciple through hard intimate training.

"Thank you. Can you explain what shiatsu is?"

"Yes, shiatsu is a massage therapy. It was developed in Japan from a massage modality called amna but it is based on concepts in traditional Chinese medicine. One applies finger pressure on various acupressure points in order to stimulate them and balance the body's energies. It helps balance the body's energy flows and consequently the process of self-healing."

"Can you explain what ayurvedic medicine is?"

"Yes, ayurveda is an ancient Indian system of medicine. Its history dates back 3,000 years ago, some even say 5,000 years and it is still the traditional health care system in India."

"How does it differ to Western medicine?"

"Ayurveda is an Indian word. Ayur means life and veda means knowledge. Ayurvedic medicine is not just one treatment. An ayurvedic doctor will diagnose an illness and then use a wide range of treatments and techniques, including massage, medical oils, herbs, and enemas or laxatives. The Western world is very reluctant to adopt ayurvedic medicine even though it has been in use in India, successfully, for many thousands of years."

"Why did you study shiatsu and ayurvedic medicine?"

"I do feel that the West ignores Indian, Chinese and other Asian medicine, whereas if they adopted them, they could solve many of West's health problems of obesity, heart disease and other illnesses.

Within a few months of going out to India, aged just twenty, I was taken very ill, possibly because of drinking untreated water or eating some poorly prepared food. For over a week I was unable to eat and was in agony with serious stomach pains. I declined all offers of help thinking that I would get better naturally, but I did not. I started to get worse. I was then seen by an ayurvedic doctor who prescribed certain ayurvedic medicines, rest and massages and within a few days I felt well again. I wanted to learn some of these techniques myself so I could help others and also so I could make a little money to help sustain myself."

"Did you make any money from practising in these areas?"

"I made a little money but most of my 'patients' were poor and could not afford to give me much. Sometimes I would settle for food or vegetables in return for giving massages, rather than money."

"Did you ever leave Kochi after you had settled there?"

"Yes, in my early thirties, I had exhausted my inheritance and although my dear late mother sent some funds for me to survive, I felt the need to return to the United Kingdom."

At David's request, Nashad did not mention his run in with 'corrupt police officers' in India that he had told David about when he first met him. The instruction was simple, 'don't lie, but you do not need to tell the jury everything'.

"What did you do when you returned to the United Kingdom?"

"I saw my mother of course and other relatives but I also embarked on a philosophy course."

"Why did you do that?"

"My mother supported me financially but I felt spiritually bankrupt in the United Kingdom. I became depressed and began drinking too much alcohol which only added to my depression."

He looked at David as if to make a comment about David, but seeing David's meaningful stare, he decided not to and carried on.

"It was during one of my drinking sessions in a public house in central London that I was fortunate to meet Joshua Christos. He was a disciple of the great philosopher, Gusho and he told me about a course that would provide for my spiritual needs. It was the 'Life and Beauty' course in Taunton in Somerset.

"I stayed there six months and completed the course. I felt truly enlightened at the end of the course and was no longer dependant on alcohol."

He looked hopeful as he asked, "Would you like me to tell you what the course entailed?"

David quickly answered, "No thank you, I am sure that the prosecution can ask you about it, if they wish."

Nashad looked disappointed; he had told David that he would like to discuss the course with the jury to show how enlightened he had become but David had told him that there was no need to go into such detail.

David moved on, "Mr Pritchard did you stay in the United Kingdom after the course?"

"I did stay with my mother for a short while but I wanted to see Asia again and see it through my new enlightened eyes."

"So where did you go?"

"I went back to Kochi to discuss my course, my emotions, my feelings and my new outlook with the Guru Darsana."

"Did you return to the United Kingdom?"

"Not for many years, I preferred the tranquillity of my base in India and I spent most of my life there, studying philosophy, religion and continuing to practice shiatsu and ayurvedic medicine."

"We know that you obviously returned to this country to deal with SLIM UK LTD. When was that?"

"I visited the United Kingdom a few times over the years. Mainly to visit my mother whilst she was alive and also to visit other relatives like my dear niece, Wendy, your partner David."

David looked at him with cold eyes trying his best not to give away that he was annoyed. At the start of the case, he had sent a note to the judge and copied in the prosecutor to mention his relationship with Nashad. Both had agreed it was irrelevant but it was better not mentioned to the jury. David had told Nashad not to mention it but for some reason he had chosen to do so much to David's embarrassment.

David tried to recover quickly.

"Apart from visiting relatives, did you return to the United Kingdom for any other reason?"

"No, not really, I did not miss the West. I preferred the simple, unpretentious life in India. The only place I have found that rivals it is Bulgaria, which I visited before starting my business of selling a miracle slimming aid. It is like India in that it has stunning countryside and generous simple people."

Except for those in the Thracian Palace, thought David reminding himself of his appalling stay there on Nashad's recommendation.

"Mr Pritchard, can you now tell us how you became involved in the slimming business?"

"Yes, of course. It was purely by accident. I went to visit some friends in Hong Kong in March 2019. They introduced me to many good restaurants and bars and it was whilst I was in one such bar that a man came up to me and sat next to me. He introduced himself as Lee Han Ong.

He was a generous man and he insisted on buying me drinks and then taking me to dinner."

David did not raise an eyebrow, Nashad had not mentioned this generosity to him before but it did not surprise him that Nashad had his drinks and dinner paid for, it was in keeping with his character.

Nashad continued, oblivious to David's thoughts.

"Lee told me how he was interested in the West and I told him how I was interested in the East and everything that I had learned there. I told him about my interest in ayurvedic medicine and shiatsu and how I felt the West had lost out by ignoring thousands of years of Eastern medical knowledge and satisfied itself instead, with a culture of simply supplying pharmaceutical drugs for all ailments."

"When did the subject of slimming pills come up?"

"Over the dinner he told me that he was investing in a company in England which he had bought and set up called, 'Slimming Inspiration UK Ltd'."

"What did he tell you about the company?"

"He told me that he had a business partner who wanted to remain anonymous and together they had chosen the name and wanted to supply a new miracle slimming drug that they had discovered."

"Did they tell you what the drug was?"

"Lee told me he was a collector of ancient manuscripts and that quite by accident he had come across an ancient Chinese manuscript in a Hong Kong market. It was apparently a few hundred years old but was a copy of a much older document. He told me that it contained an ancient formula for a slimming aid which relied on many Chinese herbs grown in a mountainous area of China. He named the area to me but I am afraid it meant nothing to me and I cannot remember the name now. He told me that the herbs only grew at a high altitude and so consequently they were very difficult to obtain."

"Did you believe him?"

"I had no reason not to, in any event I have always been a believer that many medical remedies and other useful wisdom has been lost to us over the centuries."

"What else did Lee tell you about this miracle drug?"

"He told me that his partner and he had asked a friend, a chemist, to follow the recipe and see if he could reproduce the formula.

Apparently, the friend struggled to find or identify all the herbs but he eventually was able to put together a batch of pills based on this formula.

Lee told me that he was an obese man and he had tried the formula himself and shed 15 kilogrammes of weight in just four weeks."

"When did you come into this operation?"

"Lee told me that he could not run this operation himself because he was very busy with other projects and he was looking for someone who could take over the initial running of the company, ordering the produce from Hong Kong, taking orders, filling the capsules and selling them on the internet.

He told me he was going to Bristol in May 2019 to set up the business and asked if I would be interested in working in that business.

He told me I would only have to make a modest investment and soon I would recoup my investment many times and then the company would be able to take on other staff to conduct the work I would be undertaking and then I would just be taking out a 25% profit in the business."

"Had you ever run a business before?"

"No, I was inexperienced in business but I thought I would be able to invest my few savings and then do all the work that was necessary to make the business work."

"We know the name of the business changed to 'Slimming, Limitless Inspiration and Motivation UK Ltd (SLIM UK)', whose idea was that?"

Nashad looked proud as he replied, "That was my idea. I gave it to Lee before I had the meeting in Bristol."

"Tell us about the meeting in Bristol?"

"I came to this country and stayed ...."

"David looked at him coldly, hopefully Nashad was not going to mention Wendy again!

"... with a relative. I then went to Bristol and stayed in the Imperial hotel waiting for the meeting."

"When did the meeting take place?"

"On Friday, 10th May 2019."

"Who did you meet there?"

"I expected to meet Lee's business partner but there was only Lee there.

"Why were you meeting in Bristol?"

"I don't know. It was Lee's suggestion. I assumed the business was based there but when I was there, he said he wanted to base the business in Salisbury."

"Did he give any reason for that?"

"No, not really in any detail. I believe he mentioned something about cheaper overheads in Salisbury but I cannot be sure."

"Did you have any suggestions as to where the business should be based?"

"No, apart from relatives in the United Kingdom, I have no real connection with any place, so Salisbury was as good as any other."

David had no doubt that Lee Han Ong's business had originally been in Bristol with Brian Butler who had been convicted of manslaughter, but he had to be careful in the questions he asked, to avoid referring to that fact.

"Were you aware that Lee Han Ong had been involved in other companies selling supposed miracle slimming aids?"

"No, not at all. I thought this was a new venture."

"Were you aware that people had died from pills that had been sold by Lee Han Ong's companies in the past?"

"No, not at all."

"Or that others had been charged with manslaughter as a result?"

"No, of course not."

"If you had been aware of any of these facts, would you have agreed to become involved in this business?"

"Certainly not."

That was far enough on this point for David's purpose.

"What did you discuss at the meeting?"

"We discussed my investment in the business, the product, the potential returns and matters like that."

David looked at his notes before asking, "We have heard that you invested £4,000 in the business?"

"Yes, that is right. It was all I had left from my mother's inheritance."

"What role were you to have in the business?"

"Lee told me I would be the managing director. I would be responsible for ordering the product, taking orders, fulfilling those orders, taking payment and being responsible for transferring funds to Hong Kong."

"If you were to do so much, why were you expected to invest in the business?"

"Lee explained that it was so I would show some commitment. He and the other investor were investing much more."

"Did he ever say who the other investor was?"

"No, he always said that the man wanted to remain anonymous."

"Did that surprise you?"

"No, not really. I have lived in Asia for many decades. Many people I have come across do not want all their business concerns to be widespread knowledge."

"How did the meeting end?"

"I agreed to operate the company."

The judge intervened at 11:30 stating that the defendant had been giving evidence for the best part of an hour and she asked David if that was a convenient time for the jury and his client to have a break. She meant that she wanted a break, but it was always better to suggest it was for others' benefit. David agreed as Nashad was looking a little tired as well. Before they left court David decided it was important for the jury and in particular for Nashad, to be reminded of one important rule.

"My Lady, I have informed Mr Pritchard that whilst there are breaks in the process of giving evidence, neither my junior nor myself will be able to speak to him, I wondered if Your Ladyship would just confirm that fact."

The judge agreed, "That is right Mr Pritchard, I am sure you know that is the rule."

Nashad nodded but did not say anything. With that the judge adjourned the court for twenty minutes, although it was nearer thirty minutes when they restarted the proceedings.

David began with a short recap.

"Mr Pritchard, before the break, we were dealing with your meeting with Lee Han Ong in Bristol. You have told us that you discussed investing in the company, what your role would be and that you agreed to operate the company as managing director?"

"That is right."

"Who obtained the business premises in Salisbury and your home address in Milford?"

"Lee organised the lease of the business premises in Salisbury and I obtained my residence in Milford."

"Your name was on both leases?"

"That's correct. Lee suggested that as I would be operating the company it would be better if I was named on the business lease."

"We have heard that the first order for DNP arrived in this country on 8th June 2019?"

"That is right, although I thought it was an order for a slimming drug. Lee organised the first shipment which was a 10 kg drum."

"Was that the empty drum that was found at your home address?"

"It was."

"That drum was labelled as DNP, fertiliser. Did that not make you suspicious?"

"No, Lee told me that licencing of pharmaceutical goods would take an enormous amount of time and he wanted to get this product on the market as soon as possible to help people, so he told me that the slimming drug was falsely labelled as a fertiliser."

"Why did you take the drum home with you?"

"I thought the empty drum might be useful for storage. I had a lot of items that I thought could be packed into it."

"Did you ever use the drum for storage?"

"No, I found it impossible to clean. Whenever I tried, yellow dust went everywhere and would cause yellow stains. In any event when I tried to clean it, I inhaled the dust and I did not feel well."

"Did that not cause you any concern?"

"No, not really, I suspected that inhaling any drug, as opposed to swallowing it, would make me feel unwell. I am aware of drug usage in the East and how people obtain a quicker fix inhaling drugs rather than swallowing them. I thought the same applied to this slimming aid."

"We know on 9th August 2019 that you wrote to Lee about inhaling the yellow powder when you were packaging it into capsules. Was that a different occasion?"

"Yes, it was. I was much worse on that occasion. I believe I inhaled a large amount of the powder that was in the air because I was trying to fill many orders at the same time."

"What were your symptoms?"

"I felt nauseous, very hot and generally unwell."

"Did this make you think that what you were working with was not a slimming drug but something far more toxic?"

"No, not at all."

"Why?"

"I just felt that I had inhaled too much of the powder. After that I did wear a covid mask when I filled the capsules but that was simply because I did not want to inhale any more of the powder."

"Similarly, when you sold the capsules, you labelled the packages as, 'food colouring'. Why was that?"

"Again, the same reason as to why the drums were labelled DNP. Because the drug was not licenced and we did not want to draw attention to it from the postal services."

"How busy were you working for the company?"

"Very busy. There were many orders and I found it difficult to keep up to date. I have never worked so hard in my life."

David paused, he could believe that part of Nashad's evidence, even if he struggled with believing some of the rest.

Nashad continued without apparently gauging David's thoughts.

"As I was getting so busy, I did think of employing someone but I never got around to it."

"At any stage did you think you were selling a poison or an explosive?"

Nashad shook his head from side to side.

"Not at all, I always thought it was a miracle slimming drug based on an ancient formula."

"Did you ever get any complaints from customers?"

"I had one or two but I offered refunds."

"What type of complaints did you receive?"

"One or two people said the pills did not help them lose weight."

"Did you ever have a complaint that the pills made someone ill?"

"Not ill as such. Some people phoned to say they were feeling hot and a little nauseous, but Lee had assured me that these were signs that the pills were working and these symptoms would not last long and I told people this was the case."

"We know you supplied Jensen Willmott with DNP. Do you remember him ordering the slimming product?"

"Not really, I had so many orders from so many people for varying amounts of the drug. Some people ordered a bag of ten pills to test, most ordered a bag of thirty as a month's supply and a few ordered a bag of 90 pills as three month's supply."

"We have heard that Mr Willmott ordered from you and spoke to you on the telephone. Do you recall that now?"

"I regret I do not. I did speak to a lot of customers."

"We can see from his diaries that he states that he was surprised that the first batch you sent to him was labelled, 'food colouring pigment' and he phoned you to see if he had received the right order. Do you recall that?"

"A few people phoned me about that and I always told them the same thing, we were waiting for the product to be licenced. I do not recall Mr Willmott's call specifically."

"He also stated in that diary that you phoned him back and explained that the product was not licenced in the United Kingdom but was licenced in other countries. Do you recall that?"

"I don't remember the call but, in any event, I would have said it is not licenced anywhere yet because to my knowledge it was not."

David looked down at his notes.

"We can see from the documentation that you supplied that you advised that people should only take one pill a day. Where did that recommended dosage come from?"

"Lee told me that the chemists who created the pill recommended that it was a powerful drug and people should only take one pill a day."

"We have heard that Mr Willmott ordered a total of sixty pills from you in fifteen days. Were you aware that he ordered so many?"

"I was not, I did not keep a tally of how many pills any single person ordered. I simply did not have the time. In any event we sold packages with ninety pills in which people ordered. Sixty pills was not an inordinate amount, it was two month's supply."

"Did you have any idea how many pills your clients were consuming in any period?"

"No, of course not. I assumed that people would follow the instruction and only take one pill a day. The warning was in large letters on a sheet of paper inserted in every order that I sent out."

"When did you hear that Jensen Willmott had died from taking DNP?"

"I read a newspaper article in late October 2019 that referred to his death stating it was because of him overdosing on DNP. Although I had many orders, I thought the name was unusual and I remembered it from my order book and assumed that either he had taken something in addition to the slimming pills I had supplied, or that he had died from overdosing on the slimming pill."

"What did you do when you heard the news?"

"Nothing really."

"Did you continue taking orders and fulfilling them?"

"I did."

"You said you thought the man may have taken something in addition to the pills you supplied or overdosed on your pills. Did you think of halting your supply of this product to find out?"

"No. I thought that if the young man had overdosed on the pill that was not something I could control, just like a Chemist cannot control if someone overdoses on a prescription pill or from something like paracetamol."

"Did you have any further contact from Lee Han Ong?"

"I did."

"It was within a day or two of the newspaper article appearing. He phoned me from Heathrow airport."

"What did he say?"

"He said he was flying to Hong Kong from Heathrow airport on urgent business matters. He told me to carry on with the business and to wire the bulk of the profits to Hong Kong as usual."

"Were you concerned that he was leaving the country?"

"Not at first."

"When did you become concerned?"

"When he would not respond to any of my phone calls or emails."

"Have you had any contact with him since?"

"None whatsoever."

"Mr Pritchard, we know you were arrested on 4th November 2019 at your address in Milford. Did you hesitate to open the door when the police called out?"

"No, I had little chance to respond before they smashed my door down. I told them I was coming but they immediately started smashing the locks. I shouted to stop but they continued and completely broke the door and frame and rushed into my home."

"What happened when the police arrived?"

"They grabbed me, forced me to the floor and handcuffed me."

"Did they say anything?"

"They told me I was being arrested for manslaughter."

"Did you say anything?"

"I was in a state of shock, as the police video shows, I just said 'what' and as the handcuffs were hurting, I asked the police to remove them but they would not."

"We know you were taken to the police station and you were given the opportunity to contact a solicitor to advise you before the interview. It appears from the transcript that he advised you to answer no questions but you did answer the police questions, why was that?"

"I had nothing to hide, I was happy to answer all their questions."

"You were then charged with manslaughter and bailed to appear at this court?"

"That is right."

David paused and looked down at his notes again. He decided that was enough about Lee Han Ong and Nashad's arrest, it was almost 1pm and time to bring the examination in chief to a close.

"Mr Pritchard, we have heard that you were stopped at Dover in the back of a lorry that was due to travel to Arbanasi in Bulgaria. How did that come about?"

"I was alone in Milford, I had no job, limited funds and was alone throughout the first covid lockdown period. I could not see anyone. I became depressed and worried about the trial. I obtained a forged passport for £500 and came across a young lorry driver who agreed to take me to Bulgaria for £1,000."

"You knew you should stay for your trial?"

"I did but I just panicked. I was worried that no one would believe me and that I would spend the rest of my life in jail."

"Where did you get the passport from?"

"I did start drinking heavily again. I went to a local public house, 'The Salisbury Arms' because it was close to where I lived and was cheaper than other public houses in the area. There I met a man who I would rather not name for fear of repercussions. We began talking and over the days I told him all about my troubles. He told me he had some criminal contacts and could arrange for me to obtain a forged passport and a trip to Bulgaria in a lorry. I liked Bulgaria after my visit there earlier last year and in a moment of stupidity I spent the remains of my savings obtaining the passport and the means of getting to Bulgaria. I also gave him £500 for his troubles."

"Did you flee this country because you were guilty of manslaughter?"

"No, not at all! I was scared, I was stupid and I panicked."

"Mr Pritchard you have seen all the evidence in this case?"

"Yes, I have"

"Do you now accept from the evidence you have seen and heard, that you were supplying DNP to members of the public in the form of slimming pills?"

"I do."

"At the time you supplied those pills, did you know they contained DNP?"

"No, I did not, I genuinely believed they contained a miracle slimming drug."

"Mr Pritchard, are you guilty of manslaughter?"

Nashad paused and scanned the jurors' faces before answering.

"Most definitely not."

CHAPTER 42

NASHAD CROSS EXAMINED

Nashad's evidence in chief had taken all the morning and it was 2:05pm before Gerard started to cross examine. He did not want to waste time though and went into his questioning barely giving the jury time to sit down.

"Mr Pritchard, apart from the investment role of Lee Han Ong and the mysterious unknown investor, this was your business?"

"I'm sorry I do not understand the question."

"SLIM UK LTD was your business?"

"I ran the business on behalf of myself and the investors."

"But you did everything in the business; ordering the chemicals from Hong Kong, filling the capsules, taking the orders, supplying the orders, taking the money, distributing the profits, it was all down to you."

"I do not like the word, 'chemicals' I thought this was a synthesised slimming drug, but yes, I was overworked."

"You will forgive me, but even on your case, a synthesised slimming drug was a chemical?"

Nashad looked uncomfortable.

"I suppose so."

"And you tell us you now know it was DNP, a chemical, a poison, a fertiliser, an explosive. So why do you object to the word, 'chemical'?"

Nashad looked even more uncomfortable.

"You are right, I withdraw my objection to the word, 'chemical'."

"Did you originally object because you are trying to minimise your involvement in supplying this poisonous killer drug?"

"No."

"Let's move on then and I will ask you again. Apart from being an investor, you did everything in this business?"

"Yes, as I said, I was overworked."

"Effectively, it was your business from beginning to end?"

"I suppose so."

"You sold this product as a slimming aid?"

"Yes, that is what I believed it to be."

"You intended that the product would be consumed, ingested by humans?"

"Of course, there was no other way of taking the pill."

"You realised that you owed your customers a duty of care?"

"I am sorry, I do not understand the question."

"You were supplying your customers with a product that you knew they would ingest?"

"Yes."

"You obviously owed them a duty of care not to supply them with a poison?"

"Yes."

"You agree now that you were supplying DNP?

"Yes, although at the time I thought it was a slimming pill."

"Would you agree that DNP is a toxic chemical, a poison?"

"I know very little about DNP. I believed I was selling a miracle slimming aid."

"You have heard the evidence in this case from Professor James Bulling. Would you agree that DNP is a toxic chemical and there is no safe dose?"

"I have heard the evidence of Professor Bulling, I am not sure he is right about there being no safe dose. It appears that thousands of people appear to take DNP, knowing it is DNP and only a few have died or been injured because of taking it."

Gerard paused and looked at him sternly.

"Surely one death is enough?"

"Any loss of life is tragic, but people do die if they overdose on paracetamol or on prescription drugs. No one refers to them as toxic chemicals, as far as I am aware."

Nashad looked very proud of himself with that answer until he noticed a few frowns on the faces of the jury particularly a large woman who sat in the jury box.

"You claim that you believed you were selling a slimming product?"

"That is right, I believed I was selling a product based on an ancient Chinese formula recently discovered in an ancient manuscript."

"Is that true?"

Nashad looked surprised.

"Yes, it is."

"As we have seen, you purchased drums of chemical from an industrial company based in China?"

"I believed I was purchasing a miracle slimming drug."

"Supplied in 10kg or 25kg drums from a chemical factory?"

"Yes. I did not know how drugs are supplied in bulk, I thought this was how they were supplied and I then put them into capsules using a machine that could fill hundreds of capsules at once. I presumed that is how all bulk purchases of drugs are made. Someone has to put drugs in capsules."

"The emails show that you ordered those drums of DNP?"

"Yes, but Lee Han Ong put me in touch with the company, telling me it supplied the slimming drug and that is what I believed."

"Although the drums supplied had Chinese writing on them, they clearly stated they were 'DNP' and clearly stated they were 'fertiliser'?"

"I have tried to explain that. We knew the drugs were not licenced and I believed we had to use a false description on them to avoid customs issues."

"But they were drums of DNP, fertiliser?"

"I know that now but at the time I thought they were a slimming aid."

"I suggest that all along you knew this product was DNP?"

"I did not."

"There is correspondence between you and Lee Han Ong describing it as DNP?"

"I agree, but I thought that was just an attempt to disguise the fact that this was a slimming drug."

"You knew that you were supplying a dangerous substance?"

"I did not."

"You have told us today that you became ill when you tried to clean the empty ten kilo drum of DNP?"

"That is true."

"In your email of 9th August 2019, you described to Lee Han Ong that you had become ill from inhaling the powder when you were filling the capsules?"

"That is true as well."

"From either or both of those instances, you must have realised just how dangerous this substance was?"

"I thought it was like any other drug. I imagine it would be dangerous inhaling too much paracetamol."

"What quantities of powder were you inhaling?"

"At my home it was very little because the drum was almost empty. In my business address it was more because I was there throughout the day filling the capsules and breathing in the powder."

"So, you knew from inhaling a small amount of this powder at home, that it was dangerous?"

"No, as I said, I believe inhaling any drug might be dangerous even in small doses."

"How would you describe yourself Mr Pritchard?"

Nashad looked surprised.

"I am sorry, I do not understand your question."

"At the time you were filling these orders, were you a perfect size, thin or slightly overweight?"

"I was overweight, I indulged a little too much in food and wine."

"Would you have liked to lose some weight?"

"I think most overweight people would."

"So why didn't you take any of these miracle slimming pills then?"

Nashad again looked surprised at the question. He hesitated before answering.

"I don't know. I thought it was a business. I never thought of taking them myself."

"Or was it because you knew the pills were poisonous?"

"No, I assure you I did not think that."

Gerard decided he had exhausted that subject so he would move on.

"Before this case, were you aware of the condition known as body dysmorphia?"

"No, I had never heard of it."

"Were you aware of the condition known as bulimia?"

"I had heard of it."

"Had you heard of anorexia nervosa?"

"I had heard of it."

"So, you were aware that there are people out there who have issues with their bodies?"

"Of course."

"People who would welcome a remedy to lose weight?"

"Of course, that's why we were selling what I believed to be a safe sliming pill."

"You knew there were people out there who might take more than you recommended?"

Nashad hesitated.

"I never thought of that, I thought people would read the warning note in the package not to take more than one pill a day."

"You're an intelligent man, you were aware that people overdose?"

"Of course, but I never thought they would with our product."

"You were aware that the market for slimming aids is massive?"

"Of course, that is why I thought this was a good business to invest in."

"You were aware that some people suffer from bulimia and anorexia nervosa?"

"Of course."

"You were aware that some unfortunate people out there overdose?"

"Of course."

"You must have been aware that there was a risk that someone taking your product might have bulimia or anorexia nervosa and might ignore your warning on the packet and overdose on your product?"

"I never had that thought process. I assumed people would take the recommended dose."

Gerard stared at Nashad for a few seconds, putting on a look of complete disbelief.

"Let me ask you about the recommended dose. You advised people to take one capsule a day?"

"Yes, where did that advise come from?"

"As I said earlier from Lee Han Ong."

"Where did he get it from?"

"He told me from the chemists who created the slimming drug."

"It must have been obvious to you that the suggestion of one pill a day being a recommended dose was absurd?"

Nashad looked surprised at the question.

"I don't see why. Lee said that was the figure given to him by the chemists who created the substance."

"But it did not take into account; the sex of the person taking the pill, the weight of the person taking the pill, or the age of the person taking the pill?"

Nashad looked uncomfortable.

"No but that is what I was told was the recommended dose."

"What if a ten year old was ordering your product?"

Nashad smiled, "I doubt he would have access to a credit card."

"Do you find this funny Mr Pritchard?"

Nashad stopped smiling.

"No, I just thought your question was silly."

"You had no idea how old your customers were?"

"No."

"They could be skinny teenage girls with access to credit cards?"

Nashad was looking even more uncomfortable.

"I don't believe so."

"You never checked though?"

"No."

"Surely you would accept that your pill would have more of an effect on a small underweight teenage girl than say a tall, heavily overweight muscular man?"

"I never thought about it."

"Is that because you didn't care?"

"No."

Gerard paused for a few seconds to let some of the jurors who were making notes catch up.

"Mr Pritchard, you have told us that you became aware that Jensen Willmott had overdosed on your product in late October 2019?"

"I became aware that he had overdosed on something, it might have been our product or it might have been something else?"

"Might you have become aware of his death in early October 2019?"

"I don't believe so."

"His death was referred to in the newspapers in early October 2019, not late 2019?"

"I am sure that I only became aware in late October 2019. I might have been reading an old newspaper, I do not recall now."

"In any event by late October 2019 you were aware that Jensen Willmott had died and it might be, or probably was, from ingesting your product?"

"Yes."

"And yet you carried on supplying your product to anyone who would buy it, despite his death?"

Nashad looked uncomfortable.

"Yes."

"You knew that your product was potentially dangerous and yet you continued to supply it?"

"I did not consider it dangerous if the correct dosage was taken."

"But by now you were aware that someone had died from overdosing on your product. It must have occurred to you that there might be someone else out there who might take too much of your pill and overdose?"

Again, Nashad looked uncomfortable and started to move from side to side in the witness box, shifting his feet.

"I did not think like that."

"If you had thought like that, would you have stopped supplying the DNP?"

Nashad hesitated.

"I don't know."

"You simply did not care if someone died taking your product?"

"That is not true."

"What steps did you take to ensure that no one else died?"

"I made sure there was a warning in the packet."

"You knew there was a warning in all of the packets supplied to Jensen Willmott?"

"Yes."

"Nevertheless, you continued to supply DNP to unsuspecting people who might die from taking it?"

"It was not like that."

"It was exactly like that, wasn't it?"

Nashad mumbled an almost inaudible 'no'.

"Sorry, what did you say?"

Nashad spoke loudly in reply, "No."

"I suggest you knew all along that the product you were supplying was DNP?"

"I did not."

"I suggest that your entire motive in supplying this product was greed and you did not care what risks, including the risk of death, you subjected the general public to?"

"That's not true."

CHAPTER 43

THE TELEVISION PROGRAMME

Gerard's cross examination finished at 4:30pm and the jury were sent home with the judge giving the usual warning to forget about the case, not to conduct any research themselves or contact each other overnight and to come back at 2pm the next day when she would provide them with written directions relating to the law and then they would hear from the prosecution in their final speech to the jury.

Once the jury had gone, she addressed David and Gerard and suggested that they be back at court at 10am the following day to discuss her legal directions. Draft copies of the legal directions would be sent to all counsel that night for them to consider.

It was not a great imposition to David as he had little else to do in his hotel room in Salisbury except to watch the television.

At 6:30pm the judge's first draft of the directions appeared which was eighteen pages long. Within half an hour David had considered them and phoned Sara. There were one or two directions he would like to change slightly but overall, there was nothing missing and no unfavourable directions so they could not raise any real objections to them on behalf of Nashad.

At 7:45pm his takeaway Chinese meal was delivered to the hotel and he went through the usual rigmarole of phoning the hotel staff so that they would come from wherever they disappeared to and open the front door to allow his meal in.

He was soon sat in front of his television eating his now cold beef chow main, flicking through the television guide to see what was on at 8pm when he came across a channel called, the 'Health Channel' which was showing a programme titled, 'DNP the killer slimming drug'.

David immediately switched the programme on and at the same time texted Sara to tune in on her hotel television. He soon lost his appetite for his takeaway as he watched the programme and made notes on his laptop computer.

It began with the narrator announcing that there were increasing instances of young people, bulimic young women, or body building men, who had resorted to taking DNP in order to lose weight and/or to try and sculpt their bodies.

"One such person was Jensen Willmott. He was a man who believed that he was fat, overweight and had a repulsive body. He obtained DNP from an online company run by an eccentric man, Nashad Pritchard, who had spent most of his life in Asia where the DNP is manufactured."

There was then a video of Zoe Slater telling the programme narrator how she had met Jensen shortly before his death, how they had become very close and had planned to live together and how he was tragically taken away from her by consuming this poison, 'sold to him by that evil man'.

The narrator went on to announce that since 2007 twenty-five people had died after taking DNP which had been advertised online as, 'a miracle fat burner.'

He stated that DNP was still relatively easy to purchase online and how many people who struggle with weight and self-image were turning to it as a solution to their problems, sometimes not knowing that what they were taking was a poison or knowing that it was but still willing to take the risks, because of their obsessive need to lose weight.

The programme finished with a tearful Zoe Slater saying how fortunate it was that the man who had supplied Jensen with the pills that killed him had now been caught by the police and prosecuted. She hoped he would get, 'his just desserts' and no more Jensen's would die.

On Tuesday morning the atmosphere in court was heavy and easily felt by all the advocates present. David had emailed his notes of the programme to the judge and prosecution and stated that he had no choice but to ask for the jury to be discharged and for a further trial to be listed in some months' time with a fresh jury, when the programme might be forgotten.

In Court he expanded on this submission.

"It is beyond doubt one of the most egregious examples of contempt of court to air this programme during this trial and particularly at this time. Any juror who has seen that programme could not help but be affected by the content and be prejudiced against our client just as they are about to consider their verdicts.

No doubt the court will want to hear from the producers of that programme and consider contempt proceedings against them, but meanwhile the damage has been done and, in our submission, there is, sadly, no remedy but to discharge this jury and start this trial in the future with a new jury selected from a fresh panel of jurors."

Gerard had a different approach.

"The first question we should ask is if any juror did in fact see this programme. It was on a channel which I have never heard of before called, the 'Health Channel', not on one of the main television channels that you might expect a jury to watch and it may well have been missed by all twelve of the jury.

However, even if they did see the programme, we all must work on the basis that jurors take their oaths seriously and will only try the case on the evidence they have heard in court and not on some obscure television programme. Your Ladyship warned them all about the potentially serious consequences of relying on anything other than the evidence they heard in this courtroom and there is nothing we have seen to suggest that they will not follow that direction."

David was given a right to reply which he anxiously took.

"I agree that there is nothing to suggest that the jurors would consciously breach their oaths after the serious warning that they received at the start of this case from your Ladyship, reaffirmed just yesterday. However, there are circumstances where they could be swayed unintentionally by extraneous matters and this programme is one such example. It contained facts about DNP; it specifically referred to Mr Pritchard and a witness the jury have heard from, Zoe Slater, even made comments about Mr Pritchard being 'an evil man'. The jurors may try to follow their oaths and not be consciously affected by what they saw, but subconsciously, this programme may well have influenced them and sway them against Mr Pritchard and that is a risk this court should not take and, in our submission, there is no alternative to discharging the whole jury."

The judge appeared to give careful thought to the arguments and after a few seconds she announced that she would like a little time to think about matters. At 11am she retired announcing she would sit again in half an hour.

Shortly after 11:30am the judge came back into court and announced.

"I did not see this programme myself but I have read the very helpful note prepared by Mr Brant QC and his junior. I take a very serious view about anyone airing such a programme during a trial like this and I shall want the producers of this programme and any person behind the decision to air this programme at this time, to appear before me tomorrow on the basis of potential contempt of court.

In relation to the jury, I understand Mr Brant QC's concerns and I have considered, seriously, whether I should discharge this jury. On balance I have decided not to. I have considered whether to send a note to the jury asking them if any of them saw this programme. Again, I have decided not to embark on that course as it will draw their attention to the programme if they have not seen it and might make some who may have seen it discuss it with the others. However, I have decided that I must give them a further direction in this case about trying the case on the evidence they heard in this trial and not on anything they may have heard elsewhere including this television programme.

CHAPTER 44

THE PROSECUTION FINAL SPEECH

At 11:40am the jury returned to court and as the judge had just informed the advocates, she gave the jury a careful warning about trying this case solely on the evidence and not on any extraneous material that they might have come across, whether it be in newspapers, or on the television, or through any other form of media.

Neither the Prosecution nor the defence had anything to raise about her written directions, so she then embarked on providing the jury with written copies of her directions and then proceeded to read them out slowly for the purposes of the tape of the proceedings. She completed that task shortly before 1pm and then sent the jury away for lunch.

At 2:10pm when the court sat again, the judge looked towards Gerard and asked him to give his final speech to the jury.

Gerard thanked her and then turned to face the jurors. He saw a number had taken up their pens to make notes during his speech, which he was happy about. It meant that at least a few would be listening to him!

"Members of the jury, there is no doubt that this case is distressing and it is likely to excite extreme emotions, involving, as it did, the senseless waste of life of a young man who had everything to live for. However, it is essential, as you were directed this morning by her Ladyship, that you judge the issues coldly and clinically putting aside all emotion and prejudice whether it be in favour of the prosecution or the defence.

Again, as you were directed by her Ladyship, the burden of proving the allegations made against the defendant rests entirely upon the prosecution and for you to convict the defendant the prosecution must make you sure of guilt. Nothing less will do.

It is probably useful if I now summarise the prosecution case to you before going into detail as to why we say you can be sure of Nashad Pritchard's guilt.

First, this product, DNP, was not a miracle slimming drug, it was a poison, an explosive and was never intended or expected to be ingested by humans. It was injurious to health, toxic and highly unsafe.

Secondly, Mr Pritchard accepts that he placed this substance on the market for human consumption so that it would be ingested by human beings and used as a supposed slimming aid.

Thirdly, putting this product on the market to sell carried with it an obvious risk of death to anyone consuming it.

Fourthly, it was negligent to intentionally put this substance on the market and to sell it for human consumption.

Fifthly, it was not just negligent, it was not just careless, it was a 'truly exceptionally bad' thing to do."

David noticed how Gerard quoted from the written directions on gross negligent manslaughter when he used the phrase, 'truly exceptionally bad'.

"Mr Pritchard admitted in cross examination that he had a duty of care to those who bought this product, but it is clear, we suggest, that he did not care what happened to the consumers of this product as is seen by the fact that he continued to sell it after he knew that Jensen Willmott had died from taking the very product supplied by him.

Sixthly, Jensen Willmott consumed the DNP that Mr Pritchard supplied to him.

Seventhly, Mr Willmott's act of taking the DNP was not fully free, voluntary and informed. Not only was he not aware what he was taking, he suffered from a mental disorder, body dysmorphia, which made him emotionally unstable with elements of a dependence disorder. That meant he could never have made a fully free and voluntary decision to take the DNP even if he knew what it was as opposed to believing it was a legitimate safe slimming aid. It also means that the fact he took more than the so called 'recommended dose' has no relevance to this case.

Eighthly, taking the DNP supplied by Mr Pritchard resulted in Jensen Willmott's death."

Gerard paused before adding, "Ninthly, we say that Mr Pritchard knew all along what he was supplying and never believed the fiction that this substance originated from an ancient manuscript containing the recipe for a miracle slimming pill."

Gerard paused for a few seconds to ensure that the jurors who were making notes managed to get all nine points down. He then continued.

"There can be no doubt that DNP is a toxic and dangerous chemical and is an obvious risk to life when consumed. Mr Brant QC made it plain when cross examining Professor Bulling that he did not dispute that it is toxic. His cross examination was along the lines that many prescription and non-prescription drugs are toxic if taken in large quantities. That is undoubtedly true but Professor Bulling made it quite plain that DNP is not like prescription or non-prescription drugs. They are designed to be taken by those suffering pain or illnesses, DNP is not. Taking this substance is like playing 'Russian Roulette.'

As he said in answer to questions by Mr Brant, 'You might not die from the first dose, but it will eventually affect you in some way and may lead to death.'

In answer to questions from me he went so far as to say, 'A single capsule of 250mg of DNP could be a lethal dose. Each time you take one you are dicing with death. Clearly, the more you take, the more lethal they become'.

You will recall that Mr Pritchard referred to a recommended dose of DNP to his customers. However, as you heard from Professor Bulling, there is no safe dose and the recommendations are of no clinical value whatsoever."

Again, he paused and looked at the jury. Satisfied that a few were still taking notes, he continued.

"Not only is DNP toxic, but Mr Pritchard was also aware, from his own experience, just how toxic this substance was, because he had been made ill by it when he was packing it into capsules. As he stated in that email to his partner in crime, Lee Han Ong, dated 19th August 2019.

'I inhaled some of the powder and felt very nauseous and very ill. I was really concerned for my health...'

He also knew that even a small amount of this powder could make you ill because he had inhaled a small amount when he was trying to clean the 10kg drum at his home. Yet despite this personal knowledge, he continued to supply DNP to vulnerable people like Jensen Willmott who ordered his first batch of tablets almost a month after that email, on 12th September 2019.

Perhaps the most telling evidence in this regard is that despite the fact he considered himself overweight and as he told you he wanted to lose weight, he never took this miracle slimming aid himself. There can only be one reason. He knew exactly what it was, it was a toxic substance and he was not willing to poison himself!"

He paused for affect and noticed a large lady sitting in the jury box nodding in agreement with him. Satisfied, he continued.

"DNP is not only a toxic substance, it is also an explosive. You will recall that Professor Bulling was reluctant to let us make the DNP he had brought to court into an exhibit, because it might explode. As you heard, Salisbury council would not store the DNP they recovered from Mr Pritchard's business premises because of its explosive qualities and yet Mr Pritchard was selling this explosive time and time again, delivered by the Royal Mail, by unsuspecting postmen and postwomen, for unsuspecting people to ingest!

What was the reason that Nashad Pritchard sold this poison?

There is only one reason. Greed!

This was a business pure and simple to him and his only interest was profit. The fact that he was engaged in a business which met the wishes of certain people was no good reason for doing so. To place this product on the market for human consumption is a crime and all such suppliers of this poison are engaged in criminal conduct.

Why take the risk of killing people?

Because this was a high profit business. Many people want to lose weight and slim. Many people want a way of doing so that does not involve excessive exercise and dieting. There are others who are desperate to lose weight even if they do not need to and they crave the so called easy fix that Nashad Pritchard offered. Sadly, Jensen Willmott was one of those.

This was a significant commercial operation which thrived on stealth and subterfuge. You have seen the documentation in this case, the business documents, the sales receipts, the invoices and of course, the emails.

It is clear that this poison was being sold for human consumption on a large scale and if Nashad Pritchard had not been arrested, he would have continued to sell it for the foreseeable future with untold consequences to potentially hundreds if not thousands of consumers.

The way the DNP was imported, in drums bearing that name and the reference to fertiliser, makes it clear that Nashad Pritchard knew what the substance was. He is clearly an intelligent man. He must have known what was being imported in industrial sized chemical drums.

The rebranding the capsules that he supplied as food colouring, was further designed to elude law enforcement agencies, because he knew what he was supplying was not food colouring but was a poison.

There can be no doubt that Jensen Willmott died from consuming the capsules of DNP that Nashad Pritchard sold to him. The open bag of capsules was near to him when he was found by the poor Zoe Slater. They had only arrived that day. Four of those capsules were missing. Those were the ones Jensen Willmott had taken. It appears that he vomited two of them up but not the other two which went on to complete their deadly work.

We know it was the DNP that killed him because despite the able cross examination by Mr Brant about his use of the word, 'likely', the pathologist, Dr Worthington, was adamant when he told you, "I was satisfied that it was DNP that caused his death which is why I certified that the death was caused by DNP toxicity.

Of course, members of the jury, you will want to look at the evidence in this case carefully. For the most part the prosecution evidence has not been challenged apart from what happened when the police broke down Mr Pritchard's door. You may think that whatever happened then, and maybe they did not give him time to open the door, it has no bearing on any decision that you have to make in this case.

You will then want to consider what Mr Pritchard said in interview to the police and more importantly what he said to you when he was asked questions first by his own counsel, Mr Brant and then by me. Did he come across as an open witness, telling the truth or was there an element of him attempting to pull the wool over your eyes?

Did he seem to find parts of the evidence amusing despite the fact a young man died in this case?

What did you make of his explanation for continuing to sell this poisonous DNP after Jensen Willmott had died from taking what he described as an overdose of his product?

You may think that is one of the most important questions in this case. Why did he continue to supply DNP when he knew Jensen Willmott had died from taking his product. Not from a massive overdose but as the papers reported, that Mr Pritchard read, after taking just four pills, two of which he vomited up. Two pills were clearly enough to kill him. If Mr Pritchard had only become aware then that this product was potentially lethal, he would have stopped supplying it then. The fact that he continued to supply it demonstrates that he knew all along what he was supplying and he did not care, all that mattered to him was the potential profit. Not the life of a young man, not the lives of anyone else who took this product."

Gerard paused and adopted a serious expression.

"The prosecution concede that this is not an easy case, but when you consider the evidence, carefully, clinically, coldly, we say there is only one proper verdict, guilty of manslaughter.

CHAPTER 45

A FINAL CONFERENCE

Gerard had taken just over an hour and a half to deliver his final address to the jury. As his junior congratulated him when he resumed his seat, the judge announced that she would not be asking David to give his speech today because she had to rise at 4pm for, 'urgent judicial business' and she knew David would need more than the 25 minutes that was left of the court day. She asked them all to be back for 10am the next day to hear the defence speech and then she would give the second part of her summing up dealing with a summary of the evidence they had heard. With that she dismissed them all.

The jury all left court followed by the judge who did not wait to see if the advocates had anything to raise. David turned around to say a quick goodbye to Nashad, but as he tried to Nashad indicated that he wanted David and Sara to visit him in the cells. David agreed but inwardly he was concerned. He knew that this could only mean one thing, Nashad wanted to discuss the contents of his final speech.

For forty years as a barrister David had refused to discuss his final speeches with clients. It was not out of arrogance but simply that experience had taught him that clients did not know what could be said in a final address to the jury.

Often they thought it was an opportunity to give more evidence when in fact, it was simply there to put, hopefully, persuasive arguments to the jury based on the evidence they had heard in the trial. For that reason, he often did not do any more than pass pleasantries with clients just before he made a final speech and he always did his best to avoid seeing them.

In order to avoid this, he asked Sara to go and visit Nashad and tell him that David wanted to go back to his hotel to reconsider his speech to deal with matters raised by the Gerard in his address.

It did not work for within ten minutes of David going to the robing room and changing there was a tannoy asking for Mr Brant QC to go to the cells.

Within ten minutes David and Sara were sitting in the cramped area in the cells with Nashad sat opposite them.

David nodded to Nashad and began to say, "Good evening, Nashad, what was it you wanted …."

Nashad immediately interrupted, "Why didn't you intervene when the prosecutor made all those outrageous comments about me?"

David inwardly groaned but tried to keep his cool. At least he did not have to deliver a speech today so there was a little less stress.

"Nashad, it is a custom in our courts that counsel does not interrupt another counsel's speech. If any mistakes have been made, then I have an opportunity to deal with them in my address to the jury. If any particularly serious mistakes have been made that need remedying, then I have the opportunity to address the judge in the jury's absence and ask her to order the prosecution to retract or correct something. However, I listened carefully to the prosecution speech and made notes. Although there are several matters that I want to comment on, the prosecutor merely put his case and never said anything that was not based on the evidence."

Nashad was clearly unhappy.

"David, he made out that I deliberately sold a poison and an explosive not caring what the effect on anyone was!"

David struggled to keep an impassioned look.

"Nashad, you have sat through this case and the evidence. That is the prosecution case against you. That is what they have said all along and what I have to deal with in my speech to the jury."

"That is outrageous David. I gave my account in the witness box. I have seen no evidence that contradicts my evidence. The prosecution should not be allowed to make such outrageous allegations."

David sighed, "Nashad, that is their job, that is their case. Now you should let me get on and try and persuade the jury that it is not the correct one and make them believe that they cannot be sure that the prosecution case is the only possibility."

Nashad was clearly unhappy but realising that he would not be able to persuade David to object to the judge about what he saw as outrageous allegations made against him, he decided to try a different approach.

"I am not happy David, but I assume you know what you are doing."

He paused before adding, "Very well, I would like to discuss your final speech with you David and its content."

David looked closely at Nashad and spoke forcibly.

"No Nashad, that is not going to happen. You have hired me to represent you and bring my forty years of experience of criminal trials to assist you. I make it a habit of not discussing my speeches with clients before I deliver them. It can do no good. You do not know what can and what cannot be said to a jury whereas I do."

Nashad looked perplexed.

"David, that is not acceptable to me. I am facing a criminal trial for manslaughter. You told me that manslaughter can carry a maximum sentence of life imprisonment and that the likely sentence in this case if I am convicted is probably 8 or 9 years. I insist that you take me through your speech and do not deliver it until I have had time to consider, and if necessary, amend the contents."

David paused for a few seconds before replying.

"Nashad, with Sara's assistance, I have crafted a speech that we think will be your best hope for obtaining an acquittal. You should rely on our expertise as you have throughout this case. I do not propose to discuss the speech with you as you will be tempted to interfere with it and probably reduce its effectiveness."

Nashad turned to look at Sara and saw that she was nodding in agreement with David.

"I am sorry, I know that you will have done your best for me but it is my life and I must insist on discussing your speech with you and adding or amending it when I think it necessary. That is my final word."

David looked at Sara and then at Nashad and rose from his seat and made his way to the door that was just a few feet away. Before arriving he turned around and asked, "Nashad, have you written a final speech?"

Nashad looked surprised.

"No, I did not realise I had to."

"You do if you will not allow me to deliver the speech that we have written. You see as far as I am concerned you have two choices. You allow me to deliver the speech we have written or you sack us both and deliver your own. It is entirely a matter for you."

Nashad looked even more surprised.

"David, I think you are being unreasonable. I am sure Wendy would not allow you to treat me in this way."

"Nashad, I do not appreciate you mentioning Wendy and I am beginning to think that I should take the choice away from you and treat myself as professionally embarrassed and resign from your case."

Nashad looked horrified. David saw the look and continued.

"However, I am willing to stay in your case and deliver the speech that Sara and I have written, which we believe gives you the best chance of an acquittal. Of course it is not guaranteed and the jury may find you guilty in any event, but we believe it is your best hope of walking away from this trial."

He turned to Sara who nodded and added, "Nashad I have worked with David on many cases now and I know what an excellent advocate he is and how successful he is with juries. He has crafted this speech and I have added very little to it. The main reason for that is because it is an excellent speech and in my opinion says all that can be said in your favour. You will not be disappointed."

David was a little concerned about how effusive Sara had been. It put enormous pressure on him to deliver a good speech and he was not sure he did have the material to do so. However, he was grateful for her support. He turned to Nashad once more.

"Well Nashad, it's your choice."

Nashad looked down at the small table and after a few seconds he replied.

"I am not happy David. I believe that you should be able to tell the jury everything there is to know about me, much of which they have not heard in this case, but I am not ready to deliver a speech tomorrow. It would take me at least a week to draft one and I accept that even then, it may not be as effective as one you professional lawyers have drafted. I must accede to your wishes and allow you to deliver your speech.

I only hope you are right and it is effective as you say and secures the acquittal that I deserve from this terrible charge."

CHAPTER 46

THE DEFENCE FINAL SPEECH

There was a late start on Wednesday morning as the prison van was delayed in picking up Nashad and then dropping him off at court. It might surprise some people that a prison van could be late to court but it was such a regular occurrence that David and Sara did not think twice about it. The judge, on coming into court, did make the usual comments about making enquiries as to why the van was late but no doubt, as usual, those would amount to nothing.

At 11:15am the jury came into court and David rose to make his final speech. With the permission of the judge, he moved to the witness box to address them so that he could see all of them rather than have his back to some of them. He placed his written speech on his lectern that had been set up in the witness box directly in front of him. Although his preparation these days was all on a computer, he still liked to use a paper version of his speech when he addressed a jury. It allowed him to add notations when he thought of something in the hour or so before he delivered his speech when he would read it for at least the tenth time over a cup of coffee.

David waited until the jurors looked like they were comfortable and were looking in his direction, then he looked at their faces before addressing them. He saw that an older large female juror who had sat in the jury box was scowling at him, which did not bode well. Fortunately, others were expressionless, which suggested, although an advocate never really knew, that they had not made their minds up yet.

"Members of the jury, I am conscious as I address you from this witness box that I have not seen all your faces before. Indeed, for most of this trial I have had my back to a number of you as I have cross-examined witnesses. Of course I meant no discourtesy, it is simply because of the strange times we live in that the courts have had to be rearranged so that we have more space between us with the unfortunate consequences that I have not been able to see you all and have had my back to some of you.

I should also add that counsel do not normally address you from the witness box but normally address you from counsel's row. However, in order to not have my back to some of you at this stage of the trial, with her ladyship's permission I have moved here to the witness box to address you."

He paused as if contemplating.

"It is actually the first time I have ever stood in a witness box and I should say at once, it is rather a strange feeling and again a sign of the times we live in. We often address juries on the seemingly 'long walk' that a defendant makes to a witness box to answer questions before a jury. It probably surprises you that although it is only a few yards to this spot it does feel like a 'long walk'. It may also surprise you for me to state that being here allows me to realise just how lonely and intimidating a witness box is. That is a factor I suggest that we should all hold in a witness' favour when we assess their evidence, whether they be a prosecution or a defence witness."

He noted that the female juror was still scowling. He decided that he might as well give up on her and face the others!

"Having said all that, it is now my opportunity to address you on behalf of Nashad Pritchard who faces the serious charge of gross negligence manslaughter.

I suspect there is one fact that we can all be sure of in this case and that is that the prosecution have established the gross negligent manslaughter charge so you can be sure of guilt."

David could see that several of the jurors looked surprised at this admission and even Gerard looked up from his computer where he was trying to ignore David and make notes relating to his next case.

David waited for a few seconds happy that he had now got everyone's attention, including the large lady. He also noticed that Nashad, was moving uncomfortably in the dock.

"I suggest there is no doubt that one or more persons are guilty of gross negligent manslaughter in this case..."

He paused before adding, "... they are the other investors of SLIM UK LTD, namely, Lee Han Ong and the mystery man from Hong Kong, if he existed.

You may think the fact they are not here; the fact the mystery investor kept his identity a secret, the fact that Lee Han Ong caught a plane to Hong Kong when Justin Willmott died, is clear evidence that they knew all along what they were selling was an explosive, a fertiliser, a poison. A substance that was unfit for human consumption and which should never have been sold as, 'a miracle slimming pill'.

The fact they cannot be found is powerful evidence that they knew they were up to no good. That they were selling a dangerous product and that they had no intention of hanging around when poor Jensen Willmott took the product and died as a result.

What were they interested in? This was a business, a pernicious business, but a business all the same. Their sole interest was not the people they sold this product to, it was not to assist those who need to lose weight effortlessly for health reasons, it was profit, pure and simple profit.

How do you make the maximum profit in a business like this? You obtain the product cheaply, you advertise it, you produce the pills and you sell it on the internet. However, if you are aware it is a poison you want to avoid being directly involved in all those tasks so what do you do?

You get somebody else to do all the work. Ideally you get an innocent dupe, an idiot, full of himself, a person who has no experience of business but someone who arrogantly and wrongly believes that he is capable of running a business and making a small profit for himself.

In short, you want a Nashad Pritchard."

David saw Nashad shift uncomfortably in the dock, but he ignored him and continued.

"Does he need to know all the details of what he is selling?

Of course not. Indeed, if you want to maximise your profit it is better that the person you are using as a front man does not know what is going on. If he does, he might demand a bigger percentage of the profit. If he does know what is going on he might disappear at the first sight of trouble.

In this case the mystery investor was never known, his name does not appear in any of the tens of thousands of pages that were generated in this business. Lee Han Ong's name only appears in a few emails, whereas Nashad Pritchard is mentioned on almost every single page of every document concerned with this business.

The mystery investor has never been found, Lee Han Ong, who may, for all we know, actually be the mystery investor, disappeared once Jensen Willmott died, but Nashad Pritchard remained in the country continuing to fulfil orders with his name written on all the documentation and continued to send 75% of the profit from the business abroad to Hong Kong.

We suggest that the fact that Nashad Pritchard remained in this country after Jensen Willmott's death, is strong evidence that he did not know all the details of this business and believed the lie that Lee Han Ong told him, that what he was selling was a miraculous slimming pill derived from a formula recently discovered in a long lost manuscript from China.

Of course, you know Nashad Pritchard did try to leave the country after he had been arrested and charged. That is not to his credit, but by then he knew what the prosecution case was, he knew what the evidence was, he knew the full story, he knew he alone was going to face the full weight of British justice.

Wouldn't you think that if he had known that earlier he would have fled the country when Lee Han Ong did. Surely, he would have been seated next to him on the plane, or even been on the plane before him, but he wasn't. He stayed in the country, he continued to take and fulfil orders. Strong evidence, we suggest that he had no idea what was going on. No idea that he was supplying a poison."

He paused to gauge the jurors' faces. Apart from the scowling woman most still had expressionless expressions.

"Let us look at what the real issues are in this case. On behalf of Nashad Pritchard, we accept that what was supplied to Jensen Willmott was the poison, fertiliser, explosive, DNP.

We also accept that Nashad Pritchard supplied it to Jensen Willmott for payment.

We accept that it was not fit for human consumption and should never have been supplied to anyone as a miracle slimming pill.

We accept that in this case the DNP supplied was the cause of Jensen Willmott's death.

That of course is not an end of matters as you see from the learned judge's helpful 'route to verdict'.

Although you may conclude that Nashad Pritchard was negligent and in breach of a duty of care, there is another factor that the prosecution must establish before you can convict.

The next one to consider is, 'are you sure that it was reasonably foreseeable that the breach of duty gave rise to a serious and obvious risk of death?'

As the learned judge directed you, it is for you to consider this question objectively, was there a serious and obvious risk of death in selling DNP on the internet.

It is an objective question. It matters not what Nashad Pritchard thought at the time. Nor can this question be determined by an expert like Dr Worthington. It is your view of the evidence that matters.

We suggest that there is a high threshold to meet before you can say there was a serious and obvious risk of death. It is not the same as a serious and obvious risk of harm or even serious harm but a serious and obvious risk of death.

You will recall that Dr Worthington said that DNP is not addictive like heroin or cocaine, so selling it to a person does not mean that they will have a craving for more and more and come back time and time and time again to buy it until they inevitably take a fatal dose.

Of course, there is no doubt that DNP is toxic but then many substances are if they are abused. An obvious example is paracetamol.

Paracetamol is sold in a chemist or a supermarket without a prescription. If Jensen Willmott had taken too much paracetamol and then died, no one would have thought for a moment that the chemist or the young girl or boy on the till at the supermarket who supplied him with paracetamol, would be guilty of gross negligence manslaughter, whatever Jensen's state of mind.

We suggest that is the way to approach this substance. Yes, it can be lethal just like any drug can be in excessive quantities, such as paracetamol. Yes, in the case of DNP there is no medically recommended dosage because it has not been licenced for human consumption.

That does not mean that there isn't a safe dosage.

Because the authorities have not given recommended doses does not mean the DNP community has not provided its own from actual experience of taking this substance.

It is noticeable that although Dr Worthington does not agree with the references, that some of the literature he referred to in his own report referred to people dying from 'overdoses' of DNP. In itself that suggests that it is accepted by some experts that there is a safer dosage, less than an 'overdose' whatever it might be.

One thing is clear from the evidence in this case. There have been a number of fatalities around the world from people misusing DNP, but it seems many thousands if not tens of thousands of people use it without dying or suffering serious side effects.

This is an important matter for you to decide but you may think it is not the most important question.

Whatever your view on this issue there is the next question which we suggest is crucial to this case. Are you sure that Nashad Pritchard knew that this was DNP at the time he was supplying it.

His case is that he never knew he was supplying DNP until after his arrest. He thought that all along he was supplying a miracle slimming pill not a poison.

We accept that there was negligence on his part. On his own admission he was supplying a product that he knew was not licensed to be supplied.

We accept that when he supplied it, he wrongly labelled it as 'food colouring'. However, we suggest that he was not 'grossly negligent', the standard required to convict, because he genuinely believed that this pill would assist those who were obese or were determined to slim but unable to do so by diet and exercise. As Her Ladyship has directed you, Gross Negligence is a very high bar for the prosecution to meet, conduct that was 'truly, exceptionally bad'. We suggest that the prosecution have not come near to reaching that standard when you consider the evidence in this case.

It may well be that you would not have been fooled by the story Lee Han Ong told him about finding a long lost manuscript and developing a 'miracle slimming pill' from it. However, I suspect it is likely that none of you have spent your lives in the Far East practising Ayurvedic medicine or listening to the fantastic, often farfetched tales of Gurus about the meaning of life.

That is why we suggest you look at this case not from your own viewpoint, not from people with Western cynicism but from the somewhat foolish and naive view of Nashad Pritchard.

He is a man who has taken little responsibility during his lifetime. He has not worked hard in business but has been attracted by the easy life. Travelling to the Far East when young. Staying there. Living firstly off an inheritance from his father, then receiving financial assistance from his mother and then living off an inheritance from his mother.

He has not had the wider world to contend with. He has listened at the feet of self-appointed Gurus who claim to know about the mysteries of life. He has no doubt listened to their tall stories and nonsense and lapped it up as if it were true.

It is with that background, a background of gullibility, that he was approached by Lee Han Ong who no doubt saw him as an easy target and then plied him with alcohol to make him more susceptible to the rubbish he was pedalling about ancient manuscripts.

Lee Han Ong pretended that he had found an ancient manuscript with the secret formula for a miracle slimming aid. Most people would probably have thought that nonsense or at least questioned it, but Nashad Pritchard, who had accepted the tall stories of Gurus all his life, was just the type of gullible individual to believe that story without making any personal investigation.

Nashad Pritchard agreed to start a business in Salisbury where he would invest a relatively small sum, conduct most of the business and then distribute the profits.

Did he suspect there was something wrong with what he was selling?

We suggest the answer is a resounding NO.

He had never heard of DNP. I suspect most of you had not heard of it before this trial. Even the witnesses from Trading Standards, who you might expect would have heard of it, did not appear to come across it before this case landed at their feet.

Of course the prosecution made great play of the fact that Nashad Pritchard became ill trying to clean an almost empty barrel of DNP and when he was filling capsules. However, you heard Nashad Pritchard give his evidence about that. He had inhaled the powder, not swallowed a capsule and he thought inhaling any drug, even paracetamol, would have worse affects than if you swallowed it in capsule form.

If he had known how toxic this drug was, he would have ensured that he was safe when he filled the capsules and completed the orders. There would have been filters where he worked, special clothing, masks but there was nothing save some covid masks that he later used. You may recall the words of Ms Seaton when I questioned her and asked her if she would expect someone who knew about DNP would work in that environment, her answer was, 'I suppose it depends on the individual concerned but I would be surprised if someone who knew the risks, would work in that environment for any appreciable length of time.'

We suggest that Nashad Pritchard did not know the risks because he thought this was a miracle slimming aid, not an explosive poison!

The prosecution also made great play of the fact that in an email sent by Lee Han Ong there was a reference to DNP and that the barrels supplied were labelled DNP and fertiliser.

Again, Nashad Pritchard gave evidence to you that he thought Lee Han Ong was simply trying to cover up the fact that an unlicensed slimming pill was being supplied by referring to it as DNP and fertiliser.

We suggest there is nothing in the evidence you have heard to gainsay his account that he did not know he was supplying DNP."

David paused and looked at the jurors faces including the frowning lady.

"We accept on behalf of Nashad Pritchard that his behaviour was foolish, he should never have got involved in selling this product and Jensen Willmott was undoubtedly a victim. However, we suggest the evidence demonstrates that he believed the lie he had been told by Lee Han Ong that he was selling an unlicenced miracle slimming aid. Yes, he was negligent, but we suggest his behaviour was not, 'truly exceptionally bad' and that having considered the evidence carefully, as we know you will, we suggest that the one proper verdict in this case is not guilty."

David saw that the large woman on the jury was still glaring at him as he added ironically.

"Thank you for your attention."

CHAPTER 47

AN UNHAPPY CLIENT

"David, I am very unhappy with the things you said in your speech. I am beginning to wish that I had insisted that you show me your speech in advance so that I could have edited it."

After David's speech, the judge had started her summing up of the evidence. It had been a fair and detailed summing up of the evidence that the jury had heard and only the lawyers could detect her opinion that Nashad was guilty, all other persons would have assumed that she had not formed any view of the case. It was clear to David and Sara that no appeal points arose from her summing up.

At 12:20 on Friday the judge sent the jury out to consider their verdict and David and Sara went downstairs to the cells to talk to Nashad. David had deliberately left him this long to speak to as he imagined that Nashad would not have been happy with his speech. One look at Nashad's expression and he knew he was right and Nashad had now verbally confirmed that was the case.

"Nashad, I told you that you had to allow me to deliver the speech I wanted to based on four decades of experience of conducting trials as an advocate. There was never any prospect of you 'editing' my speech. I gave you your choices, either let me deliver the speech I wanted or you would have to sack us and deliver your own.

You may not be happy with the speech I gave; it was never designed to make you happy but it was constructed in such a way as to give you the best chance of an acquittal. If I had to deliver my speech now after your comments, I would say exactly the same."

Nashad shook his head, "Then I wish I had delivered my own speech. Your speech made me look like an idiot. You attacked and rubbished my life experience of searching for some meaning to life. You attacked the teachings of the great Gurus who have inspired so many and given many people, including myself, spiritual enlightment and a greater understanding of the cosmos, that people like you, with your cynicism simply cannot understand.

I chose you as my advocate because my niece, Wendy, said you were one of the best. I cannot believe that you gave your best for me David. I do not know if you have some residual dislike of me for reasons that I cannot fathom, but I believe that you used your speech to simply attack and denigrate me."

David remained calm. It was not the first time that a client had been unhappy with his speech, it would probably not be that last. Most clients appreciated what an advocate said about them but a few, like Nashad failed to understand why advocates like David presented them as naive, fools to a jury.

"Well Nashad, we can discuss this on another occasion. The jury have gone out to consider their verdict. We do not know how long they will be. They could come back with a verdict today, although it is more likely to be early next week as this is not an easy case and they do have a lot to think about.

I have no idea what the verdict will be, although we must prepare ourselves for the worse and consider what mitigation we can put forward to reduce any sentence that might be passed."

"David, I am not sure I want you to deliver any 'mitigation' on my behalf. If I am found guilty you might persuade the judge to increase my sentence!"

David's polite friendly expression changed.

"Nashad, I told you before I gave a speech on your behalf that you were welcome to sack me and give it yourself. If you would rather deliver your own mitigation in the event of a conviction, I am happy for you to do so. You are welcome to sack me now and I shall leave court now and go home. I will warn you that if you do, you are likely to make matters worse for yourself as you will have no idea what mitigates a sentence and what might aggravate it. The choice is yours!"

Before Nashad responded Sara added a few words.

"Nashad, this is a difficult case and David has done his very best to secure an acquittal for you.

I consider his final speech addressed every issue in your case and clearly made most members of the jury think. If you are convicted, you must allow David to mitigate on your behalf. There is a real danger that if you dispense with his services, and mine, because I will not stay if David is sacked, your sentence could be higher than it should be. It simply is not worth the risk."

Nashad was silent for a few seconds before he answered.

"David and Sara, I am not happy with the way this case has been conducted and the final speech was disappointing but having reflected, I consider it might be foolish to dispense with your services at this late stage so I shall not do so."

It was David's turn to pause before replying.

"Thank you, Nashad, although your response was not particularly gracious. Having considered what you have said, I am wondering now whether I can continue to represent you. You seem to have no confidence in your representation. It may be that Sara and I should leave the case now on the basis we are, 'professionally embarrassed'."

Nashad started to look alarmed. He quickly added, "I am sorry David and Sara, I have perhaps spoken hastily. These proceedings have been very stressful and I am worried about being convicted of manslaughter and the possible sentence I might face. I do have confidence in you both and wish you to continue to act for me."

David and Sara agreed that they would and left the cell area. As they did so David turned to Sara and commented, "A pity really, it means we have to come back to Salisbury next week and its depressing hotels. I almost wish he had sacked us!"

CHAPTER 48

JURY DELIBERATIONS

As David and Sara made their way to the cells to see Nashad, the twelve jurors entered the jury room and took their seats around a table. Geoffrey Simpson a chartered surveyor took the lead when he said, "So much for keeping us apart during covid. They give us lots of space divided up by plastic in court but here we are crowded again and it's not easy discussing a case with these masks on!"

There were a few groans among some of the others who were rather tired of listening to Geoffrey's gripes. They had listened to them throughout the trial during adjournments and were now bored of listening to him.

William Tyler, a local council employee, voiced the majority opinion when he said, "Well let's get on then. If we can deal with this case quickly, and of course fairly, we can all get out of here."

William addressed all the jurors when he added. "The first thing we must do is elect a jury foreman or forewoman. I've chaired quite a few meetings in my life and I'm happy to act as foreman if you like or I'm happy for anyone else to do the job."

Daphne Philpot, a housewife and a rather large lady who had frowned at David throughout his speech and through most of the trial, now turned her attention towards William.

"I think we should have a woman to act as a foreperson. There are seven women on this jury and only five men so it makes sense to have a woman foreperson as we outnumber the men!"

There was a further groan from a few women as well as men. In order to move matters forward, William asked, "Do you want to chair the meeting and deliver the verdicts in court then Daphne?"

Daphne reddened at the thought. "No, I am happy to simply take part in the deliberations but I was wondering if any of the other women would like the role?"

She looked at each woman in turn who avoided her gaze. None of them fancied taking on the role of foreman in this case.

Janice Walters, a civilian working for the Crown Prosecution Service spoke up, "I suggest we appoint William as foreman and just get on with our deliberations."

Daphne could see the mood in the room and she said nothing more about the subject meaning that William was appointed as jury foreman. He took his seat at the head of the table glancing at Malcolm Barrett. In his conversations with Malcolm, the latter came across to him as quite intelligent and he had thought that Malcolm might put himself forward for the position of foreman but he could see that Malcolm just quietly took a seat and looked quite contented.

Malcolm Barrett was a practicing criminal barrister. He knew the Bar Councils instructions on barristers sitting as jurors. For centuries barristers had not been allowed to sit on juries along with judges and certain other professionals. However, since section 21 of the Criminal Justice Act 2003 came into force on 5th April 2004 that 'immunity' had been removed. Accordingly, the Bar Council had issued an edict which Malcolm had read and reread when he received his jury summons through the post.

Malcolm was aware from that guidance that he was acting in his capacity as a private citizen and not as a barrister. He was aware that he should not be afforded any special status. He was further aware that; he should not lie about his occupation, but that there was no need to volunteer what he did for a living unless asked and he was also aware that he should follow the judge's directions on law even if he thought they were wrong. Accordingly, he decided it would be prudent not to put himself forward as jury foreman and he would try not to dominate discussions in the room.

Once everyone was seated around the table William produced the judge's written directions and then addressed his fellow jurors.

"I think we should use this document as a blueprint for our deliberations. The judge has written out a number of questions for us to answer under the part called 'Route to Verdict'."

Daphne immediately interjected, "I don't think we need to spend a lot of time over this, he's obviously guilty. I've tried to lose weight several times and tried many, 'miracle slimming aids' and I can tell you they are all rubbish and anyone pedalling that trash is guilty in my eyes!"

There was an adverse reaction from most jurors to this comment. Even Geoffrey groaned and Malcolm could not resist saying.

"Daphne, you cannot just say he is obviously guilty because he is pedalling trash. We all must discuss the evidence and the judge's directions. This is a serious charge, a manslaughter charge, it's not simply about pedalling trash but whether we can be sure he is responsible for killing someone."

Daphne visibly bristled, "It's obvious he killed that poor man. He sold him this trash and that man died. That's enough for me!"

Malcolm spoke up again, "That's not enough Daphne, we have to follow the judge's directions and the route to verdict."

Daphne would not surrender her position, "Didn't you see that programme on TV just before the judge gave us these directions. That programme made it clear he's as guilty as hell."

Malcolm shook his head, "I'm happy to say I didn't see any programme and you should put it out of your mind. The judge directed us that we were only to rely on evidence we had heard in court and nothing else and certainly not some television programme that has its own agenda."

Daphne bristled, "How can I ignore it. It covered all the evidence there is in the case."

Malcolm realised he was becoming exasperated and he tried to calm himself. He had addressed well over a hundred juries in his practice at the Bar, in all that time he never thought for one minute that jurors may act like this. He turned to the other jurors.

"Did anyone else see this programme?"

Three other jurors admitted that they had. Malcolm raised his eyes to the sky before asking, "Do any of you intend to be influenced by what you saw?"

All three said they did not, confirming that they were going to follow the judge's directions on this topic. Malcolm then turned to Daphne.

"You've heard that, Daphne. Are you going to breach the judge's directions and rely on what you saw in this programme in order to come to a decision?"

Daphne looked a little sheepish, "What if I am?"

Malcolm was aware of another piece of guidance from the Bar Council. He recalled it said that if he had any concerns about anything said or done by another juror, he should not remain silent or take matters into his own hands but should raise it with the judge. He had already technically breached this by raising it directly with Daphne but he wanted this trial to conclude so he could get back to his practice. He looked directly into Daphne's eyes.

"If you tell me that you are going to ignore the judge's directions and rely on something that was not part of the evidence in this case and which the defence never had a chance to challenge, then I am duty bound to report it to the judge."

Daphne now deeply reddened, "What do you mean, 'duty bound'?"

"I mean I have a duty to mention it to the judge with a view to her discharging you."

William intervened, "Forgive me Malcolm, I thought we were not supposed to discuss what happens in a jury room."

Malcolm nodded, "Generally that's right but as the judge directed us, if we have concerns about what other jurors say or do, we should bring it to the attention of the judge and I feel duty bound to do so."

Geoffrey looked at Malcolm closely, "Why do you feel 'duty bound' to raise this with the judge?"

He then had a thought, "What do you do for a living Malcolm?"

Malcolm hesitated but as he had been asked a direct question, he felt he had to answer it. "I am a criminal barrister."

Daphne's mouth visibly dropped. It took her a few seconds to recover, now worried as she remembered the judge's comments about prison if jurors did their own research. She looked coldly at Malcolm as she said, "All right then. I'll ignore what I saw in the programme and rely on what I saw in court."

Malcolm nodded but then she added, "I still think he's guilty though."

William felt he had to get control of this jury before the whole thing got out of hand.

"Ok, let's all calm down. No one is reporting anyone to the judge. Let's concentrate on the questions the judge asked us and upon the evidence we heard ..."

He quickly added for Malcolm's benefit, "...in the courtroom."

Malcolm sat back. He had done his duty. He thought Nashad was probably guilty as he had been struck by the cross examination of Nashad when he had been asked why he had not tried the 'miracle slimming aid' when he considered himself overweight. However, the concept of a 'reasonable doubt' and 'being satisfied so that you are sure', were ingrained in his psyche and so he had not made his mind up whether to find Nashad guilty or not guilty. He intended to take a back seat now although he would give his opinion if he felt it became important to do so.

William continued, "To me the most important question in this case is, 'Are we sure that Nashad Pritchard knew he was selling DNP?'

If he knew he was selling it then I think he's guilty, if he didn't and he believed some silly story peddled by that crooked Chinese bloke, then he's not guilty."

He suddenly looked up remembering that one of the jurors looked like they had Chinese heritage, he hoped he had not offended him.

"Sorry Peter, I don't mean to offend you."

Peter Wang looked surprised, "Why would your comments offend me, they have nothing to do with me, you were referring to Lee Han Ong who clearly is dishonest and presumably from China. I was born in Salisbury!"

William smiled, you were never too sure these days what words might offend someone. Happy he had in his own mind, 'dodged a bullet', he continued.

"Does anyone have anything they would like to add to the discussion involving this question?"

Daphne spoke up, looking in Malcolm's direction as she did so.

"It's obvious he knew. He was buying the stuff in massive barrels labelled, 'DNP' and 'fertiliser'. That's good enough for me!"

Deirdre Long was not certain.

"He gave his explanations for that. They had got no licensing in place to sell the drug in the UK so he thought they were disguising what it was."

Daphne was annoyed to see that another woman was arguing with her. She noted that Deirdre was quite thin. She had probably never had to take any slimming aids so she clearly did not know what she was talking about. She would try to explain it so even Deidre understood.

"He knew it was poisonous. He was ill himself when he tried to clean that drum and when he was filling the capsules. They said on that programme...."

She stopped herself as Malcolm stared at her. She decided not to finish her sentence and not to add anything else to the conversation. Someone else could take over the discussion. Maybe Ruth Collier. She was a large lady and she had confided to Daphne during the case, that she had taken many 'miracle' slimming aids in her time and none had worked and she didn't trust people who sold them.

Daphne stared across the table at her but noticed that Ruth was avoiding eye contact, she was remaining quiet and was looking out of the window. Daphne sat back in her chair wondering how the idiots around her had made it onto a jury. She had tried her best, as far as she was concerned, Nashad Pritchard was guilty and no one was going to change her mind.

CHAPTER 49

THE JURY RETURNS

The jury left the courtroom on Friday at 12:20. They deliberated that day until the judge sent them home at 4:20pm. They returned at 10:00am on Monday and they were sent home at 4:15pm after a full day's deliberating. The same had happened on Tuesday. On Wednesday morning at 11:45am a tannoy told David and Sara that the jury were returning to court.

As the barristers took their seats the judge came in. "Mr Smedley and Mr Brant, the jury have been out eighteen hours and fifteen minutes, deliberating on this charge. They have just sent me a note which I am afraid is one that I cannot show to counsel."

That immediately told all the barristers what the note contained. Normally a judge would show a juror's note to counsel unless it was a note telling the judge they were deadlocked and revealing the numbers for and against a verdict. The latter type of note was never shown to counsel.

The judge continued, "As the jury have indicated that they are deadlocked I propose to give them a majority direction and see whether we can make any progress, unless anyone objects to that course at this stage?"

Of course no one did, there was nothing to object to.

Five minutes later the jury came into court. Some of them looked ashen and tired as if they were exhausted from arguing with each other.

The judge waited until they were seated and then she commenced with her majority direction.

"Thank you, ladies and gentlemen, for your note. I have read it and although I have not shown it to counsel, they are aware that you have sent a note and the nature of what it contains. The time has now been reached when I can give you another direction. What is called a 'majority direction.'

In a moment I will ask you to return to your jury room and continue your deliberations. It is important that you continue to try to reach a verdict on which you all agree. But if you find you really cannot all agree on your verdict, I may now accept a verdict upon which eleven or ten of you agree. That means I can only accept a Guilty or a Not Guilty verdict where there is a majority of ten to two or eleven to one. Please will you now return to your rooms and continue with your deliberations."

All the barristers looked closely at the jurors faces to see how they reacted to this. Often a juror will show frustration on the basis that they are nowhere near a ten to two or eleven to one verdict, other times they let nothing away. On this occasion the large lady who frowned throughout David's speech was frowning again at Nashad. David wondered, did that mean she was in a minority or was simply annoyed that it had taken this long to persuade the others of his guilt. David could only guess at the answer.

An hour later, just before the luncheon adjournment they were all called to court again. Once they had all taken their seats the clerk of the court asked the jury foreman to deliver the verdict. William stood up and the question was asked by the clerk of the court, "On count one on the indictment, do you find the defendant guilty or not guilty?"

William looked straight at Nashad and said in a clear voice.

"Not guilty, My Lady."

The clerk continued, "And is that the verdict of you all or by a majority."

"By a majority my Lady."

As it was a not guilty verdict the clerk did not ask how many jurors were in favour of an acquittal and how many were against, only the jurors knew that and they also knew they had reached this verdict on Tuesday afternoon but Daphne had held out refusing to give a not guilty verdict and continued with that stance until the rest of the jury decided to deliver the majority verdict. The final result had therefore been an eleven to one verdict in favour of an acquittal.

Once the verdict was delivered David stood to ask that Nashad be released from court in relation to this charge. The judge nodded.

"Of course Mr Brant there is the question of breach of bail and the passport offence that your client was charged with. I understand that your client pleaded guilty to both at an earlier hearing and should be given maximum credit for that plea. I propose to deal with those offences now by passing a sentence of immediate imprisonment that will allow for his immediate release. I will therefore pass a sentence of 8 months imprisonment of which he will do half. In view of the time he has waited for this trial in custody, that means he will be released immediately unless, of course, you seek to persuade me differently?

"No, My Lady, I have nothing to add."

Although Nashad was free there were still a few administrative matters that had to be carried out in the cells before he was fully released and as it was lunchtime there were no visits in the cells until 1:45pm.

At 1:45pm David and Sara went down to the cells to visit Nashad, hoping that at least now he would be happy that he was going to be released.

They walked into the cell and Nashad followed them. David spoke first.

"That's it Nashad, you can put this horrible incident behind you and continue with your life."

Nashad stared at him with a frown that was not dissimilar to Daphne's.

"Of course I am happy that justice was finally done. I expected an acquittal when I gave evidence. I thought I did a very good job and that it was unlikely that anyone but the most jaundiced juror would convict me. However, I am still not happy with your conduct of the trial and the fact you made me look like a complete fool!

Wendy told me you are one of the best criminal barristers there is. Having seen you, 'in action', I was not impressed. You failed to tell the jury the real story about me and my life's work and there was a real danger I could be convicted because of your conduct of the trial and characterising me as a fool. I love my niece and her daughter but I regret David I will not be visiting them again whilst you are there. I trust you will tell them both it is nothing to do with them, it is entirely to do with you!"

David tried to keep his best poker face, "Nashad, most people would be grateful having been acquitted on a serious charge which could have resulted in them getting between 8-10 years in prison, but obviously you are not one of those. I will pass your best wishes onto Wendy and Rose but for professional reasons I will not say anything to you further. Goodbye."

David marched out of the cell with Sara closely following behind him. Sara could not resist saying, "What an ungrateful bastard after all you did for him."

She noticed that David had a big grin on his face. "David are you alright?"

"Absolutely perfect thank you. It's been a great day, another acquittal to put on Chambers website for a bit of self-promotion and at the same time I won't ever have to see that insufferable fool again. What could be better!"

CHAPTER 50

CHRISTMAS COMES EARLY

It was the afternoon of Saturday 12th December 2020 and all was good in the Brant household. Christmas was around the corner and David had just been notified by his clerks that he was going to be paid for Nashad's case before Christmas and Roger Cooper's traffic case was going to start on 13th January 2021. After the lean effects of Covid, the payment of Nashad's case would be a relief to the family's finances before Christmas and the Roger Cooper case meant that the New Year was looking up to. It also seemed now that the courts were keen to try the considerable backlog of cases that had mainly been built up before covid and then increased when covid closed the courts. As a result, David looked forward to a fruitful and rewarding 2021. What could be better.

David was in the kitchen with Wendy who was preparing a meal for Rose who was happily sitting at the kitchen island playing with her soft toys. He was happy, nothing could be better than spending a few weeks at home with Wendy and Rose, relaxing and putting Nashad, Cooper, his clerks and chambers behind him.

He looked around the kitchen and his eyes were drawn to his wine rack. There was a particularly good bottle of Malbec begging to be opened, but he turned away. With all his health scares this year which had slightly increased when the doctors booked him in for a liver scan in the New Year, there was a new regime in the Brant household.

Although he could not guarantee reducing his alcohol intake to the Government's recommended fourteen units a week, he intended to continue to cut his alcohol consumption down, reduce the amount of food he ate, (save of course for Christmas lunch that just had to be celebrated in a traditional way) and do a lot more exercise.

Indeed, he was thinking of going to his gym now to swim a few lengths in the swimming pool. If he went before 3pm, he could probably get in 50 lengths and avoid the water aerobics class which he detested. It meant he was forced to swim in one lane with all the other lane swimmers whilst fifty or so women and the odd man, took up the rest of the pool. They caused enormous waves with their excessive gyrations, whilst very loud music was played that reverberated around the pool walls and to him, was quite deafening.

He was just about to go upstairs to get his swimming gear when the phone in the hallway rang. Wendy was nearest to it and she asked David to keep an eye on Rose whilst she answered it.

He waited in the kitchen as he heard Wendy say, "Hello stranger, I was hoping I would hear from you before Christmas, it's been such a long time."

David was glad, for a horrible moment he thought it might be his clerks asking him to conduct a trial the following week in some far flung place like Newcastle or Carlisle. Fortunately, it was not and was presumably some friend of Wendy's whom she had not seen for some time.

At that moment Rose started laughing loudly as she had moved on from her soft toys and was watching her tablet. As a result of the noise Wendy closed the kitchen door meaning that David could not hear any more of the conversation.

David went over to Rose to see what was so funny and saw that she was watching some cartoon with hectic characters running all over the place. He watched for a few seconds before taking a seat next to her at the kitchen island.

Ten minutes later Wendy entered the kitchen. She was smiling but he could see by her expression that she had some additional news that he would probably not want to hear.

"What is it love, why are you looking like that?"

Wendy came over and took his hands in hers.

"Well, its good news really."

David nodded and replied, "Good, glad to hear it, and what is the good news?"

"Well, that was Uncle Robert."

David immediately removed his hands from hers and his expression changed to one of deep concern. Wendy ignored his look and continued.

"He told me he has reflected on the case and believes that you did as good a job as you are capable of and he feels that he forgives you and ought to apologise to you."

David could see that was not all of the message.

Wendy continued, "He regrets saying some of the things he said to you after the trial and wants your forgiveness."

David could not wait any longer, "And?" he asked laconically.

"He wants to apologise to you in person. He says he would like to come here and apologise to you. He said he would also like to see Rose and me. He asked if he could come here and spend a couple of weeks with us over Christmas."

David's face turned an ashen white. "You did tell him that's not necessary, didn't you? He can apologise over the phone and face message you and Rose?"

Wendy was silent so David pleaded, "Oh please, you did tell him it's not necessary to come here?"

"Well, I did tell him there was no need to apologise in person, but he insisted. He did say he does not know anyone else in the country and if he cannot spend it here, he will be alone at Christmas. After the ordeal he has been through this year I did not think that you would object ..."

She paused before adding, "... too strongly."

"You are kidding. You know I can't stand the man and representing him on a manslaughter charge for close to three weeks did not change my opinion one bit. If anything, it strengthened it. He was rude and obnoxious during the trial and ungrateful even when he was acquitted of manslaughter. I will be quite happy if I never see him again!"

Wendy nodded, "I understand all that David. He should never have acted the way he did and should have been grateful on the day he was acquitted. I know you did your best for him even though you cannot stand him. But Rose does not see many of her relatives. She does not see your children for example, except on increasingly rare occasions and it is nice for her to see Uncle Robert. He does make a special effort around her."

That was it, David had tried his best to persuade Wendy that Uncle Robert's coming was a bad idea but his advocacy skills had failed him.

He turned his back on Wendy and started to make his way to his study muttering, "Where is that bottle of Malbec and where did I put that blood pressure medication?"

Suddenly another thought hit him and he turned back to face Wendy and coughed.

"You know Wendy, I'm not feeling very well. I have developed a cough and I am feeling very sweaty. I think I might be coming down with covid. I ought to take a test. That's annoying, we might all have to go into isolation for the whole of Christmas!"

Books by John M. Burton

THE SILK BRIEF

The Silk Tales volume 1

The first book in the series, "The Silk Trials." David Brant QC is a Criminal Barrister, a "Silk", struggling against a lack of work and problems in his own chambers. He is briefed to act on behalf of a cocaine addict charged with murder. The case appears overwhelming and David has to use all his ability to deal with the wealth of forensic evidence presented against his client.

UK LINK

http://amzn.to/16QwwZo

US LINK

http://amzn.to/1bz221C

THE SILK HEAD

The Silk Tales volume 2

The second book in the series "The Silk Tales". David Brant QC receives a phone call from his wife asking him to represent a fireman charged with the murder of his lover. As the trial progresses, developments in David's Chambers bring unexpected romance and a significant shift in politics and power when the Head of Chambers falls seriously ill. Members of his chambers feel that only David is capable of leading them out of rough waters ahead, but with a full professional and personal life, David is not so sure whether he wants to take on the role of *The Silk Head*.

UK LINK

http://amzn.to/1ilOOYn

US LINK

http://amzn.to/1iTPQZn

THE SILK RETURNS

The Silk Tales volume 3

David Brant QC is now Head of Chambers at Temple Lane Chambers, Temple, London. Life is great for David, his practice is busy with good quality work and his love life exciting. He has a beautiful partner in Wendy Pritchard, a member of his chambers and that relationship, like his association with members of his chambers, appears to be strengthening day by day.

However, overnight, things change dramatically for him and his world is turned upside down. At least he can bury himself in his work when a new brief is returned to him from another silk. The case is from his least favourite solicitor but at least it appears to be relatively straightforward, with little evidence against his client and an acquittal almost inevitable.

As the months pass, further evidence is served in the case and begins to mount up against his client. As the trial commences David has to deal with a prosecutor from his own chambers who is determined to score points against him personally and a co-defending counsel who likewise seems hell-bent on causing as many problems as he can for David's client. Will David's skill and wit be enough this time?

UK LINK

http://amzn.to/1Qj911Q

US LINK

http://amzn.to/1OteiV7

THE SILK RIBBON

The Silk Tales volume 4

David Brant QC is a barrister who practices as a Queen's Counsel at Temple Lane Chambers, Temple, London. He is in love with a bright and talented barrister from his chambers, Wendy, whose true feelings about him have been difficult to pin down. Just when he thinks he has the answer, a seductive Russian woman seeks to attract his attention, for reasons he can only guess at.

His case load has been declining since the return of his Head of Chambers, who is now taking all the quality silk work that David had formerly enjoyed. As a result, David is delighted when he is instructed in an interesting murder case. A middle class man has shot and killed his wife's lover. The prosecution say it was murder, frustration caused by his own impotency, but the defence claim it was all a tragic accident. The case appears to David to be straight-forward, but, as the trial date approaches, the prosecution evidence mounts up and David finds himself against a highly competent prosecution silk, with a trick or two up his sleeve.

Will David be able to save his well-to-do client from the almost inevitable conviction for murder and a life sentence in prison? And what path will his personal life take when the beautiful Russian asks him out for a drink?

UK LINK

http://amzn.to/22ExByC

USA LINK

http://amzn.to/1TTWQMY

THE SILKS CHILD

The Silk Tales volume 5

This is the fifth volume in the series, the Silk Tales, dealing with the continuing story of Queen's Counsel (the Silk), David Brant QC.

Their romantic Valentine's weekend away in a five-star hotel, is interrupted by an unexpected and life-changing announcement by David's fiancé, Wendy. David has to look at his life afresh and seek further casework to pay for the expected increase in his family's costs.

The first case that comes along is on one of the most difficult and emotionally charged cases of his career. Rachel Wilson is charged with child cruelty and causing the death of her own baby by starvation.

The evidence against Rachel, particularly the expert evidence appears overwhelming and once the case starts, David quickly notices how the jurors react to his client, with ill-disguised loathing. It does not help that the trial is being presided over by his least favourite judge, HHJ Tanner QC, his former pupil-master.

David will need all his skill to conduct the trial and fight through the emotion and prejudice at a time when his own life is turned upside down by a frightening development.

Will he be able to turn the case around and secure an acquittal for an unsympathetic and abusive client who seems to deliberately demonstrate a lack of redeeming qualities?

UK

https://goo.gl/YmQZ4p

USA

https://goo.gl/Ek30mx

THE SILKS CRUISE

The Silk Tales volume 6

This is the sixth volume in the series, the Silk Tales, dealing with the continuing story of Queen's Counsel (the Silk), David Brant QC.

After a difficult, exhausting but highly remunerative fraud trial, David and Wendy decide to take their young daughter Rose on a cruise to Norway to get away from cases, chambers and city life.

A chance meeting leads to David being instructed in a particularly difficult murder trial. The case appears straight forward at first, even though the defendant's own friends give evidence against him. However, a series of surprising developments in the case make David wonder what his strategy should be and whether he should ever have taken the case on in the first place.

UK LINK

https://amzn.to/2VD6bPh

US LINK

https://amzn.to/2VfZoMo

SILK DILEMMAS

The Silk Tales volume 7

Following a lengthy, but lucrative fraud trial, David takes his family on a much needed holiday to Turkey. On his return David is instructed in a multi handed murder trial for a defendant called Iqbal Bhutta. The case alleges that Iqbal was involved in a revenge attack on a drugs dealer who had attacked him.
Soon David finds the case has extraordinary difficulties. Not only is the evidence seemingly overwhelming, the client seems determined to make the case against him stronger and is constantly assisted by co-defending counsel in this regard.

As the trial progresses, David faces a series of dilemmas including tricky questions involving his case and his junior. As he deals with these increasing difficulties, he receives surprising and disturbing news about a close relative, only adding to his Silk dilemmas.

UK LINK

https://www.amazon.co.uk//dp/B0B1CBVN4K/

US LINK

https://www.amzn.com/B0B1CBVN4K/

PARRICIDE

VOLUME 1 OF THE MURDER TRIALS OF CICERO

A courtroom drama set in Ancient Rome and based on the first murder trial conducted by the famous Roman Advocate, Marcus Tullius Cicero. He is instructed to represent a man charged with killing his own father. Cicero soon discovers that the case is not a simple one and closely involves an important associate of the murderous Roman dictator, Sulla.

UK LINK

http://amzn.to/14vAYvY

US LINK

http://amzn.to/1fprzul

POISON

VOLUME 2 OF THE MURDER TRIALS OF CICERO

It is six years since Cicero's forensic success in the Sextus Roscius case and his life has been good. He has married and progressed through the Roman ranks and is well on the way to taking on the most coveted role of senator of Rome. Meanwhile his career in the law courts has been booming with success after success. However, one day he is approached by men from a town close to his hometown who beg him to represent a former slave on a charge of attempted poisoning. The case seems straight forward but little can he know that this case will lead him on to represent a Roman knight in a notorious case where he is charged with poisoning and with bribing judges to convict an innocent man. Cicero's skills will be tried to the utmost and he will face the most difficult and challenging case of his career where it appears that the verdict has already been rendered against his client in the court of public opinion.

UK LINK

https://goo.gl/VgpU9S

US LINK

https://goo.gl/TjhYA6

THE MYTH OF SPARTA

VOLUME 1 OF THE CHRONICLES OF SPARTA

A novel telling the story of the Spartans from the battle of the 300 at Thermopylae against the might of the Persian Empire, to the battle of Sphacteria against the Athenians and their allies. As one reviewer stated, the book is, "a highly enjoyable way to revisit one of the most significant periods of western history"

UK LINK

http://amzn.to/1gO3MSI

US LINK

http://amzn.to/1bz2pcw

THE RETURN OF THE SPARTANS

VOLUME 2 OF THE CHRONICLES OF SPARTA

"The Return of the Spartans" is a sequel to "The Myth of Sparta" and continues from where that book ends with the capture of the Spartan Hoplites at the battle of Sphacteria.

We follow their captivity through the eyes of their leader Styphon and watch individual's machinations as the Spartans and Athenians continue their war against each other. We observe numerous battles between the two in detail, seen through the eyes of their most famous and in some instances, infamous citizens.

We follow the political machinations of Cleon, Nicias and Alcibiades in Athens and see how they are dealt with by the political satirist at the time, Aristophanes, who referred to all of them in his plays.

Many of the characters from "the Myth of Sparta" appear again including the philosopher Socrates, the Athenian General Demosthenes and the Spartan General Brasidas whose campaign in Northern Greece we observe through the eyes of his men.

The book recreates the period in significant detail and as was described by one reviewer of

"The Myth of Sparta", is, "a   highly enjoyable way to revisit one of the most significant periods of western history".

UK LINK

http://amzn.to/1aVDYmS

US LINK

http://amzn.to/18iQCfr

THE TRIAL OF ADMIRAL BYNG

Pour Encourager Les Autres

BOOK ONE OF THE HISTORICAL TRIALS SERIES

"The Trial of Admiral Byng" is a fictionalised retelling of the true story of the famous British Admiral Byng, who fought at the battle of Minorca in 1756 and was later court-martialled for his role in that battle. The book takes us through the siege of Minorca as well as the battle and then to the trial where Byng has to defend himself against serious allegations of cowardice, knowing that if he is found guilty there is only one penalty available to the court, his death.

UK LINK

http://goo.gl/cMMXFY

US LINK

http://goo.gl/AaVNOZ

TREACHERY – THE PRINCES IN THE TOWER

'Treachery - the Princes in the Tower' tells the story of a knight, Sir Thomas Clark who is instructed by King Henry VII to discover what happened to the Princes in the Tower. His quest takes him upon many journeys meeting many of the important personages of the day who give him conflicting accounts of what happened. However, through his perseverance he gets ever closer to discovering what really happened to the Princes, with startling consequences.

UK LINK

http://amzn.to/1VPW0kC

US LINK

http://amzn.to/1VUyUJf

Printed in Great Britain
by Amazon